The Awakening
of
Khufu

A novel

Les Lester

Kanefer Books
Minneapolis-St. Paul

Kanefer Books
2015

Author's Note

The election of Barack Obama, as the first black president of the United States, reminds us that the U.S. is not a static nation and that it continues to evolve towards its ideal as a pluralistic democracy.

This unprecedented event has brought all Americans together, as never before. And as black Americans, we are indelibly assured that we have allies, across the board, who echo Dr. Martin Luther King Jr.'s mantra that individuals should be judged by the content of their character not by the color of their skin.

Meanwhile, the dialogue among characters in this first edition of *The Awakening of Khufu* certainly reflects a time-specific era in American history, which may in future years be considered as pre-Obama. And, hopefully, just as the dialogue of Huck Finn and Tom Sawyer, today, reflects a bygone era, we in this moment of history may conclude that we are emerging into a more inclusive culture that respects and reflects the best of all of its citizens, as never before.

Les Lester

Prologue
2560 B.C.

From the upper terrace of the Great House, Pharaoh Khufu casually swatted away an insect with his flail as he watched the construction of the Great Pyramid going ahead in the distance. Thousands of noble Egyptian men joined in what was one of the most unifying efforts in the kingdom's history. In the process, its golden crest and polished limestone finish were beginning to gleam in the sunshine.

The work of constructing this largest man-made structure in the world had required that they erect an earthen ramp around its perimeter as they went ever higher. And now, they disassembled the sloping causeway as they worked downward, capping limestone siding onto the pyramid's surface.

But after nearly twenty years of construction, its luster had waned somewhat in Khufu's eyes. Perhaps due to the persistent quelling of the venomous rumor on why the pyramids had begun to be built in earlier dynasties, he thought. Hearsay arose, ever-so-often, poisoning the workers with a false quote attributed to Imhotep, the great scholar of the Third Dynasty. Essentially it said that the colossal projects were created to keep the people occupied, that they would be too tired to think of weightier matters such as overthrowing the throne.

Certainly not true for my era, Khufu mused smugly. Lower and Upper Egypt had now cemented; their union more than merely a physical joining, as in earlier periods. Now conscripts from far and wide made their way to Giza, the necropolis, with the unified aim of contributing to the kingdom's welfare. Admittedly, he tired of the occasional need to purge the land of unscrupulous troublemakers, but it was the price of rulership, he conceded.

Overall, the historical condition of war and turmoil, common to earlier periods, had subsided. And he comforted himself in the reality that under his rulership the kingdom had done more than build pyramids. Now canals linked farther outlying fringes of the dominion than ever before, and the food supply was unrivaled in all the world. Only in Egypt are poor men fat, he mused. The natural supply of fish, meat, dates, melons, grains, beer and wine were the envy of the world. This land of the blacks, resting along the Nile, is Amen Ra's wonder to the uncivilized heathens, he surmised.

"Queen Henutsen is here to see you, Son of Amen," a voice from the door guards rang out, bringing him back to the present.

"Yes, send her in, I'm expecting her."

Queen Henutsen, a consort queen selected in early childhood by his mother, Queen Hetepheres, and his father, Pharaoh Snefru, entered the room gracefully, her handmaidens accompanying. They followed demurely as she approached him, her translucent fine-linen gown swaying regally; her braided locks, luxurious shoulder-length tresses, interwoven with golden threads.

"Henutsen, the radiance of Amen Ra consumes you," Khufu said admiring her beauty as she came nearer.

"And the light of your countenance reflects his wisdom, your majesty," she responded.

6

"What favors may I bestow upon my queen?" Khufu asked, his hands securely taking hers as she joined him on the terrace overlooking the bustling city.

"It is Kewab and Dedefra. Pharaoh's eldest sons are leading Khafre into a life of waywardness," she said. "They've taken him on hunting expeditions as far as the first cataract, an area we have forbidden them to venture due to the rapids." She looked up at him steadily, with expressive black-lined eyelids, her ebony face radiant: "Just a month ago a boat capsized near there and three men drowned."

Khufu was admittedly concerned about the escapades of the young striplings. The Nile could indeed be dangerous. And he was pleased with Henutsen's diligence in rearing Khafre. The seventeen-year-old was already a natural leader with good people instincts.

Pharaoh could remember his youthful days, as a prince of Egypt, hunting hippopotami and wild game along the Nile. Indeed, navigating the far reaches of the waterway was a rights-of-passage into manhood—something Henutsen could not readily concede. Her nurturing tendencies overshadowed the fact that Khafre had come of age.

"I will talk with the boys myself," Khufu said, mindful that she would be further discomfited by his decision. He clasped the edge of the ledge firmly, his mahogany arms outstretched. "I'm going to assign them to military training regiments in different nomes. They're men now. They need constructive work to occupy their time."

He marveled at the passing of the years as he gazed out at the grandiose construction. It represented a paradox of colossal beauty, yet impending finality.

The Awakening
of
Khufu

1

The Twenty-first Century

P rofessor James Hannibal III peered into his microscope and examined the samples of DNA with the routine stare of a scientist long past his quitting time for the day, but mindful that one last observation might reveal the hoped-for outcome of many hours of investigation.

Suddenly, he stood from his stool and stepped backwards in astonishment, wiping his hands on his lab coat as if to wipe away his findings. At last, he'd found what he'd wanted, but now he weighed the ramifications. "Incredible," he mumbled.

Since the discovery of a frozen wooly mammoth in Siberia, in 1999, scientists had pondered the possibilities of resurrecting bio-cellular matter from ancient DNA. In addition, his groundbreaking research, which revealed the presence of human-memory prints in the cell nuclei, had fostered discussions of the previously unthinkable.

Actually, James couldn't believe he was conducting such research. He had always been conventional in his scientific views, and cloning had definitely been off limits.

It all began after the Egyptians had pursued him relentlessly in the wake of his breakthrough findings on cell memory prints. His gradual warming to their overtures came with the realization that DNA sequencing was indeed feasible.

Now, alone in his lab, he reflected on the chain of events that had led to this day.

≈

Dr. Hannibal had been in Chicago as a visiting professor at Chicago State University from Tuskegee U., in Alabama, where he headed the genetics department. He was also engaged in a medical student recruitment initiative with a physicians' association.

One evening, while driving through the West Side on a return from one of his recruitment engagements, at a local high school, in an area he was quite familiar with from his college years, he gazed out of his car window to view a scene he had witnessed all-too-often.

The activity on Madison Avenue could have been mirrored thousands of times in cities across the United States. Several black men ranging from eight to middle-aged passed around a wine bottle in front of a liquor store, some asking passers-by for loose change.

Hannibal, meanwhile, accelerated his burgundy Jaguar sports coupe as the stoplight changed, shaking his head in chagrin. He'd likely see the same scene at the next red light.

The genetics professor had climbed up from those mean streets. But he admittedly had had it much easier than many. He had been reared by a hard-working upwardly mobile Southern family. Still, somehow, paradoxically, the glamour and allure of the big city culture had drawn him in after he'd moved to Chicago as a student.

At the next light, another pre-teen stood taking in street knowledge as older boys and men unwittingly played the roles of teachers, tutoring another ghetto scholar. Similar goings on awaited him throughout the urban sprawl.

Up ahead, however, out of the blight of the ghetto, pro basketball's NBA United Center arose like a majestic beacon of hope. Indeed, some did make it out. In front of the huge stadium a bronze statue of the legendary Michael Jordan, stretched in his trademark Air Jordan flight-routine was proof positive—or was it? Hannibal mused. Of the over five hundred thousand high school males playing basketball in the United States each year, fewer than sixty would make it to the NBA, he had read. Yet every kid on every court in America had dreams of beating those odds.

As he continued to reflect on the streets around him, he was keenly aware of how the music had changed over the years from soul, to hip-hop, to rap. But the realities had remained the same. Black boy and girl grow up in the ghetto looking for happiness in a world that had written them out of the script, in many ways.

Finally, he reached the South Side, at 35th Street, and headed towards the lake. The whole area was turning for the better, thanks to forward-looking redevelopment and the historic Bronzeville-area concept targeting tourism. His block was a stretch of totally remodeled brownstones. Chicago greats like Negro League Baseball founder, Andrew Rube Foster; America's first black woman airplane pilot, Bessie Coleman; activist-journalist Ida B. Wells; and jazz great Louis Armstrong, among others, had lived and worked in the area. In fact, it had been the only area that blacks could live in during the 1940s. And, interestingly, during that period, due to the close proximity of successful and grass-roots folk, it had become a breeding ground for African-American culture, business and community. Later, following integration, however, most of the upwardly mobile blacks had moved out to the suburbs and other areas of the city, leaving the masses of poor behind, creating a solid underclass in that section of town. But what a difference redevelopment makes, he mused.

He turned into the driveway and clicked the garage door opener, steering directly into the university-owned brownstone's attached garage. His wife, Marika, was there with the lights on. She was indeed his Rock of Gibraltar. She'd stuck with him through thick and thin. Now, despite what went on in their workaday worlds, they were there for each other.

They'd had their backs against the wall early in their marriage, twenty years ago. But they had remained together and withstood the test of time.

He entered the house and she waved cheerfully from the study while talking on the telephone and apparently engaged in surfing the Internet. James went into the kitchen and found that she had brought Chinese food. They'd been having Chinese pretty often on this stay in Chicago, and he was becoming rather accomplished at using chop sticks.

The microwave beeped that the food was hot, and he retrieved the shrimp fried rice and broccoli, before heading towards the dining room where his wife met him in the hallway dressed in a new long, flowing satin night gown. She stretched her arms high and exuberantly; then posed like Miss America. James winked approvingly—his hands full—happy that she was with him in Chicago.

It was their usual type evening at home. They would talk of each other's day, share insights and cuddle in each other's arms, before falling asleep when they retired for the evening.

"Something has got to be done about this hopelessness affecting the people," he told her as he expertly utilized the chopsticks to grasp a stalk of broccoli.

"The mass media parades the low test scores among many black students as indicative of our cultural inefficiencies, without attributing the residuals of colonialism into the discussion. The seed beds of the past are impacting us today," he said philosophically, chomping hungrily at his meal.

"But *you* are doing something, honey. You're a world-renowned scientist, a living, breathing role model—there's just so much one man can do."

"Scientist? Kids don't respect scientists, Marika. To them a scientist is the antithesis, the polar opposite, of cool."

"But how could they not appreciate scientists, sweetheart?" she asked. "They use cell phones. They drive automobiles. They listen to weather reports."

"Okay, maybe I'm over generalizing, Marika. There are some sharp young people out there. Folks in society said the same things about you and me, but look at us now."

He pushed the food to the center of the table, signaling that he was through, and arose taking his wife and pulling her close to him.

"You smell like shrimp and broccoli, Casanova," she said pushing James away playfully. A new tube of Aim is on the sink, and I'll run your bath water.

≈

Fifty or so pre-med students crowded the front rows of the Chicago State University lecture hall, taking in the undergraduate class with the intensity of finals time; despite that it was still early in the semester. Dr. Brooks Edwards knew how to bring out the best in students; and in this session, he riveted their attention, with every graphic illustration he could muster, on the subject of cell mitosis. In his white lab coat and armed with his instructor's pointer, he effectively simplified the students' understanding of bio-cell separation.

"Mitosis is a process of cell division where duplicated chromosomes separate from each other, resulting in two nuclei," he pointed to the chart. "The genetic potential is identical in both new cells."

"Professor?" a student called out raising his hand eagerly. "How does mitosis play into the discussion of stem cells and the current debate of stem cell use in organ development?"

"Stem cells inherently reflect the mitosis process, Stan," he responded, turning to the students squarely. "Scientists describe them as the rudimentary component in the makeup of protoplasm. And since the process of differentiation is not yet reached in stem cells, they can be regulated to mature in many different directions.

"Okay, 10:45 AM. That's enough for today," he said putting down his pointer. "In next week's session we will look further into mitosis and the stem cell connection. Read chapters ten through twelve over the weekend and be ready to discuss what you've learned when we return on Monday."

Edwards was admittedly fulfilled in his chosen profession. As a medical researcher and teacher, the professor subsumed himself in his work and enjoyed interacting with his students. Several of them remained around his lectern asking questions about assignments or waiting to mull over a question they wanted to discuss further. And he patiently addressed them as best he could despite his need to leave for an 11:00 AM lunch meeting in the student union's grill.

He was about to meet with his old pal Dr. James Hannibal. They were both members of NAP, the National Association of Physicians, and had worked diligently in efforts to bring more African and African-American students into the medical profession. They had worked together for fifteen years, since joining the organization. Edwards had grown up in Tuskegee, had lots of relatives there and visited often, which helped to cement their friendship.

Both were visiting professors at Chicago State and had timed their tenure in the Windy City to facilitate their recruitment efforts of qualified students.

He finished placing his things in his briefcase, hung his lab coat on a corner hanger and headed out the door accompanied by admirers and hangers on who slowly dissipated as they walked across the campus. By the time he reached the student union he was alone, and as he entered the grill he could see Hannibal mulling over paperwork at a table.

"How're your recruiting efforts?" Hannibal asked, preoccupied, not looking up as Edwards sat down. Hannibal grasped the rim of his eyeglasses with his right hand, apparently focusing on something he didn't want to miss.

"Excellent," Edwards responded, peering over to see what his friend was engrossed in. "And yours, James?"

"Outstanding," Hannibal said, finally looking up from the paper. "Chicago is a mecca for young talent; the sheer numbers guarantee success." He resumed looking at the papers in front of him. "There is only one African-American doctor for every nine hundred and five African-American patients," he said looking up again, shaking the findings that were apparently in the documents he held. "Ludicrous. Just plain ludicrous," he ranted, offering the papers to Edwards.

Edwards took them and began to read the findings for himself, tuning out the busy eatery around them.

"So much for the talented tenth," he murmured returning the study to Hannibal, when he had finished.

"The talented tenth," Hannibal said with a note of reflection in his voice. "W.E.B. Dubois had a point during his era. He advocated that ten percent of the African-American populace needed to act as the vanguard for black America's masses, leading the way to a more affluent society."

"And what of Booker T's masses?" Edwards asked.

"Booker T.," Hannibal responded, in the same tone as before. "Booker T. felt that the masses needed to learn vocational skills that would facilitate grassroots building efforts and a resulting solid cultural foundation of achievement through individual hard work.

"The problem was that they both failed to factor in the very real aspect of negative forces working to curtail their efforts. Stepped-up economic and social oppression thwarted what were workable strategies, given a perfect world."

"So, Mr. Teflon Professor," Edwards said in half jest, "What is *your* proposal for uplifting the huddled masses?"

"All we can do is our best in our sphere of influence, I suppose," Hannibal said yawning, as if his thoughts on the matter had exhausted. "Your and my contribution is our physician recruitment efforts," he said rising. "Let's eat and get on with our meeting, brotha."

2

Hannibal peered at himself in the full-length mirror in his bedroom. *Not bad for forty-two*, the tall, mustached professor mused. He straightened his bow-tie and congratulated himself for having gone out and purchased a tuxedo. Marika had chided him about it for years.

"What do you think?" a cheerful voice rang out. It was Marika in her trade-mark pose—arms outstretched, palms facing skyward.

"As pretty as you were at nineteen," James said suavely turning around to admire his elegant wife of some twenty years. Her lovely honey-colored complexion, framed by flowing braided tresses, and knowing brown eyes, gave her a look of an Egyptian queen. Her dress was black, with shining glitter-like starlets. And it hugged her figure in all the right places.

They would make their grand entrance at the Museum of Science and Industry awards ceremony in style. The handsome, articulate professor was one of the awardees of the night. He had written his short acceptance remarks on a five-by-seven index card. He always wrote the names of those who had helped him in some capacity, just in case he overlooked someone in his litany of acknowledgments. It was his way of remaining humble and remembering that his success had not come from his efforts alone.

His research on human-memory prints in the nucleus of human cells had rearranged science's conception of what was possible in the realm of human biology. He had found that the body essentially reproduces itself on the micro level. All of the potential for a complete human being is inherent in each tiny cell, his research had proved. And to top it off, the storage segments for memory in the brain were also preserved in each cell.

The study had been quite simple, he reflected. He had merely inserted color-coded fluorescent dye into the nucleus of single cells, much like physicians do on the macro-level with colors that differentiate organs within the human body.

And as he had theorized, the segment within the cell that reflects the brain color-coded to the exact sequence in his study as on the macro level. But the real leg work had been done by Japanese scientists, who had cloned primates from single cells and documented the results alongside of his memory tests.

"Okay, Doctor, I'm ready when you are," Marika said enthused. She knew this was a special night for him, and she wanted to do her best to make him happy.

They drove over to Lake Shore Drive and headed south to Fifty-fifth Street where they exited and turned into the parking lot of the white marble and granite Greek-styled classical structure. James pulled up in his Jaguar and gave the valet a sizable tip, instructing him to leave the car out front, as he and his wife might leave early.

Inside, clusters of Chicago's, and America's, Who's Who stood in small groups chatting as waiters and waitresses, dressed in black and white, served hors d'oeuvres and drinks. More guests sat at large round tables with white tablecloths.

Up front, at special tables reserved for honorees and their guests, Edwards and his wife Jheri waved greetings to James and Marika, who nodded occasionally at recognizable faces as they headed towards the Edwards' where they would be sitting. Finally, they reached their table and were met by greetings from two other couples.

"James...Marika, I'd like you to meet Jerome Jerrod and his wife Margaret. You've heard of Syntec Software, haven't you?" Edwards asked.

"Yes...the pleasure's mine," Hannibal said shaking hands with the well-known computer software tycoon. Jerrod looked just as he did in the newspapers and on TV. He was built like an NFL linebacker, but graying around the temples with gray bristles in his moustache. He was fifty or so but had maintained his physique and was apparently still ruggedly athletic.

His wife, meanwhile, reflected his suave bearing. Sveltely built, she had maintained her girlish good looks and flashing personality.

"I understand your husband is some kind of a guy in the medical world," Margaret said to Marika, flashing a cool smile that immediately put others at ease.

"Yes, I'm proud of him. He works hard, and it has certainly paid off."

"Honey, you haven't met the Studenmachers," James said gesturing to a young white couple across the table. "Todd and Jan Studenmacher, they're buyers for the Harvard Feld stores."

The couple, in their early to mid-thirties, smiled graciously. Could be cousins or close with the billionaire Feld family, James figured. Well pedigreed folks in their early thirties have a way of emerging at settings such as these, he mused.

A mix of ethnic and cultural groups populated the hall. This was the kind of event where Democrats and Republicans, Muslims and Christians, conservatives and liberals all came together for a worthy cause. The event themed: 'Science Makes Cents' was a fund-raiser to help the museum in its new expansion project.

James scanned the one thousand or so strong gathering and noted the many well-heeled movers and shakers.

"Ladies and gentlemen," a voice rang out getting the crowd's attention. "You've probably noted that the fare this evening is finger food," a cherub-looking man, with a salt and pepper mustache, declared from the podium. "Many of us can afford to miss a full meal," he said hands on his ample mid-section.

The crowd roared in laughter.

"If you haven't had your fill, there is plenty left at the buffet area; or our first-class servers are here to help you. If you will, just mingle for the next ten minutes or so and then we'll get on with the evening's program."

Two servers converged on both sides of their table.

Marika began her order: "I'll have the salmon, mix the cheeses—"

"Mr. Hannibal," a foreign-accented voice rang out.

James turned to see two well-dressed Arab-looking men standing over him.

"If we could have a moment with you please, Mr. Hannibal?" One man handed James his business card, while the other stood genteelly alongside him.

THE EGYPTIAN MINISTRY of SCIENCE and TECHNOLOGY, the card read.

"How might I help you?" Hannibal said rising—wondering what the men could possibly want with him.

"I'm Ahmed Salih," the man who had handed him the card said as they walked.

"And I'm Reshef Ottah," the other man said.

They walked toward the buffet area and the man who had handed him his card began.

"Our scientists in Egypt have looked into your cell-memory research, and we believe that you are just the scientist who can assist us in developing an unprecedented study in DNA sequencing."

"DNA sequencing?" James asked.

"Yes. DNA sequencing. Our scientists believe technology has reached the point where we can actually clone an ancient pharaoh."

The word clone sent shivers down James's spine. He had made up his mind years earlier that he would never get involved in the science; even though he realized, given his background in genetics, that he was as prepared as anyone to accomplish bio-cellular cloning. In fact, he had stopped his cell-memory research just short of validating his memory theory because he did not believe in cloning.

But the Japanese had no such reservations and had documented his assertions through their primate studies.

"Yes. Let me explain, sir," Ahmed continued. By now they had exited the noisy hall and were standing in the concourse area where it was quieter.

"Mr. Hannibal, our government is willing to pay you two million dollars to help us clone the DNA of an Ancient Egyptian pharaoh."

James was startled. He half wondered if the guys were part of some practical joke that was being played on him. But they remained solemn.

"We are serious, Mr. Hannibal. I know this seems far out, but we've been asked to make this offer to you with our government's backing."

James looked at the men incredulously. What they were suggesting was a radical break with what, theretofore, had been the domain of God and nature.

"Why has your government asked me and not the Japanese?" he asked pointedly.

"Unfortunately, we are just the messengers, Professor. You have our employer's card. Please think about our offer, and we will get back with you. Or, you can call Mr. Raheem Nadat—the Egyptian High Consular of Science. That is his name and phone number on the business card. Enjoy your night, sir."

James still held the card in his hand as the men returned inside. He understood the science of DNA sequencing well. But he recognized the potential offshoots of the science, and its possible impact on society. He put the card in his cardholder and proceeded to re-enter the hall.

The program had just begun, and Marika looked up at him with a supportive smile when he reached their table and sat down next to her.

"You haven't eaten a thing...What did those guys want?" she whispered.

"I'll tell you later," he mumbled.

The key-note speaker was now being introduced, and he stepped to the podium amid avid applause from the assembled guests.

He talked about new scientific discoveries and their impact on modern life. He lauded the advent of the Internet and its role in accelerating the flow of information across vast physical and intellectual borders. He championed scientists for not allowing themselves to settle for the status quo, praising them for using their innate talents and skills to help make the world a better place.

After the speech, awards were given in a number of categories ranging from philanthropy to invention. James's name was called and he walked to the podium genteelly amidst applause and a standing ovation. He accepted his plaque, posed for pictures, and pulled out his five by seven, ensuring that he didn't leave anyone out. Lastly, he mentioned Marika and her steadfastness despite the obstacles they had faced together. He left the podium amidst another standing ovation, and a teary-eyed Marika welcomed him to his seat.

3

S *aturday morning in Chicago...so much to do, so little time*, James mused as he rolled over groggily on his side of the bed, while Marika slept. This was their last weekend in the Windy City. By this time next weekend, they'd be back in Tuskegee.

The phone rang, jarring the morning's stillness. And James blankly answered to the sound of a foreign accent.

"This is Ahmed Salih. Sorry to disturb you at home, Professor Hannibal. I got your number through the university. Did you think over our proposal?"

"No," James said perturbed that Salih had called his house unsolicited. "In fact, I hadn't thought anymore about it...What makes you guys want to clone an ancient pharaoh anyway? Don't we have enough things to think about in this world than wasting it on some far-out design like cloning a mummy? No. Forget it. I'm not interested," James said perturbed. "And don't call my house again," he shouted, abruptly slamming the phone.

"James. What's wrong...?" Marika asked startled, rising amidst the ruckus.

"They want me to clone a freakin' pharaoh, Marika. What is this world coming to? They want me to clone a freakin' pharaoh."

She got out of bed and walked around to his side. She sat down beside him and chuckled. "Clone an ancient pharaoh?"

He chortled. "A pharaoh, can you believe what they asked me to do? A pharaoh...I'm supposed to raise him from the dead," he chuckled again.

They both laughed deliriously at the thought of it. She laid her head on his shoulder, and they fell back on the bed losing it in laughter.

≈

Raheem Nadat combed his straight salt and pepper gray hair to the side, his usual part on the left side. Smiling, he acknowledged that he, indeed, epitomized the average Egyptian male. Westerners often reminded him of that fact. Many Arab men, across Arab countries, looked a lot like him, he realized. Perhaps it was the consistency of the region's gene pool. For the past thousand years, or so, Arabs had sealed their imprint on Egypt.

Meanwhile, he acknowledged the passing of the years, as he noted the subtle aging lines on his face. He was a young sixty, but sixty, nonetheless. The mirror didn't lie.

Yesterday, it seemed, he had been a boy on the streets of Cairo. And just as recently, it seemed, he had been a good student preparing to attend university in America. He turned from the dresser and walked over to the window overlooking the nearby newsstand, where the vendor hawked papers and magazines like a desperate worker ant amidst its unconcerned peers, all engrossed in their own assignments. The Egyptian people worked hard, but they never seemed to earn enough. The inheritors of a renowned culture, they were now relegated, in many ways, to a hand-to-mouth existence in the twenty-first century.

He turned soberly and walked over to his closet. Opening the door, he assessed his pick of Westernized suits, alongside his Egyptian wear. He had been taught, or rather indoctrinated as a young man, that the Western way was the way of sophistication and charm; and like his heroes on television and in the movies, he exhibited a debonair style polished through his years of international travel.

His only regret was that he had never married. His career, he admitted, had been his marriage. He'd almost made the commitment at one point, but it was a sore area in his life now. He didn't like to think about it. Frankly, no woman had ever taken the place of his ongoing affair with science and governance. He had envisaged a modern Egypt on the cutting edge of scientific research, with a populace that understood the benefits of scientific thinking. But alas, the conservative tide of fundamentalism had prevailed, and unfortunately, still held its sway over the masses, he mused. They were a good people, but too content for his taste, too pragmatic to recognize the benefits of planned growth and change within a society.

Raheem Nadat wanted his people to recognize, for-the-most part, that science was merely a series of controlled experiences that proved valid when reproduced under consistent criteria—that science had proved effective for Ancient Egypt. And that it had propelled the West ahead of the rest of the world today.

≈

Back in Tuskegee, everything was business as usual. Hannibal managed his university department, taught classes and conducted research, settling into his normal day-to-day routine. It had been several months since his Chicago trip, and he hadn't thought much more about the encounters with Ahmed Salih and Reshef Ottah. Then out of the blue, while retrieving a stray history textbook that had been left in the lab, he flipped open the pages to find pictures of ancient Egyptians—all white-looking Egyptians.

They looked nothing like the afro, cornrow-wearing, ebony-colored people he had seen on the tomb walls when he had visited many years ago as a college student. He looked closely at a picture characterized as Rameses II, also known as Rameses the Great. The text book had him depicted as lily white. He then walked over to his computer, sat down and pulled up more likenesses of Rameses the Great on the Internet. Mostly, he found only statues and busts. Finally, he pulled up sites of Nefertari, the wife whom Rameses called, "The Beautiful One." And there on the walls of her tomb was the likeness of her husband, the king—Rameses the Great—a black man. He explored the Internet more. There was Rameses's grandfather Seti, an undeniable black African on the tomb wall paintings.

Leaning back in his chair, he thought about what he already knew about Ancient Egypt. One, they had used black basalt rock in sculpturing lifelike figures of their pharaohs and nobles, while the Greeks and Romans—two millennia later—had used marble. Two, on the tomb wall paintings, the skin-tone of the people covered the spectrum, of color, from jet black, to chocolate, to cream colored—like many black people he knew so well.

He acknowledged he wasn't a scholar on Ancient Egypt. But he did know the images that had been perpetuated by Western culture were tainted. Granted, the Greeks had taken control of Egypt by 332 B.C. But the textbook displayed the Ancient Egyptians as exclusively white, of so-called Caucasian stock, throughout the country's history.

What would happen—he dared to think—if someone really did bring back a black pharaoh? For one thing, textbooks would have to correct their depictions of Ancient Egyptians, that's for sure, he realized. He reached across his desk and retrieved a copy of the Tuskegee student newspaper. He had noticed earlier something about a conference coming up in Cairo, Egypt. Yes, that was it—a conference on human biology, he mused, when he found the posting. He still had the business card of the Egyptian scientists in his cardholder.

THE EGYPTIAN DEPARTMENT OF SCIENCE & TECHNOLOGY, RAHEEM NADAT...He dialed the number.

"This is Professor James Hannibal. I'd like to speak with Mr. Raheem Nadat, please."

He had decided to look into the cloning issue, mostly out of curiosity. "Hello, Mr. Nadat. I'm Professor James Hannibal of Tuskegee University, in the United States—"

"Yes, Professor Hannibal. I have heard a lot about you," Nadat said at the other end of the line.

James continued: "I was offered a substantial sum of money, by two gentlemen claiming to represent you. Are you familiar with what I'm referring to?"

"Yes. Yes. Mr. Ahmed Salih and Reshef Ottah; but after their report, I didn't think I'd be hearing from you, Professor."

"Well, is the offer still open? I'm going to be attending a conference in Cairo in a few months and thought we might discuss the matter."

"Yes, I'd be delighted," Nadat said ecstatically.

James gave him the calendar dates for the conference and agreed to meet with him when he arrived. He knew his research merited representation at the event and felt it wouldn't be difficult to get on the presenters' list. With that, he explained that he had to work out the specifics, but assured Nadat he would be calling him back as soon as possible.

"Goodbye, sir," James said amazed that he had set in motion something he had barely dared to ponder.

He sat back in his chair and thought about what his decision might lead to. One thing was for certain; if he pulled it off, the world would never be the same—that was for sure.

Now, the issue was how he would explain things to Marika. He hated to keep things from her, but he'd already made up his mind to go to the conference in Egypt. It was slated for early December—so he would be returning home before the holidays. He'd explore the Egyptian offer more thoroughly while there. He knew he'd eventually have to tell her. So finally, to assuage his own mind, he decided to let the proverbial cat out of the bag.

So there he was, about to take her on a drive into the Tuskegee countryside. She liked taking rides into the rural terrain. They rode alongside cotton fields and passed by shotgun houses. In some parts, it seemed like they were still in the early twentieth century.

She put on one of her favorite oldie CD's by Marvin Gaye, and they grooved to the beat not talking much, just taking in the music and the scenery.

"You're thinking about the Egyptian offer, aren't you?" Marika asked out of the blue, catching James off guard. He was startled. She never ceased to amaze him with her penetrating insight.

He tightened his grip on the wheel, looked at her and simply nodded. The music continued to play, and they continued the drive not talking much, just enjoying their time together in the rustic countryside.

4

T he Pyramids at Giza formed the backdrop of the terrace window in James's suite at the Mena Hotel. The ancient necropolis was literally the hotel's front yard. The surrounding encroaching city was at the foot of the Pyramids—unlike postcard renderings—a shocking revelation for most tourists. But James had traveled to Egypt before and was long over this modern reality.

Jet lag was his concern at the moment. He had landed the night before but had barely been able to sleep. Egypt was seven hours ahead of Central Standard Time, and his body had simply decided not to cooperate with the time change.

Despite his preparation through sleep deprivation while still in the States, he was beginning to feel drowsy when it was time to get up. He arose anyway, though, his enthusiasm for exploring the exotic sights and sounds of the foreign land overriding his body's impulses to sleep.

The conference planners had selected the hotel because of its picturesque location, and since the presentations were to be held on site, the daily logistics were uncomplicated for the presenters. He would have the opportunity to give his talks, freshen up and then explore.

He dialed Raheem Nadat, and the affable Egyptian eagerly agreed to attend the first of Hannibal's presentations. James was slated to do three for the week. And following Monday's session, they'd decided to meet and discuss in detail Nadat's proposal.

Marika had stayed home. She had already taken off enough time from her job at a small public relations firm in Tuskegee. She had spent her vacation and additional time with James, while he was the visiting professor at Chicago State, earlier in the year. He would be in Cairo for only a week, anyway. And since it was the first week of December, he would return in time for the Christmas shopping season. The holiday would be spent with his family in Mississippi.

He walked over to the terrace door and opened it, deciding to forgo the air conditioning for the fresh morning breeze.

The Pyramids were every bit as awe inspiring as he'd remembered. The Great Pyramid soared some forty stories and covered thirteen acres. Already, lines of tourists were beginning to assemble at the edifice.

When he had checked in the night before, the desk clerk had mentioned that a courtesy copy of the English-language newspaper would be dropped off in the morning, so he opened the door and retrieved it.

The headline read: "REMAINS OF PHARAOH KHUFU FOUND VIA ELECTRONIC IMAGING DEVICE."

James could barely believe his eyes. On his first day in Cairo, they find the mummy of Khufu—the illustrious builder of the Great Pyramid. He stared at the paper in disbelief, as he sat down in a chair by the open terrace, and proceeded to read. It seemed that the imaging device worked through refracted sound. It had digitally decoded sound waves into video, revealing a facsimile of a hidden room discovered beneath the King's Chamber. Now, after over forty-five hundred years, the builder of the Great Pyramid of Giza's body had been found incredibly preserved.

The newspaper story explained that the "so-called King's Chamber had only been a veneer to fool thieves. And it had worked splendidly." The concealed lower room had held the true sarcophagus and additional priceless treasures, which had remained untouched until now. Grave robbers had apparently breached the upper-level, in antiquity, stole an abundance of gold and other precious items and left satisfied. An empty, broken granite sarcophagus on the upper floor had possibly served as a decoy resting place for the pharaoh. Whether it had ever actually held a body, or any other particulars, was unknown.

James showered and decided to order breakfast in, so he could work out his plans for the day and the coming week. He wanted to familiarize himself with his presentation room and look over the other research topics to see which ones he might attend as well.

His talks were scheduled for eleven AM on Monday, Wednesday and Friday. He would explain how the selenium, he used in his study, worked to stimulate the areas in the cell where memory is stored. And he would delineate how the color coding, he used in his research, matched all of the prior science community's findings of general organ color-coding. Japanese scientists had actually confirmed his studies, so he would provide summaries of their reports for the conference attendees.

Following his presentation on Monday, he would be chauffeured with Raheem Nadat to the Egyptian official's office in downtown Cairo and get a better understanding of the Egyptians' aims and goals concerning the cloning proposal.

He vowed to listen carefully to what the scientists were really interested in doing. After all, if they pulled it off, the pharaoh would be a living, sentient human being with desires and needs like any other individual—needs that should be protected.

The following day Hannibal presented his findings to a room of a hundred or so academic scholars. He utilized a PowerPoint presentation to show graphically the accuracy of his color-coding technique; and underscored how the area which represents the brain becomes charged when selenium is added. He displayed the Japanese findings on how various animals performed in memory tests—with and without the selenium superimposed into their cellular memory. The selenium acted as a stimulant, activating recall. Non-use of the element appeared to render the animal oblivious to prior experiences.

James was satisfied with how his presentation had gone. He had learned early on as a research scientist that the more simplistic findings could be presented—the more easily they could be diffused into the general culture of the scientific academy and society-at-large.

Raheem Nadat seemed to have retained the findings well. He walked up to James and introduced himself and even began to elaborate on the research. James could tell Nadat had given the study a lot of thought—probably for quite some time.

Nadat looked just like his pictures on the Internet; broad-shouldered, graying hair, a kindly sort. He exhibited a generosity of spirit that conveyed that he was trustworthy, and Hannibal could tell that he loved his country and its history. All told, James's instincts said that Nadat was someone he could work with.

Meanwhile, Nadat was apparently assessing James as well. "You look just like your pictures, Professor Hannibal. Good to meet you."

"The pleasure is mine," James replied.

Nadat escorted the American scientist out of the hotel into the waiting limousine.

"Have you seen this story, yet?" he asked James, handing him a newspaper as they settled in the car.

"Yes, I read it this morning," James answered.

Nadat continued with a gleam in his eyes. "There are over a hundred pyramids scattered throughout Egypt, yet Allah has allowed us to find the builder of the crown jewel right here in Cairo—and at this juncture in history."

James looked out at the Great Pyramid. It was now closed to tourists. What he had seen from his hotel window earlier were scientists, workers, and security personnel, not tourists.

The limousine headed away from the necropolis east into Cairo. The landscape was like no other. James marveled at the contrast of desert and palm-tree-shrouded terrain—at the uniqueness of the Egyptian topography. It was a river oasis, cut through the desert, creating an ideal lifeline for arguably the most fascinating ancient civilization in the world.

"I suppose you wonder why we want to clone a pharaoh, eh professor?" Nadat asked, bringing him out of his thoughts.

"I'm sure you have rational reasons," James replied. "But, yes, I *would* be interested in hearing them," he said unassumingly.

"Egypt has lost her bearings as a great nation," Nadat said. "The people view her as a has been—like an old man with stories of his youth, but flaccid in his actions today."

"I see," James nodded knowingly, in a tone that invited Nadat to continue.

"With a great pharaoh to look to, we can retain the fervor of our land and regain our stature in the community of nations."

They rode for awhile without speaking. Soon, the limousine was pulling in front of Nadat's office. The chauffeur got out and opened the door letting the men exit.

They entered the building and took the elevator to Nadat's floor and stepped off into a small lobby area walking just a few feet to the left before entering Nadat's suite. It served as the nerve center of several other offices that could be entered from the corridor also. His secretary looked up with an amiable smile and warm brown eyes. She wore the hijab, the Muslim head scarf, and khamar, an Islamic upper garment for women.

"Hello Anat, this is Professor James Hannibal from the United States. We'll be in my office...hold the phone calls, please," Nadat said. He then spoke momentarily in Arabic, before heading into his office and closing the door behind them.

His classically decorated office touted highly polished mahogany furniture accented by executive brown leather chairs. Numerous awards and plaques adorned the walls along with a picture of him shaking hands with the Egyptian president.

"Please be seated," Professor Hannibal, Nadat gestured, walking around to his side of the desk. "Anat, could you bring tea, please?" he said into the intercom.

Leaning back in his chair, Nadat continued: "Tell me about the amniotic gestation chamber that is used for embryos, Professor Hannibal?"

James had anticipated in-depth discussions about the chamber. It indeed had the potential of revolutionizing their plans.

"Well, I gather, Mr. Nadat, that you are aware that the Japanese used the gestation device when they corroborated my research?"

"Yes, yes. Please call me Raheem," Nadat interjected.

James nodded and continued. "Dr. Nailah Ali, a Harvard School of Medicine classmate of mine, who happens to be Egyptian by the way, introduced me to the gestation chamber a few years ago. The unit was designed initially to save the lives of embryos that had difficulty surviving in their mothers' wombs. Although it has not caught on globally yet, it is slowly emerging as the solution for women plagued with miscarriages. They simply transfer their otherwise healthy embryos into the chamber. Medical practitioners then monitor the babies to full term. Dr. Ali, a pediatrician by training, has worked with the developers of the chamber since its inception over a decade ago.

"A few years ago," he continued, "she had consulted with researchers who studied animals that required longer gestation periods than humans. So when the Japanese informed me that they were set to conduct research that might corroborate my findings on memory prints, Nailah's expertise came to mind."

Anat entered with a silver heirloom-looking teapot on a matching silver tray and summarily began to pour both of the men a cup.

"Sugar, Professor Hannibal?" Nadat asked as she poured.

"Just one cube, thank you," James said.

"Of course," Nadat nodded graciously.

Anat walked over to James presenting him his tea and then brought Nadat a cup.

"Professor Hannibal, we got wind of your research and realized you are the one scientist who has the specialized skills and background necessary to carry out our wishes," Nadat said, getting back to business.

"We have also heard that you consulted with the Japanese on the food industry's market-place acceleration processing of food-source animals, which speeds up their maturation process."

James modified Nadat's observation. "Not just me, Raheem. As a result of the food industry's breakthroughs, the science academy, in many Western countries, has been adopting techniques that direct cells to copy the rapid growth common for embryos and fetuses to continue until we signal them to shut off. I talked with the Japanese because they utilized the process in their study with amazing results."

Nervously, Nadat asked: "So this will allow us, in our case, to maintain an accelerated gestation into adulthood for our pharaoh?"

"I see no reason why not, Raheem. We could feasibly gestate from embryonic to adult stage in a matter of months. We couldn't have done this a few years ago, but the technology just keeps getting better."

"Yes. It's really incredible how fast science is moving," Nadat concurred, leaning forward. "It was just at the dawn of the twenty-first century—not many years ago, if you think about it—that they cloned Dolly the lamb."

They talked about the laws for and against cloning throughout the world; how pork farmers were already reproducing prized pigs through the science and channeling them into the food supply; how agriculturalists had been the first practitioners of genetic engineering through cross pollination, cross germination and pruning centuries ago.

"And you, Professor," Nadat asked candidly—looking James squarely in the eyes. "Why did *you* suddenly become interested in this project?"

"Frankly, Raheem," James said maintaining Nadat's gaze. "The rich heritage of the black man has been stolen by Western culture, which basks in our legacy as if it's its own. To rationalize the slave trade and colonialism, two thousand years of our heritage was usurped—we were whitewashed out of history. But the paintings on those tomb walls tell me a different story."

"Enough said," Nadat nodded knowingly, extending his hand for a handshake. "Welcome back, brother."

5

The snow fell on rural Mississippi uncharacteristically like one would expect of a Minnesota snowfall. The fluffy-blanketed countryside exhibited post-card-like charm.

Children rushed out to salvage a snowman out of what would be melted in a few days. And big snow plows hurried down the roads clearing away the slippery slush.

James and Marika were home to see his folks in Blackston. His brother, Mack, was there, and his sister, Candace, had driven up from Orlando, Florida, with her children.

The grownups sat in the living room around the fireplace drinking eggnog and reminiscing about their growing-up years. They also discussed their current lives and dreams. But James shied away from mentioning his current research.

His younger brother, Mack, was doing well. He had started his own catfish farming business up state in Sardis, Mississippi, and had become rather well off, the family was oft to say. Never the scholar, that James was, he had seen a niche in the freshwater fish-market and never looked back.

His wife Saundra was from Sardis, and he had been fortunate to marry into land. She had inherited lots of acreage that had been used for cotton in earlier years, but neither of them had a mind for traditional agriculture. They had, instead, researched the freshwater and farm-raised fish market, resulting in his putting all of his energies into the business, while she taught school.

She had remained at home for the holidays with her family and their two boys, who were engaged in basketball tournaments during the Christmas break.

Marika, meanwhile, had begun to reveal a coolness concerning James's Egyptian plans. She had initially played the role of dutiful wife, but now she was making it clear that she didn't go for his research one iota. And when he'd mentioned that they might have to stay in Egypt for a couple of years, she had lost it.

Hands on her hips, letting her backbone slip, was how James had characterized it to Mack. Meanwhile, his dad and mom upon hearing he was considering moving to Egypt for two or more years supported his wife. He knew he didn't have a chance on God's green earth when those two teamed up against him, so he didn't even try for a defense. He simply remained polite and looked at the big picture; he'd learned to pick his battles wisely. Furthermore, he wouldn't dare tell what the research was about, even if he were at liberty to do so, which further exacerbated the situation.

"James, what's gotten into you?" his father asked, as he pulled the tempered-glass screen from the fireplace to add wood. "You're living a good life, got a committed wife...and a good position over there at Tuskegee," he said, sparks flickering from the logs as he prodded the poke iron into the flames. "What's this about going off to Egypt for two years? For what?" He turned looking at James squarely, now that he had finished.

James knew, even if he could, that it was no use trying to explain his research to his father. Any explanation would leave him dead in the water. His mom and dad had very definite beliefs about certain things, and he knew there was no use going there with them. Marika, meanwhile, felt he and the Egyptians were going too far; that they were stepping on sacred boundaries. So in the midst of such an atmosphere, James didn't have much he could elaborate on. His wife's attitude in the last week had gone from anger, to sour, to total shutdown.

Mack and Candace, on the other hand appeared objective not rushing to conclusions. They were generally supportive of James's decisions. But as not to offend Marika, they withheld any opinions that veered from neutrality.

"You two certainly know how to live," Mack said, to the both of them, trying to ease the tension. He sat in the matching chair to Marika's on the opposite end of the couch from her. It was clear she was not in a good mood, but he pretended not to notice.

Candace, for the most part, was easy going and believed in live and let live. She had lost her husband, Jamaal, in a boating accident nearly a year ago. This was her first Christmas without him. They had been together for twenty-two years, and the ordeal had taken its toll on her. She wasn't of the mind set to intervene in the affairs of others anyway.

She sat in a chair positioned near the Christmas tree, in earshot of everyone but just far enough away to tune out when she felt like it. She and Jamaal had been close, and now she was left with the challenge of carving out a new life for herself and their three kids. Life had slowly mellowed her. She had been pretty headstrong as a teenager for awhile, but those were the days when she was just trying to find herself, Mrs. Hannibal often said.

Mom, as excited as ever that everyone was home, rose cheerfully from the couch to check on the turkey. She always cooked it last so that it would be fresh out of the oven when dinner was served. She had worked full time as a secondary school counselor and raised her family without missing a beat. It was her nature to be efficient, warm and nurturing.

Meanwhile, as intelligent as his father was, James Hannibal II had not been able to be all he could be in life. He had the smarts of an engineer, but had only risen to the level of a building engineer. James thought about the military recruiting slogan often flashed on TV—"Be All You Can Be." That reality had not been an option for his dad. The society in his generation, in Blackston, had no room for progressive Coloreds, as they had been called back then. They only left room for blacks to work as preachers or teachers, in the white-collar world. And blue-collar jobs were generally at the mercy of the economy. His dad had eventually settled for a position as the head high school janitor, but not without considerable assaults to his ego.

His wife was one of the school counselors across town, and he forever felt the sting of people's shallow minded social-class comparisons whenever the question of his and her professions arose. On a couple of attempts he had tried to go into business for himself, but the marketplace in rural Mississippi just wasn't there for an upstart black businessman. He had started a clothing store once, but could never get the lowest wholesale prices for clothes, since he couldn't afford to buy in large enough bulk. His futile attempt in the restaurant business hadn't gone well, either. He simply didn't have the natural inclination needed for food service. He wasn't a cook, and the only help he could keep for any length of time were short order cooks, who were generally unskilled laborers in reality—and the small town folks knew this. Thus, James II's Soul Food Diner went down ignominiously. He'd been bruised but not defeated, he always said. Meanwhile, he'd joined wholeheartedly in the civil rights movement and worked to create better opportunities for his children.

His generation had knocked down segregation in public accommodations in the United States. The harsh black versus white restroom facilities and white's only hotels were a thing of the past. He took pride in the role he had played in that critical era of American history. He had fearlessly led-up registration drives and had been one of the first black men to vote in the county. And despite having had only a high school education, he could communicate with the best of them. He had always chalked it up to a family gene. His father, James Hannibal I, had been a preacher and a fiery spokesperson in the county in his own right.

So, Professor James Hannibal III chalked up *his* current endeavor as a continuation of service for the public good. He had just three months to assemble a team for his Egyptian project. He decided to enjoy this time with his family while he could, despite Marika's mood—he was about to be a very busy man.

6

Raheem Nadat leaned forward at his desk, stroked his goatee, and sighed. He was pondering the potential fall out of the media and, subsequently, the populace upon learning of his department's attempts to clone a cell from Pharaoh Khufu's mummified remains. After all, Why not begin with Khufu? he figured. He would be a more interesting figure than even Rameses the Great. Meanwhile, not only would he receive flak from the world scientific community, but religious leaders and governments, fearful of the repercussions, would also challenge the research.

It had been four months since his first meeting with Professor James Hannibal III. He was admittedly impressed with the geneticist's natural grasp for the science of cloning. The professor was, frankly, tailor made it seemed to head the off-the-beaten-path scientific breakthrough. An African American and a key researcher on the Human Genome Project, the Harvard School of Medicine alum and professor of genetics at the renowned Tuskegee University was highly respected in his field.

Nadat reflected on how he himself had worked in the Egyptian scientific bureaucracy for most of his adult life; how now he was graying and considering the prospects of retirement. That's why he'd decided to reach beyond the tried and true. How could he not? he acknowledged. This was the chance of a lifetime. Songs and tales had been written throughout Egyptian history about the great Khnum-Khufwy, more commonly known as Khufu—or Cheops, by the Greeks.

Meanwhile, the voice of his secretary on his intercom beckoned.

"Raheem? Professor Hannibal is here to see you."

"Thank you, Anat," send him in, please.

Hannibal entered and shook hands with Nadat in a warm grasp. They were becoming fast friends. As he had expected, he and Raheem worked well together. Nadat gestured for James to take a seat and anxiously returned to his in anticipation of the professor's report. The research of a lifetime had begun:

"We simply placed the pharaoh's DNA into the empty nucleus of an irradiated human egg, which became the host for Khufu's genetic material," James explained. "The irradiation kills off the foreign DNA, as you know, leaving the stripped ovum as the perfect home for nature to take its course. So, we positioned the egg within the uterine cavity of the gestation chamber, and it quickly began to develop as we expected," James pointed out.

"How long will it take to complete the process, Professor Hannibal?" Nadat asked.

"Well, the first nine months of the birth cycle will be pretty normal. But the challenge will be to nurture him in the gestation tank for an additional twenty-seven months, to ensure his cellular age matches the age he had attained when he died.

"As you're aware, Raheem, earlier studies of animal clones taught us that the cells perform best if the subject is allowed to forestall consciousness until it—he in this case—reaches the maturity level he had attained at death. Otherwise, it seems an incongruity in the cell's kinetic output and the body's physical age results in unaccounted for cellular breakdowns, fostering disease."

Nadat twiddling a pencil interjected: "Similar to the Dolly sheep-clone case."

"Exactly. Dolly was a newly born lamb with a mature sheep's cells. And biologically that doesn't work well in some species," James explained.

"So will it—he—be a clone? Or will *this* be Khufu?" Nadat stammered.

"In every way," Raheem, "this will be the pharaoh, Khufu. You've read my studies which indicate that each cell contains a complete blue-print of human memory in the nucleus. By turning this segment of the cell on at physical maturity, the organism returns to the conscious state it had attained before it shutoff at death. So, this will be the authentic pharaoh, with the exception that his body will be as new as a baby; no war wounds; no scars—a physically perfect adult."

The thought of meeting Khufu face to face brought chills down Nadat's spine. What tales might he hear from the distant past? What new insights might be learned about the ancients? he wondered.

James was also moved by the possibilities of meeting Pharaoh Khufu. He remembered the first time he had visited Egypt, as a college student, and noted with awe the ebony-skinned kinky-haired Egyptians on the tomb wall paintings; so unlike anything he'd been taught in America's schools— *beautiful, classical and black African.*

What had possessed them to leave such lucid, colorful renderings within their tombs? he wondered. Meanwhile, he shuddered to realize that had they not, their memory might have been lost forever. But now, he had a chance to make the link complete—to perhaps talk with Khufu—to grant this great African's wish for a veritable afterlife.

James reflected back to the moment he realized the DNA of Khufu would, in fact, clone. Now, here he was in the midst of a historic nexus.

"So, the embryo is nearly one-month-old? When can I see it?" Nadat asked eagerly.

"Well, certainly *you* can drop in, Raheem, whenever you'd like. But overall, we're limiting visits to the research lab in the immediate future, because this is such a tenuous time in the study. But how about we set up an inspection for a couple of your staff within a month when it...," he said, clearing his throat, "will be closer to fetus stage?"

"Yes, that sounds reasonable, professor."

James realized he was now walking on uncharted terrain. After nearly two decades of research in genetics, he was finding that the deeper he looked, the more there was to discover. And to think that they had a healthy embryo already. No, he would not allow visitors into the laboratory just yet. A truly spectacular, yet tenuous, miracle was in the making.

Meanwhile, he thought about the apparent foresight of the Ancient Egyptians. *They were on to something*, he mused. They believed by preserving their bodies, they'd be able to use them in the afterlife. Maybe they knew something about eternity that we're just beginning to ponder, he marveled.

7

J ames left Nadat's office and joined the bustling tapestry of downtown Cairo; a smorgasbord of twenty-first century modernity amidst medieval timelessness. People dressed in Western clothes pressed among others in ages-old galabayyas, the flowing gown-like attire. Donkey-drawn wooden-wheeled carts plodded along in traffic oblivious, it seemed, to the horns of impatient automobiles.

James enjoyed the exotic sights and sounds of this city. In fact, it was one of the cities he most enjoyed in the world. He had become an accomplished international traveler over the years. In addition to Egypt, he had visited West Africa's Ghana, and Nigeria; Europe, where he had spent time in Britain and France. And in the Americas—Canada, Mexico and the Caribbean had been frequent destinations.

He'd decided to make up to Marika by taking her to Asia and the Pacific Rim when the project was completed. She had remained in the States and, frankly, he was concerned about the state of his marriage.

He pointed to the curb Egyptian style to hail a taxi and hopped into the front seat when one of the myriad of black and white fiat cabs pulled up, horn honking. Drivers often needed passenger space to pick up other riders who might be going in the same direction, so he followed the local custom by getting up front. *When in Egypt do as the Egyptians*, he quipped to himself.

"The American University, please," he said to the galabayya and skull-cap clad cabbie.

"The Amerrikkan Universetee," the driver responded tautly as he pulled into the slow-moving traffic.

The strong accent was a signal to Hannibal that the cabbie likely didn't speak English well. Thus, he braced himself for a psychological duel. Sometimes the operators would attempt to use their lack of proficient English, or better, *his* inability to speak Arabic, as a leeway to overcharge a foreigner. Although the taxis had meters, the cabbies seldom used them because the government-set rates were much too low for them to make a reasonable living.

James, meanwhile, knew he'd have to settle the score early concerning the price; otherwise the driver might concoct some outrageous fee at the end of the journey. So he immediately began his interrogation.

"How much will the trip cost?"

"My English is little," the driver said with question marks in his eyes, as if he didn't have a clue what James had asked.

"How much will it cost me?" James repeated glumly, reaching into his pocket pulling out a modest roll of ten, twenty and fifty-pound notes. Twenty pounds is three or four U.S. dollars James calculated to himself.

"Oh! eighty pounds for you, sir," the driver responded.

James looked at him dryly: "Fifty pounds."

"Seventy-five pounds low as can go," the driver said haltingly, with an air that he was at his limit in price talks.

James had read enough tourist manuals to realize that seventy-five pounds was still a little too high. Egyptians, as part of their culture, had made the ancient practice of negotiations into an art. They always began high in hopes of catching the straight shooter, who might give them the first price asked for.

"Fifty pounds," James said succinctly, with an air of finality. And since they still hadn't gone far in the bumper-to-bumper traffic he feigned preparation to bail.

"For you, fifty-five pounds," the driver said quickly in his Egyptian accent, realizing he might lose a decent fare.

"Okay, fifty-five pounds," James agreed satisfied, as he wiped his perspiring brow with a handkerchief, leaning back in the seat to relax.

Today would be his first fencing-match workout with his long-time friend and confidant, Professor Brooks Edwards. He hadn't seen Edwards since Chicago.

A tenured professor on the staff of Fisk University Medical School, Edwards had jumped at the opportunity to join James in such a ground-breaking undertaking. He and his wife, Jheri, had recently divorced, so he also saw the endeavor as a chance to get away for awhile as he settled into his new solo lifestyle. The dissolution of their marriage had come as a shock to James and those who knew them. The two had always been able to work through things it seemed. Despite the unfortunate impetus, however, he was glad Brooks was there with him.

They'd made plans to meet twice a week at the university facilities to ensure they engaged in a regular exercise regimen. While the two had never sparred with each other, Hannibal did have the advantage, since he had learned the art several years before he had recommended it to Edwards. James knew he'd be in for a competitive dual, though, since Edwards was a natural warrior. By nature, the burly professor was relentless in any competitive endeavor and didn't take losing easily.

James, meanwhile, admitted that he himself was more of a tactician. He picked his moments, then flurried for quick points.

He settled back more comfortably in the cab and thought about what was in store for his life in North Africa for the next thirty-six months or so. The Egyptian government had provided him with a nice house in the affluent district of Zamalek and had laid out the red carpet in regards to his lab west of Cairo, which had additional sleeping quarters for him and his staff.

But moving to Egypt was a steep price to pay in his personal life, he admitted. His marriage was decidedly on the rocks. Hopefully, he and Marika wouldn't end up like Edwards and Jheri, he mused.

Marika had been skeptical about his research early on, and as he'd gotten more involved in his preparation for Cairo, she'd drifted further and further away. He looked blankly out the taxi window toward the urban sprawl of some twenty million people, but his personal life commanded his thoughts now.

She had decided to remain in the U.S. Perhaps she would follow later after she'd ironed out her feelings. Meanwhile, James tried to assess what might have been done to keep the relationship stronger. A miscarriage early in the union certainly hadn't helped. And now, she felt her biological clock was running down. They had agreed to hold off having children following the miscarriage—but now, he wondered if they'd waited too long. For her, later might be too late. Yet his ongoing research was so controversial, she feared the prospects of carrying a child.

He could feel his pulse quicken as he thought about it, now.

I've backed you in everything you've done, James, she'd said, tears streaming down her pretty cheeks—her mascara-smudged brown eyes peering deeply into his from between exotic cornrow tresses.

But I just can't carry a child under these conditions. The media frenzy that will follow this cloning research is more than I can handle right now.

At age thirty-nine, she was even more beautiful than she'd been two decades earlier when they'd met in Chicago; she, a junior at Columbia College, and he, a senior in pre-med at DePaul. They'd hit it off instantly and had been like peas in a pod ever since—until now. And she had helped him, with her degree in mass communications, to better publicize his research and become well known in the science academy. Her only shortcoming was that she could be emotionally volatile at times. He had learned in medical school that, that was just some women's inherent malady each month. But he had to admit that it was hard to live with.

She had tried to get better at restraining herself, though. Maybe a break would do them good. And at least he did trust her. She had come from a good family; no tradition of infidelity that he was aware of. Her mother and father had been married for forty-seven years. They were grounded, church-going folk. Maybe their strengths would rub off on her more, in time. For the most part, she'd proven to be all he needed or desired in a wife. She was culturally attuned, statuesque and emotionally available—most of the time, at least. She was simply being pulled in two directions at that point, and he understood that, because he wanted children too.

Meanwhile, his research had taken on a life of its own— something beyond perceptible human reasoning. It was as if his experiment had unfolded like some cosmic puzzle that urged him to look deeper. And now, he knew there was no turning back. The genie had been let out of the bottle, and he was obligated to see the process through.

"You are Amerrikkan?" the driver asked, bringing him back to the present.

"Yes," James responded, focusing on the driver again, whose big hands gripped the steering wheel as if they were just as comfortable handling a horse-drawn carriage. He was just being friendly, so James returned the gesture, "You from Cairo?"

The driver simply laughed, nodding his head. But James knew that was about the extent of his English. The Cairenes were just like that, paradoxically friendly and accommodating to tourists, yet formidable when it came to daily money matters. But he understood. The weekly income of the people was far less than that of the average tourist. They did have to survive.

The taxi was now pulling in front of the university campus where Edwards was standing near the steps of a building talking with a group of students. James paid the agreed upon fare and tipped the driver a twenty-pound note. He'd decided to ensure the driver still got the seventy-five pounds he'd asked for.

"*A salome alaikum*," peace be unto you, he said as he got out.

"*Wa laikum salome*," and peace be unto you, the driver said nodding with a broad smile before he sped away.

"James," Brooks waved. He was apparently in an animated discussion with the students. "They're trying to ascertain whether Brother Malcolm or Martin King's strategy was best during the civil rights movement back home," he said as James approached. "Share with us, my brotha."

"What's up, man?" James said greeting Brooks with a shoulder-level high five, maintaining it in a clasp and smiling knowingly at his good friend. "I'd say both of them were effective," he began, eyeing the group for their response. Everyone quieted, waiting to hear more.

"You see, Malcolm and groups like the Black Panthers were the alternative to the peace movement. It was a matter of deal with them, or deal with us. Dr. King was the rational voice," he explained, now focusing in on the students individually; three Arab-looking guys and two Anglo females. "The two civil rights leaders actually played off each other."

"But don't you think Malcolm X had a point when he said, 'By any means necessary?'" one of the guys asked, straightening his sunglasses as he awaited a response.

"Oh, no question about it, the man on the street was ready for some redress to the second-class-citizenship issue, and Malcolm hit home with the issues for many of them."

A horn tooted from a car that was pulling up. It was apparently the students' ride. "Hey, see ya," they chimed merrily. "Maybe we'll talk with you guys later," the guy who had asked the question said as they made their way to the car.

James and Edwards waved goodbye and headed towards the fencing gallery. They entered to the clang of metal swords as men, and a few women, in white uniforms and dark wire screen-protection masks, parried and thrust foils, epees, and sabers in the ages-old art of sword fighting.

"Fencing began here in Egypt," Edwards pointed out, as they made their way past a few rows of fencers being trained by coaches, while others were sparring in twos.

"Really? I didn't know that," James said surprised.

"Yeah, there's a relief at the temple of Madinat Habu in Luxor that shows black brothas with helmets covering their ears and swords with the tips blunted for sparring."

"One can never stop learning about this land. Incredible," James said.

He thought gloomily about all of his years in America's schools and not a whimper had been taught about black Egypt. America purposely marginalized blacks not only in the world's eyes but in our own eyes, he thought begrudgingly.

They got their equipment, changed and headed to their sparring area. James had worked out a deal with the facilities manager that provided use of a private gallery adjacent to the large gym. They had their very own piste to spar on. It was a six- and-a-half-foot wide by forty-five foot long strip where they could duel unencumbered.

James had picked up the sport while in medical school at Harvard. Fencing provided excellent cardiovascular exercise, and it satisfied his competitive nature.

Edwards had decided to try the sport after James had informed him of its health benefits and the relative ease at becoming proficient at it, compared to a sport like golf. At fifty-three Edwards was in excellent condition, and he credited his commitment in part to fencing as an exercise regimen.

They saluted with slight nods of the head, put on their masks and faced each other in the on-guard position; legs outstretched and slightly bent, while the left arm formed a right angle to the rear. They then crossed their foils which echoed a metallic sound throughout the room. James could tell by the feel of Edwards's blade that he was in for a duel. There was a certain firmness to it that signaled determination.

Edwards immediately lunged in quarte, but James parried in tierce and double feigned before responding with a quarte thrust, which ended just short of its mark. Edwards came back with a reposte in prime trying effusively to disengage James's foil, but James held on while retreating, waiting for an opening to reposte in time.

To James, fencing was a science. He would shut out all distractions and begin to flow, parrying impeccably and lunging in an instinctive display of the technician that he was. Edwards, meanwhile, had one thing in mind and that was winning, which forced James to utilize every tactic he had learned in his years of training.

They were both purists and followed the straight-line format of sport fencing, which consisted of advancing and retreating rather than the circular motions that occurred in true sword duels.

By now, they were both breathing heavily, but equally gratified that their opponent had not scored a point yet, while aware that the inevitable would soon occur. One of them would exploit an error or the other through fatigue, allow an opening. Edwards lunged, provoking James to perform a counter double—his foil brilliantly encircling his opponent's in a tight curl, finishing in a lightning thrust to Edwards's lower rib cage. "*Touché*," James chimed.

They returned to the on-guard position and resumed the bout trading thrusts and parries until they were both sweating profusely despite the air-conditioned room. Finally, Edwards's slashing in prime dislodged James's foil, allowing him to score on his disarmed opponent. Later, their accuracy began to wane as they both became winded and their thrusts fell short. The all-out exertion was taking its toll.

"*No mas*," Edwards said at last, taking off his mask, he'd had enough for one day.

"I second...the motion," James breathed heavily, cupping his hands on his knees. "It'll be awhile before we get into really good shape," he sighed, taking off his mask. "Believe it or not, that was a forty-five minute workout."

"How time flies when you're having fun," Edwards said gasping for breath.

≈

The laboratory facilities the Egyptian government provided James matched his requirements perfectly. And he was satisfied that all was going according to schedule. He had handpicked his three staff members and at least three other medical professionals provided by Nadat's office would be integrated into the team as the need arose. He was further comforted by his staff's familiarity with his work, aims and research history.

His cohort, Brooks Edwards, had logged in many hours in cardiovascular research and practice. In addition, the two long-time friends could work together for hours without uttering a word, totally comfortable in each other's presence. Edwards's job was to monitor the respiratory levels, heart rate and general health of the clone.

Meanwhile, Dr. Nailah Ali, the Harvard School of Medicine classmate of James's, was a pediatrician and an expert on the gestation chamber.

She was intimately familiar with the unit and had overseen various births utilizing the mechanism. In addition, she was a native of Aswan, in Upper Egypt, and was personally familiar with the local culture; assets that would prove invaluable in the volatile mine field of public opinion that would inevitably await them.

His executive assistant, Felicia Maxwell, meanwhile, was a nursing student from Chicago State University, in the Windy

City. She had been recommended by an old friend. The cheerful twenty-five-year-old was responsible for the smooth day-to-day operations of the research facility. She was detail oriented and possessed the basic medical knowledge necessary to assist the team in a general capacity. The staff had nicknamed her Maxie. Now gestating, the embryo was healthy and growing rapidly.

"How're the vital signs, Brooks?"

"Blood pressure's normal, James," Edwards replied, clipboard in hand and peering at the embryo through the clear glass of the chamber, along with James and Ali.

"The chamber is doing everything it's designed to do," Ali said in her truncated Egyptian accent. "It's a healthy embryo, that's for sure."

"As healthy as any I've ever seen," Edwards chimed in.

They all basked in the miracle that was unfolding before them.

"We're on the brink of introducing the world to a whole new paradigm," James opined in almost speech-like fashion. "The increase of our collective knowledge about the past will be phenomenal. For Khufu, it will be literal time travel."

"That's for sure," Edwards said, his head nodding in agreement, and wonder. "It'll probably seem to him like he just closed his eyes, but he'll open them in the twenty-first century."

While James marveled at the embryo, he also weighed the problem areas that would inevitably crop up for the reborn pharaoh. He would have the knowledge-base of a man from the twenty-sixth century B. C., yet he would encounter jet planes, television and cell phones. "He'll probably think we're the gods," James surmised. "He spent his entire life preparing to meet them...we'll need to bring him along slowly."

Ali agreed. "Perhaps we should construct his initial surroundings like his tomb was designed. That might help in his transition of understanding who we are," she suggested.

"Good point, Nailah," James nodded. "Initially, he won't be able to communicate with us—we'll need to have Raheem bring in specialists in Old Kingdom hieroglyphics and religion to formulate what we'll say to him. I'll have Maxie begin working on that now."

8

The crème-colored young woman in the light blue SUV maneuvered the Cairo traffic like a veteran of the legendary congested streets. Felicia Maxwell had learned to drive on the busy avenues of Chicago and enjoyed the challenge of navigating Egypt's crowded thoroughfares.

She was happy with herself and realized she was fortunate to be living the lifestyle she had always envisioned. She had come a long way from her lower-middle-class upbringing on Chicago's South Side—she was "Livin' large in Cairo," she mused out loud, snapping her fingers while rocking her head to the beat of the music from the CD player. Meanwhile, she turned up the volume and sang along with one of her favorite singers Whitney Houston, belting out the lyrics like a miming disc jockey on urban contemporary radio. The professor would be leaving his meeting at the Ministry of Science in just moments, and with only a few blocks to go, she felt she had managed her time well.

The research center was only thirty minutes away in mid-morning traffic, and the drive had become routine for her.

Outside the SUV, Cairo was bustling as usual, so much of the old interspersed with the new. A mule-drawn wagon with two men on board clanged out-of-step, it seemed, beside her automobile in the bumper-to-bumper traffic. Here and there a Muslim woman was dressed in all black, enshrouded in a burqa, a full-length covering from head to toe, with only an opening for the eyes. Maxie could not imagine living under the constraints imposed on some Arabic women. She was young, single and free—American style. And she liked it that way.

Street vendors were everywhere. And in Cairo, there appeared to be no traffic rules. Cars trudged on despite red lights, and mules and donkeys often became stubborn without warning. But she made it with time to spare, and a familiar concierge of the building pointed her to a good parking spot.

"*Shukran*" thank you, she said through the open SUV window in Arabic, giving a thumbs-up as she pulled in front of the building. She was glad she had purchased an English-Arabic dictionary; that helped her to communicate somewhat in the language. She put the vehicle in park and reached into her purse to give the concierge a tip as he approached her. This executed with a discreet backward turning of the hand, money tightly folded—the expected way of handling such transactions in Egypt.

"Lady, lady," a voice rang out, as a man, unshaven but friendly, poked a handful of dates from his fruit cart into her window. "The best dates in Egypt. Try one."

"*La shukran, la shukran*," no thanks, she managed to say quickly, pressing the automatic window button to discourage further negotiation attempts. She hadn't meant to be mean, but experience had shown her that she had to be firm with the many street vendors. They would usually attempt to wear a person down. And despite her wish to help a persistent salesman, she had learned to be final when necessary.

Meanwhile, she thought about the here and there media reports concerning Americans working with Egyptians to clone a cell from the DNA of an ancient pharaoh. The stories had missed the mark for the most part, but they had continued to resurface anyway. The government of Egypt had refused to comment on the story and not much had been made of it in Cairo.

Thus, things remained relatively quiet in the huge third-world metropolis. In the past month, there had been one small protest outside the Ministry of Science building, but it had been quelled quickly by police, and nothing else had been noted publicly in the aftermath. Raheem Nadat, meanwhile, seemed quite secure in his job; and with support from the government to stay the course, he labeled the media accounts as Western sensationalism.

"What have I gotten myself into?" Maxie said quietly.

Finally, Dr. Hannibal arrived, and she steered the SUV back into traffic and headed towards the research facility. They didn't talk much during their drives, as he was often preoccupied with notes on the many issues and decisions he was faced with. So as usual, she quietly tuned the radio to the English-speaking news station he enjoyed. Maxie, meanwhile, studied the ancient landscape as she drove and only said something when she was certain he was disposed to talk.

They traveled west, crossed over the Nile and headed up the road leading toward the laboratory. Up ahead, she could see the Pyramids on the horizon. She had visited the structures over a year ago, now, and still marveled at how the massive tombs evoked feelings of awe in her. She made herself a promise that she'd ask Dr. Ali about accompanying her on a trip up river soon, to Luxor. There, she would visit the Valleys of the Kings and Queens, where she could see some of the Theban sites. Luxor was located in what was called Thebes in ancient times, the capital during the New Kingdom. Since Ali had grown up in the area, she would probably serve as the best tour guide one could ever find, Maxie figured.

"What's your take on the *Time* magazine article concerning our research?" James asked, matter-of-factly, bringing her out of her thoughts.

"Well, it wuz amazing how much the writer nu," she answered in her cheerful Chicago accent. "They know we're here, they're just a little inaccurate concerning the dee-tails. They seem to think an Egyptian woman is carrying the child."

"Yeah, that's what's puzzling," James wondered aloud. "If someone from the Ministry of Science, here in Egypt, had been their source, it seems they would have mentioned the gestation chamber. But since they're assuming traditional pregnancy methods, I'd have to imagine the informer is just someone connected with the general science community, somehow."

Maxie nodded her head in agreement and accelerated the utility vehicle on the open road. "They're also assuming that several embryo's and fetuses have miscarried," she added after a pause. "They know we've been at this for over a year now and suspect we've had problems, since we haven't introduced a baby to the public."

She slowed as they neared the research site and turned into the entrance of the compound where guards with automatic rifles stood on post. The government housed the facility in an enclosure owned by the Ministry of Antiquities that was used to protect important artifacts that were not currently on display. The armed security personnel manned a checkpoint some distance from the buildings, and two additional guards were posted outside the doors of the structure to ensure proper screening of anyone who entered. Inside, two other personnel were stationed at a front desk. The research staff used scanner cards as an extra precaution to gain entrance to the lab area.

"*Al salaam alaikum,*" peace be unto you, Maxie said to the guard in Arabic, as the SUV stopped at the gate of the compound. James looked up with a smile and resumed reading his paperwork.

"*Wa alaikum salaam,*" and peace be unto you, the young man replied with a pleasant look. "Whut you guys doing heer in Egypt?" he asked in a heavy accent.

"Oh, just a little research on antiquities," Maxie replied off handedly.

"Ahways good to see you," he said, pressing the button that lifted the barrier pole.

Maxie drove into the compound past the buildings at the entrance and made her way around a bend that led directly to the research facility. Once inside, she made her way to the office area to gather the latest reports on the clone for Dr. Hannibal. He, meanwhile, went immediately to the lab to take a look at the growing miracle. Now, fourteen months into the gestation cycle, and continuing in embryo-like hyper growth, Khufu was the size of a five-year-old. Honey colored and resting snugly, his sometimes fetus-like movements, paradoxically, alarmed and comforted the staff. He seemed comfortable enough in the man-made birth chamber, but they were well aware that any anomaly could spell disaster.

"Hi James," Dr. Ali said, as she walked in from her office scribbling notes on a pad, her reading glasses resting low on her nose. She was dressed in a traditional Arabic galabayya covered up by her white lab coat. She also donned sandals. But like many contemporary Arab women, didn't wear a hijab, its absence a statement of independence. A divorcee with two adult-aged children, both studying in the U.S., she was, nevertheless, the picture of a self-assured professional and exuded an air of dependability and efficiency.

"How's it goin', Nailah?" James asked with arms folded looking earnestly for feedback.

"Oh everything's going according to schedule, it seems," she said, raising her head and repositioning her glasses farther up the bridge of her nose.

"Well, I'm concerned whether he can make it full term," James said frankly, looking intently at the gestating pharaoh. "We're talking about another twenty-two months in that chamber. We've had him on sedation since he made nine months, you know. And we can't predict how his system is going to respond when he begins to enter realm dream-states, if he hasn't already. What are the readings?"

"The charts from Dr. Edwards's shift did show increases in his respiratory and heart rates last night," she said, her eyes asking should she be concerned. "But I suppose we would *expect* him to begin dreaming at this stage," she continued, answering her own question.

Little did they know, inside the chamber, Khufu *was* dreaming. The child king was in some ways reliving his past, while he grew in the man-made womb:

"You are a son of Pharaoh Snefru," Nefermaat, the vizier, reminded him, as the boy studied the hieroglyphics text on the papyrus scroll lying across the table. "The kingdom's destiny may someday rest in your hands. Read further," Nefermaat instructed, his arms folded across his bare chest.

"Kemet arose out of the waters of the...abyss," the five-year-old read, looking up triumphantly.

Outside the gestation chamber, they were still assessing Khufu's state. "Let's remember, he's growing at a hyperbolic rate," James said. "The images in his dreams could be much more vivid than might be expected. Analog television pictures used to operate at thirty frames per second. I'd imagine his mind is moving that fast at least due to his rapid growth. We should be concerned about how that might affect his respiratory system," he continued.

"Yes, I've been thinking the same thing," Ali said. "I suspect he's already begun to dream. It's probably an issue of how intense an episode could become."

James paced to his right, his hands clasped behind him, then back to his starting point, pondering the matter; "I was able to cause the memory prints to surface in his donor cell by introducing trace levels of selenium into the nucleus," he noted slowly. "By neutralizing the selenium, in his system, we *might* be able to cause the memories to become dormant. That might curtail any major dream episodes. What do you think, Nailah?"

"Makes sense to me, Professor," she nodded. "Where do we start?"

$\approx$

From the beginning of the project, Dr. Brooks Edwards had selflessly volunteered to oversee the night watch, to closely monitor the rapidly growing pharaoh. He was confident the team could nurture the embryo through the birth process, and now his enthusiasm surged as Khufu continued to grow healthily and thrive. Edwards had also shared the staff's concerns about the possibilities of the clone miscarrying. But the neatly bearded, balding professor had brought his experience as a cardiologist into the initiative to help prevent such a disaster.

His well-attuned sensitivity to the heart and respiratory system were tantamount to a race-car driver sensing an irregularity in his vehicle. Thus, he continuously focused on preventive maintenance. If the gestation chamber held its own, he and the team would do their part, he maintained.

Edwards had felt all along that the clone would have a good chance of survival if it reached the normal nine-month gestation point. And it had succeeded with flying colors. By nine months it had been the size of a two-year-old.

And while opponents to cloning had pointed out that too many embryos were generally lost in cloning research. And that the potential loss of human life was too great to justify experimenting with human subjects. He saw the opportunity to resurrect the ancient pharaoh as too profound to pass up—this was more than a basic scientific experiment, he reasoned. There were cultural ramifications for Africans the world over. He reflected on how the English-speaking world had not published a picture of a black pharaoh in any of its mass-appeal publications for the first fifty years of the twentieth century. And when word had begun to circulate about the King Tut discovery in 1922—that he was a black pharaoh—all mention of color had been eliminated from the public discussion.

Instead, museum exhibits of black pharaohs consisted of sterile non-racial epithets. Thus, blacks under Western influence were quietly denied the knowledge of ancient African achievements.

Now was the time to assert the black classical story that had been stolen by the European usurpers, he mused. This would help to wake up the sleeping masses to claim their rightful places in the world. And if it takes a clone to do it—so be it, he maintained.

Working alone at night gave him plenty of time to think. And the more he thought about it, the more he realized the research was significant, extremely significant. While DNA analysis had already proved, along with tomb wall paintings, that the pharaohs were black Africans, the cloning of Khufu would provide a media sensation that would satiate the literature on the matter.

Now, black youth would learn of not only American history, but the classical Africa that predated the West's story. They would learn about Kemet, the *real* name of Ancient Egypt.

In addition, they would learn of Khufu's ancestors, his contemporaries and his descendants: Ancestors like Imhotep, called Asclepius by the Greeks—and lauded as their god of medicine. To think that today, the symbol of Asclepius—a serpent entwined around a staff—is the symbol of the American Medical Association and most people aren't even aware of its history "is criminal," he murmured. *This research will raise black consciousness to its rightful place*, he surmised pensively.

Now, eighteen months old and the size of a young adolescent, Khufu was thriving. And Edwards could readily see—he was a black African.

≈

The spectacular progress put the staff on major alert, however. And they were prepared to induce delivery at any sign of trouble. Furthermore, no one had ever attempted to use a gestation chamber beyond eighteen months. So James had, as a precaution, called in two additional physicians from Nadat's team to help monitor the pharaoh around the clock. At least two doctors would be on duty, thereafter, prepared to deliver the pharaoh at a moment's notice. Edwards would work with Dr. Abubakar Mosi, and Ali was assigned to work with Dr. Layla Urbi.

Ali, meanwhile, compared notes from her earlier studies on gestation chamber births and was careful to mark the current development against the projected range set for his growth at specified stages. At twenty-four months, he would have the body size of a twenty-year-old, and at thirty-six months, the targeted birth month, he would reach the maturity of a forty-year-old.

She sat with notepad in lap and the gestating Khufu just a few feet away and took in the potential of it all. *The great Khnum-Khufwy, right there,* she mused, delineating his full name; *unbelievable, but true.* Meanwhile, a conscious realization that they were succeeding sank-in deeply for the first time.

To her right, Dr. Layla Urbi sat in a well-padded chair quietly ruminating over her own assessments of the remarkable study. Her countenance revealed thoughts of incredulity, fear, amusement and a barrage of incomprehensible phases. The two did not talk while on the laboratory floor, however. Current conditions dictated that they maintain silence in the lab if they wanted the pharaoh to reach full term. Any major noise could jar him—and a premature birth could likely result in an unhealthy physical specimen, at best; or worse, an aborted birth.

Ali, born and reared in Aswan, Upper Egypt, was beginning to become more concerned about the impact of the research and its broader implications now also. At the start of the endeavor, everything was just a concept—now it was real.

The rebirth of Khufu would be a break with the past in terms of what it had, heretofore, meant to be human, along with man's conception of the afterlife. Her ancient forefathers had held an unrivaled fascination with the hereafter. And now, she was poised to be a part of a new nexus between the past and eternity.

Ali reflected on the history of her nation. She knew it like the back of her hand. *Khufu was of the Fourth Dynasty—the son of Snefru who had before him built the Red Pyramid and the Bent Pyramid at Dashur. Khufu's son Khafre and grandson Menkaure had built their pyramids on the Giza plateau, alongside his Great Pyramid.*

Khafre's structure was the second-largest pyramid at the site. And Menkaure's was also an imposing edifice. Although hotly debated, it was said that Khafre's likeness was represented on the Sphinx, the large lion-man figure on the eastern end of the Giza necropolis.

Her nation, Egypt, had continuously held a major place on the world stage for nearly three thousand years, since the unification of Upper and Lower Egypt in around 3150 B.C., until the Greek conquest in 332 B.C. And now, she had a chance to play a major role in its history by making the afterlife of Khufu a reality. This would be her contribution to her ancient nation, she reasoned.

Meanwhile, she considered the American anomaly on the race issue. Ali was a dark-skinned Egyptian. But, frankly, skin color didn't play a major role in her life or her nation's life. The American over-emphasis on race was foreign to her social reality. *Was she not the same pigmentation as former Egyptian President Anwar Sadat? Had Egyptians ever even considered his skin color? No. Modern Egyptians recognized that they were the descendants of a mixed heritage of Africans, Persians, Turks, Greeks and Romans. They were a special race, the Arab race.* And she was uncomfortable with the emphasis Americans placed on the issue.

She remembered that as a college student in the United States, she had often been mistaken as an African American by whites, and at first made no issue of the matter. Over time, however, the American culture eroded her comfort with the designation, and she had begun to feel stigmatized. As if because of her skin color, she was somehow different. So she understood the plight of the American blacks and respected their cause.

Meanwhile, she realized that many uneducated, and unenlightened, Egyptians would be uncomfortable with the new movement by non-Arabs to claim Egypt as their *own* classical heritage—and she understood that too. The Arabs had been in Egypt since 640 A.D.—it was their home. And most of them now had the direct bloodlines of the pharaohs through intermarriage. Any outside influence would be felt as an unwarranted intrusion, she admitted.

Ali was still in deep thought as she blankly read the vitals concerning the ancient pharaoh. The project was progressing beyond her wildest imagination and thoughts of seeing Khufu face-to-face preoccupied her now.

"Hi ya?" It was Maxie whispering humorously. "The king needs his rest," she quipped, as she looked into the nearby viewing glass.

"Oh, Hi Maxie," Ali whispered, covering her mouth with both hands to keep from laughing at Maxie's funny facial expression. She muffled a snicker, but rose and hurried to the administrative office to keep from laughing out. Maxie followed behind her whispering rapidly and stifling her own laugh. "I'm sorry, Nailah, I'm sorry," she repeated, as they both headed to the office, which had a huge floor-to-ceiling window that covered the entire front area and allowed a total sweep of the lab. It was also the place where the staff relaxed and enjoyed their down time. They often surfed the Internet, watched television or read.

Ali tried to feign a serious composure, but realized Maxie really had made an offhand quip not intended to be hilariously funny.

"I'm really sorry, Nailah," Maxie chuckled, patting the professor nervously on the shoulder as they entered the room.

"Oh, I know, Maxie. Sometimes we need to break the monotony in there. I was in deep thought, I suppose, and *needed* a laugh, actually," she said. "It makes my head spin just to think about what's happening here," she added, flopping onto the couch. "It's like history is being made but we can't tell which way things will go from here on out—you know?"

"Uh-huh. Like what kind of personality will he have?" Maxie shrugged.

"Well...Maxie, he's been described in two ways in Egyptian history. One: as the good-willed pharaoh who repented to Amen-Ra for his shortcomings earlier in life; and thereafter, righted his ways and became a benevolent ruler. Or, he has been described as a tyrant who closed the temples because of his deep conceit and evilness, forcing the people to worship him as the son of Amen-Ra. One thing we can be certain of is he seemed to believe he was the son of Amen-Ra," she exclaimed.

"That's deep," Maxie responded, looking out into the laboratory. "Well, I hope he was the good one and not the evil one," she said with a gaze of wonder in her eyes.

"Seems we may find out soon enough, Maxie," Ali quipped, getting up from the couch. "But we've got to be heads up from here on out. We just don't know when his body might reject remaining in the gestation chamber, and we'll have to induce birth. Also, remember, too much noise could jolt the clone's system, and the whole project could go down the drain," she whispered, closing the office door quietly behind her.

James, meanwhile, sat in his office reading charts, concerned that his decision to reintroduce small amounts of selenium into the pharaoh's system might lead to the earlier feared hyperactive dream state. He had decided that the need to resurface Khufu's memories outweighed the former fears, now, since lack of selenium could result in the pharaoh's cognitive development lagging. In addition, Khufu had been in the birth chamber for over twenty-four months now and was fully developed, which led James to wonder what toll that might take on an adult body lounging in the man-made birth sac.

All was going well, though, from what he could deduce— no problems to speak of. But he knew each additional day added to the risk of losing all they'd gained. The ancient pharaoh was an adult, and alive. And who knows how many untold secrets he could share with modern man? James wondered.

Maybe we should induce birth now, and all the waiting will be over, he pondered constantly. The selenium should have taken hold, he figured. And forestalling his birth through the complete thirty-six months was becoming riskier each day. Khufu had reached the physical maturity of a young adult, and at least now he had some semblance of a life before him. While it would take several months to learn to communicate effectively with him, at least the world would see what had been accomplished, James thought. Meanwhile, the pharaoh inside the gestation chamber was quietly developing cognitively and dreaming again:

"Son of Ra, your father, Snefru, the pharaoh is dead," the priest of Memphis said, holding out a golden scepter to the twenty-something year old. Khufu received it dispassionately; resigned but prepared to reign on his newly ascended throne.

"Snefru has transcended to the gods, and in your hands the scepter of Kemet now rests."

Next, in Khufu's dream-state, *he stepped upon the Nile's banks—accompanied by the funeral party—his royal barge followed by the boats of the priests and nobles. In the foreground, the stunning Red Pyramid of his father rose majestically against the horizon.*

To James, Khufu was now more than a scientific experiment. He was a living human being. And the possibility of an unhealthy birth resulting from the staff's eagerness to complete the process was unacceptable, he'd decided.

Hannibal considered himself a genetics-research physician, first and foremost. But he had to admit that the black-white cultural debate had to be addressed, whether Khufu pulled through or not. Afrocentrists maintained that the Ancient Egyptians were a black African culture. A position that had been obscured by academia under a number of guises—but now they would have to face the facts. The guy in the birth chamber was, unquestionably, a black African. It would settle, once and for all, the issue of the African origins of Egyptian civilization, and that was important.

Furthermore, the cloning of Pharaoh Khufu would play a crucial role in the emerging construction of a new black classical culture and consciousness. Although this had been a major part of his intent, when he had begun the research, it figured to be an all-consuming result of this new reality that had emerged.

≈

Maxie liked her job, or at least she liked the glamour of international intrigue it represented. But, paradoxically, she had to admit the research was too far-fetched for her liking—this cloning of a long-dead pharaoh. The doctor was just asking for trouble, she figured. Meanwhile, she'd been able to hide her conflicting feelings. She was careful to maintain a good working environment by being pleasant and engaging. But in her heart of hearts, she knew the cloning research was not something she agreed with.

She filled her day filing the study's various reports in the appropriate order and made sure that all was running efficiently in the lab. She took phone calls, which came in infrequently from the staff and Mr. Nadat and monitored the media from the Internet to see what might be said about the research project online.

In fact, this is what prompted a major turn of events. She hadn't seen or heard very much speculation in the media on their research for awhile, so she'd decided to telephone an old acquaintance, who now worked for a Chicago daily newspaper, with a little tip to stir up some interest. He'd done a pretty good story with the limited information she'd fed him earlier, and with a more definitive story, other media would certainly bite as they'd done before. And yes, they could *all*, that is all of the staff, become instant celebrities. No sense in the professor getting *all* of the spot light. In fact, this might defray some of the negative scrutiny of him, she reasoned.

In addition, she rationalized that the rest of the staff could give their perspectives on why cloning the pharaoh was a good idea. She hadn't actually figured out what she'd say. But she'd do her best to make the professor and the research appear responsible. After all, he *had* hired her for the job—and she wanted to please her Aunt Naomi who had recommended her for the position. During the job interview Maxie had simply told the professor that she agreed with his research, because it was a *black thing. Why shouldn't we confirm our roots in this very confirmable way*, she'd said matter-of-factly.

≈

77

The sound of computer keystrokes in the newsroom of the *Chicago Daily Defender* clacked incessantly yet went unnoticed by the young reporter who scrolled the AP wire service for the day's news stories. He was beginning to make his mark as an investigative reporter, and thanks to Maxie and the earlier lead on the clone, the editor was beginning to give him more bylines on the front page. Things had slowed down now, but he figured it was just a matter of time before Maxie got back with him.

The phone rang like any number of rings he would get that day, and he answered expecting a routine lead.

"*Chicago Defender*, how might I help you, please?"

"This is Maxie. What's up, sugar pooh?"

"*Maxie!* What's up? I was wondering what was going on over there. Are you still in Cairo?"

"Yeah, that's why I'm calling you...block head. Do you want this lead or not?" Maxie began breathing in labored breaths as if she wasn't sure she should say what she was about to say, but went ahead anyway.

"You want a free trip to Egypt?"

"Egypt? What! Is that clone ready to be born, Maxie?"

The young reporter listened intently as Maxie gave him the plan. He would tell his editor a story too incredible to pass up. And the nail in the scheme was that the source in Egypt would only allow *him* into the research facility to get an exclusive and pictures. He would also be able to get video footage of the clone, which was being gestated in some newly advanced fetus incubator.

The top is about to blow on possibly the biggest story in history, and I'm the one's going to cover it, he grinned as he hung up the phone.

9

Back in the States, Marika's only concern was that her family had begun to talk. She had moved back to Chicago and had taken a good job with a small but prestigious public relations firm there. One of her female friends, a doctor, and divorcee, had decided to move to Ghana and had offered to rent her house out; so Marika had taken her up on the offer.

Her family, meanwhile, would prod her about James's doings in Egypt and couldn't figure out why he would leave her alone in the States for so long. Her sister Melody had even insinuated that James had abandoned her.

But Marika was secure in her relationship with her husband and disregarded the aspersions for what they were—idle chatter. Unfortunately, the less people knew about a matter, the more hurtful their remarks could be sometimes. She retrieved a bottle of diet cola from the refrigerator and headed into the living room—her diva figure was still there at least, she mused.

She'd actually never doubted James's love for her, not for one moment. He was a one-woman man. And when he said he loved her, as he often did, she knew it was true from the bottom of her heart. After all, she had visited him a few times and could easily be on a plane for Egypt, at the drop of a hat—

and into his waiting arms. What she and James had was special, and gossip couldn't change that.

But it did rattle her a little, how James could expect her to just pull-up and move to Egypt on such a far-out notion. Knowing him, the venture would succeed, though. She had to admit, when he set his mind to something, he generally got what he wanted. James didn't take losing easily. And at least he was high minded. *He wanted to help raise his black brothers and sisters, collectively, to the top alongside himself.*

She flipped the pages of a new copy of *Essence* magazine, sipped her cola and perused an article on black moms, as she crossed her honey-colored legs along the length of the beige leather couch. Would she ever experience the joy of having her own child, she wondered? She wasn't quite beyond childbearing age, yet, but she knew that time could sometimes be unkind in the conception process at her age. She was no longer a spring chicken. Suddenly, she remembered her promise to her nieces Shanti and Karli. She had told them they could spend the weekend at her place and that she'd take them shopping. Marika enjoyed doting over the precocious eight- and nine-year-olds.

She quickly grabbed her leather jacket and was out of the house, into the car, and found herself nearing their residence in no time. She then dialed the girls on her cell phone as she approached her sister Melody's address. The girls ran out as soon as she entered the driveway. And they were off to the Near North Side to do some shopping on the Magnificent Mile. They would shop for awhile and then enjoy a bite to eat before heading back to her house for a game of Scrabble or a DVD movie.

As she drove, they talked about school and family matters. Indeed, ironically, she realized that she cherished being in Chicago with her loved ones. And, paradoxically, she thought about how she had hated to leave Tuskegee. Its rich tradition of Booker T. Washington, George Washington Carver and the Tuskegee Institute, engendered a fulfilling cultural life that had resulted in rewarding experiences for James and her. They hadn't sold their house—they were simply renting it out to a visiting professor until James finished his project. After all, they had lived there for fourteen years and had made many friends and acquaintances.

But being in Chicago had allowed her to spend lots of time with her family, and she was getting to know her nieces better. They were a close-knit clan, and despite the occasional banter over personal concerns, they all loved each other.

Admittedly, she had done well for herself from a financial standpoint. And she enjoyed lavishing gifts on them. She and James had prospered in their respective careers. And currently, the Egyptians were making hefty disbursements into James's account. And upon completion of the project, if he achieved his goal, he'd be a very wealthy man. And what was *his* was *hers*. They were simply like that in money matters, she mused.

They pulled into a parking garage, and she tipped the attendant a nice amount to ensure the car would be close when they returned. They then walked down breezy Michigan Avenue and people-watched and window shopped, before reaching their destination. Next they entered a ritzy, polished gray, marble building with a wide, modern concourse and rode the escalator to the second floor. Karli and Shanti talked excitedly about the things little girls talk about. And Marika corrected them in a subtle but stern way, on a few occasions, when they began to argue or banter one another mercilessly.

Their mother, Melody, often went shopping with her and the girls. But at other times Marika enjoyed the solace of being alone. It somehow brought her in deeper touch with herself. And after a busy day at work, she didn't mind being alone sometimes. After all, she talked with Melody everyday on the phone, and her eldest sister, Darla, always had good suggestions about what she might do in this or that situation. Thank God, she had a large family, and her mom and dad were still healthy and alive. There were five siblings, including herself.

In addition to her sisters Darla and Melody, Marika had two brothers; Raheem, who was a guard on the CBA basketball team in Indiana, and Bruce, a commander with the Chicago Police Department, on the city's South Side. Bruce's and Darla's kids were young adults now.

She had known from the moment she laid eyes on James that he was the man she wanted to marry. He was as kind hearted as he appeared. And he had always looked out for her best interests and had done his best financially even when they were students and didn't have much.

Now, the more she thought about him, the more she realized she wanted to see him and be with him. She did have her passport, which she always kept up-to-date. Maybe she should surprise him, she mused. That would be memorable. He loved surprises. She wouldn't stay long, though. While she admired his commitment to his work, she felt the cloning research was just too far-fetched. Her husband was engaged in scientific inquiry that was simply too much for her to comfortably deal with on a day-to-day basis. And now he had told her that the pharaoh was gestating successfully in a see-through glass incubator.

The girls got her attention as she realized they were leading her into a store with board games. She had already gotten them board games on previous outings, so she wondered what could possibly be the newest rage. They quickly found one, however, that they said was popular, and she bought it because she knew it would make them happy.

They then left and decided to have pizza at a parlor just off Michigan Avenue.

As she sat and talked with the girls in the dimly lit establishment, with the red and white checkered tablecloths, she realized that the true joy of life was being with loved ones and sharing what one had—that was the key to real fulfillment—to have someone to love and to love them in return.

The girls, meanwhile, were head-over-heels about all the attention their Aunt Marika showed them. They even began to mimic the subtleties of her behavior—they began to act rather proper, like her. Marika saw the outings with the girls as opportunities for bonding; critical defining moments that would shape their future relationships and expectations about life. Yes, she would visit James soon, but she realized she was engaged in an unexpectedly profound project of her own.

≈

James spent the day alone at his house in the district of Zamalek resting. Maxie and the crew would hold the fort down in his absence, he'd decided. He would return to the lab on tomorrow in revived spirits. *Even the chief needs a rest every once in a while*, he quipped. He felt guilty about not being at the lab, however, since he also had sleeping quarters there. But he needed a break to clear his head, and he was confident the staff could handle whatever came up, anyway.

Maxie's immaturity *was* beginning to show through, though. But with Ali, Edwards and Nadat's two staff members there, everything would be okay, he figured. They had gone over all the contingency plans in the event of an emergency.

And yet he still worried more than he wanted to. He went into the kitchen, opened a packet of Alka-Seltzer and watched it fizz in a half-glass of water. He then drank it and returned to the bedroom to relax again. Still, all he could think about was the clone. Now twenty-eight months into the process, it might miscarry at any moment. They were so close and yet so far from completing the research.

Perhaps he should allow the press and outside scientists to come in, now, to take pictures and conduct tests. At least they would know the study wasn't a farce.

But all-the-while a parent-like responsibility to the man in the gestation chamber nudged at him. He knew that too much disturbance might cause problems—he had to hold to his decision to wait.

Snoozing, here and there, but mostly awake in some midway point between sleep and consciousness, he reflected on how even Nadat was getting antsy. Nadat wanted to bring more of his people in and had suggested that they induce birth now in order to salvage all they could from the clone information-wise. James countered that Khufu was a sentient person and deserved all they could muster to give him a healthy life. Besides, he maintained, it would take several months, or longer, to learn to communicate with the pharaoh, so rushing really wouldn't help matters.

He then reflected on his and Marika's relationship and opened his eyes to look at the picture of them on the nearby bed stand—they were all smiles, happier times. Things weren't too bad now though. She had visited him a few times, and they'd talked daily over the telephone. In fact, he realized she was presently contemplating a visit to spend some time in Egypt—he knew his wife well.

She was still his Cookie, his special moniker for her, and he was still her beau, despite this transition period in their lives. She only had to access their joint checking account at will; that counted for something, he figured. And the Egyptian government was paying him a pretty penny, he had to admit.

The phone rang, and he toppled the receiver trying to get to it.

"James?" His wife's voice made him wonder if she had been reading his mind.

"Marika...I was just thinking about you, honey. Yes, I'm half-asleep," he admitted.

Then she dropped the bomb.

"James, I thought you weren't gonna release the story until the project had reached full term? There's footage on all the morning's TV stations that show the clone in the gestation chamber. And an exclusive in the *Chicago Daily Defender* with quotes from Felicia Maxwell that say Pharaoh Khufu could be birthed any day now."

James could feel his blood-pressure rise but had learned to calm himself when his body reacted faster than his mind. Marika simply held the phone. She knew her husband well. He was gathering his thoughts. In addition to just waking up, he was considering his next move.

"I'll call you back later...on your cell phone, James, okay?"

"Okay, talk with you later, baby," he said, hanging up, still assessing the situation before him.

Immediately, the phone rang again. Professor James Hannibal was about to be a highly sought-after man, it seemed.

"Hello?"

"James, we've got trouble." It was Edwards with a tone as serious as a heart attack. "The world media is outside the gates of the compound, and everyone is waiting on you to get here."

85

"Ok, no problem, I'm on my way," James said, trying to sound relaxed. His stomach had knotted up inside, and his countenance was as tight as a drum. But he began to meditate on positive affirmations to turn his mind away from the incensed thoughts he had about Maxie and her juvenile deed.

Next, he went into the bathroom and took a quick shower. He then returned to his closet to find suitable clothing. The whole world would be watching. He'd need to be at his best—a classic tan Diaspora suit; that would do it.

The phone rang again. It was Raheem. Nadat told him about the explosion of news stories that were running in all of the media and asked what he might do to help.

They discussed the need for security personnel to escort James through the gates and into the facility; and decided to hold a press conference at 6:00 PM that evening.

James purposely didn't have a television in the house, because it was his get-a-way place. So he turned on his radio and listened for the breaking news on an English broadcast, as he got dressed.

James Hannibal was a pragmatist in his thought processes and seldom made rash moves. He had already come up with a contingency plan, in case anything went wrong with the experiment, and had a well-honed strategy for contending with the media.

He had often appeared on television, so this was nothing new for him.

Ready, he walked outside, settled into his SUV, and headed toward the bridge to Giza and out to the research center. Meanwhile, he was satisfied that his study was already a quantitative success. As a black man in a Western-dominated world, he was helping to reorder what was, indeed, a stolen legacy. Yes, he was a medical professional, but now, more than ever, he was committed to a broader cause.

The professor drove leisurely out to the research facility and soon approached the horde of media trucks, onlookers, and gawkers in cars at the gate of the compound. He had imagined such events all of his life, and it would be like his other media talks—a reasoned, rational approach.

Nadat had dispatched the police personnel, and James was able to drive through the gates without a hitch. He waved to the security personnel who returned quizzical smiles. On the compound grounds, a few TV vans, trucks, and media people had somehow gotten in also. And about a hundred or so people who apparently worked in other buildings, crowded the entrance to the facility. But the police, maybe a hundred strong, formed a human barricade for him from his car to the lab door. He got out and walked to the entrance of the building untouched. Upon reaching the door, he stopped to issue a statement indicating he would be available for the press at 6:00 PM that evening. Shouts of displeasure rang out in the crowd amid heckles of "mad scientist." They would simply have to wait, though. He would prepare an official statement.

Felicia Maxwell, meanwhile, had fled after the horde of reporters had begun to descend on the premises. She had made barely intelligible remarks to them that the clone was inside— then she had vanished.

Maxie had engaged in her proverbial fifteen minutes of fame, but thought better of talking to live broadcasters in depth. A flight had been booked for Chicago. She would be headed back to the States to lie low for awhile.

10

O nce inside the facility, James did a three hundred- and sixty-degree turnaround that stunned the staff—he inexplicably said he'd let the media in. He would open the research lab for the entire world to see.

The fuzzy pictures from the newspaper reporter were just a primer, he said to their amazement. Khufu would now be unveiled to the world in vivid, living color.

The professor, meanwhile, found he was unexpectedly emotionally drained. He had spent twenty-eight months in Egypt. He was ready to go home.

Whatever happened, happened. He had done his deed for humanity. Future generations would have to assess whether he was right or wrong.

He dialed Nadat.

"Raheem, I'm letting 'em in."

"You're what? What's up with you, James? I thought you said you'd wait until the clone made full term?"

"Calm down, Raheem. Trust me on this, okay? Listen," he whispered. "When I walked in a moment ago, I saw the clone make a sudden shivering motion. It's ready to take leave of that gestation chamber. Trust me," he whispered emphatically.

"I'm on my way out there, James," Nadat said nervously, hanging up.

Al-Jazeera, CNN, Nippon, the *SABC,* the *BBC,* the *AP, Reuters*; the global media were outside the doors of the research center—and Professor James Hannibal had decided to let them march in. He would crowd *all* the *big* boys in to record history.

He realized something might go wrong with the birth, but at least the world would see that Khufu had really been brought back to the twenty-first century.

≈

Cairo was six hours ahead of the American East Coast time zone, and pictures from the press conference started to stream into the U.S. at 12 noon Eastern Standard Time.

Locally, in Egypt, the national stations and Al-Jazeera were broadcasting the information live, also. And thousands pressed the gates of the compound in amazement. It was like a science-fiction movie, but real, and with profoundly impactful and far-reaching ramifications. A sense of awe best described the energy of the crowds. And surprisingly, they were rather mum, waiting to hear more.

Meanwhile, Nadat and other officials of the Egyptian government, including President Fadil Hamadi, made their way into the compound and gave obligatory comments to the media, which added to the buzz of the story. Hamadi was a progressive's progressive and an optimistic thinker, but even he was amazed at how far the research had succeeded.

Old Kingdom Egyptian speech specialists, who had been tapped through the Department of Antiquities and universities in Cairo, also began to serve as media pundits. They speculated on how long it might take Khufu to learn to speak a modern language, and pointed out that he likely had proficiency for several tongues, due to the preponderance of tribal idioms and dialects spoken in the region during ancient times.

Single file, the journalists began streaming into the lab. Digital cameras clicking; spotlights from TV cameras beaming. Subdued whispers, magnified by so many people, erupted as rumbles. And then came the inevitable; the jostling inside the lab took its toll.

Khufu began to rotate restlessly, subtly at first, then faster; turning this way and that, as if having a nightmare. He reached out as if suddenly awakened from a deep sleep, his eyes opening startled like, and his lungs suddenly requiring air over amniotic fluids. The several doctors on hand now went into action. Dr. Brooks Edwards pressed the five-number code to release the fluids from the man-made birth sac and out flushed the pharaoh onto the soft, synthetic reception chamber, coughing and wheezing loudly, but alive and well.

The doctors then cut the long umbilical cord, applied anesthesia to the area, bandaged it, and wrapped the new arrival in a huge towel. The mahogany-colored clone lay on his side in a fetus curl and looked out at the lights of the cameras and the horde of a hundred or so people without discernable expression in his countenance.

Everyone, meanwhile, tried to converge on the birth area at once. Khufu now looked out at them confused, then blinked and sat up with what appeared to be a triumphant smirk on his face.

A frenzy of cameras began to flash in an incessant blitzkrieg. Meanwhile, a barrage of noisy chattering in various languages rose to a feverish pitch.

There he was. His skin was smooth rich chocolate, and his expressive eyes struck a balance of wisdom and terrestrial adventure.

James then sauntered slowly toward Khufu and issued the Old Kingdom phrase for hello: "*Hotep!*"

Khufu leaned his head sideways, perhaps to translate through the accent, and then responded: "*Haatep!*"

The media people went wild. Khufu looked around warily, not knowing what to do. And Nadat gave James a big hug as they danced in jubilation.

Meanwhile, Edwards and the other doctors began an EKG and other tests to ensure the pharaoh was functioning properly. Next, they helped the apparently healthy Khufu onto a motorized wheelchair and steered him to his quarters, where a Jacuzzi had been installed, for a steamy, sudsy bath.

The media had seen what they'd wanted to see for now, and James ordered a reprieve until later, asking them to file out of the laboratory until an unspecified future date. The world had seen it all—live on television. It was enough to keep the press abuzz until the hereafter.

In the pharaoh's quarters, they all stood around the sudsy Jacuzzi and looked. The doctors, the speech specialists, and a few security people—they all just stood and gazed at him, mesmerized. Khufu, meanwhile, smiled triumphantly. It was apparent that he thought he had arrived in *Duat*, the Egyptian Heaven. He slid down to his neck in the sudsy Jacuzzi and relaxed as if fulfilled that he had reached his celestial home.

Then President Hamadi, followed by Nadat and Hannibal, entered the room just when Khufu spoke the words: "*Heker, te, shabew em Duat?*" I'm hungry, got any food here in Heaven? Everyone looked at each other stunned. They'd never heard a language that sounded quite like that.

"What did he say?" Nadat asked turning to the speech experts.

"We're not sure," a short, light-skinned Egyptian said, looking quite confused. "Seems to be a question of some sort, but I can't be certain. Old Kingdom Egyptian hasn't been spoken in thousands of years—can't pick up the accent. Let's see...*Horem Ipy Ankwa*," he said, in what was apparently a feeble attempt to speak Old Egyptian.

Khufu sat impassively. It was evident he had not understood. He then yawned and laid the side of his head on his forearm, along the flat marble ledge of the Jacuzzi. He had apparently tired.

"We should be able to communicate through written hieroglyphics, though," the speech expert said excitedly. "When we dry him off, we'll need something to write on."

"That'll have to wait, it seems," Edwards replied. Khufu had already begun to snore. "Looks like after so much time in the womb, the pharaoh is used to a lot of sleep; let's just let him relax for awhile," Edwards suggested.

The room had been furnished with many of the items discovered in the tomb where the well-preserved mummy was found. With the exception of the Jacuzzi, vial-like covered lamps, and curtains designed to look like leopard skins to cover the bathroom entrance and the shower, the quarters would remind him of the twenty-sixth century B.C. But now, James had in mind to transform it into a personal learning center. He would bring in television, a radio and other modern conveniences to begin the gradual acclimation of the pharaoh into the modern era.

Nadat turned toward James, along with President Hamadi, jarring James out of his thoughts. "Professor, the president would like to thank you for your services," he said smiling smugly. The affable chief-of-state stretched out his hand and they clasped in a warm handshake.

"We'll be taking over from here on out," Nadat continued, with a self-assured grin. "Any particulars you'll need during the transition please let me know." He then looked around at the assembled scientists and spouted out instructions in Arabic. His team gathered around him, some nodding affirmatively, while others took notes.

But James didn't understand any of it. In fact, he couldn't quite understand his own feelings at that point. In some unfathomable way, he had come to feel paternalistic toward Khufu. He knew it wasn't fully rational. But the two years and four months of nurturing the clone from inception to birth had brought about an attachment that could only be explained in the parent-child model of relationships.

While a couple of the men led the pharaoh to his bed, James thought about the situation, unsteadily. The Egyptian government had hired him to conduct the study, but the follow up was inherently theirs to administer as they pleased. He was dead in the water. The future of the project was in Nadat's hands. The exchange of power had been fairly executed.

The pharaoh, he realized, in the long term—if he proved cognitively functional, would dictate the parameters of his relationships with all of them, anyway. He was an independent individual.

Still, James felt like he was being torn away from the project he had given two years of his life to. Sure, Raheem had pursued him on the matter, but he had given his heart equity to the project on a daily basis.

He admitted, reluctantly, that he felt a surge of emotional dissonance—that feeling of being pulled in two directions on the inside. The adage, "old habits die hard" had some merit in this case, he realized. While he was ready to return to the States, it was going to be hard to pull himself away so abruptly. But he resigned himself to the reality of the matter. Khufu was the responsibility of the Egyptian government.

"James?" Raheem said emphatically, walking across the room towards him with the hieroglyphics expert in tow.

"I'd like you to meet Mr. Abasi Masud. He'll be heading the transition team and will probably have some questions for you from time to time. Meanwhile, I suppose two weeks should be enough for us to finalize matters. What do you think?"

"Sounds great," James said trying to appear unaffected. "Anything I can do to help, let me know." He felt like his voice had come from some other person. It felt like the death of a child or sibling had occurred.

He turned to look at Khufu, now stretched out across the bed asleep, and wondered with guardian-like apprehension, what might become of this ancient king—the pharaoh whom he had snatched from what was there-to-fore the land of no return.

11

N adat placed his people in their new posts immediately. Masud was now the head of the lab. He would consult with two onsite psychologists who would assist him in ascertaining Khufu's mental state. He also placed four medical practitioners and two other specialists in hieroglyphics on site as well.

Dr. Brooks Edwards and Dr. Nailah Ali both seemed relieved that it had all come to an end. Edwards vowed to take some time off, but offered to return to Egypt to help in any capacity needed. He also agreed to assist the pharaoh in a tour of the U.S., when Khufu became proficient enough in English. Ali would remain in Egypt for awhile, but she also had plans of returning to the States to do consulting work surrounding the gestation chamber. They would finish the two-week transition period and start their lives anew.

≈

Dr. Abubakar Mosi and Dr. Layla Urbi monitored the pharaoh closely during the night and were pleased and relieved that he was functioning as might be expected of any healthy thirty-two year old. They were met the next morning by Mr. Masud along with Dr. Brooks Edwards.

A slight, middle-aged man in his mid-fifties, Masud was a graduate of Cairo University and had worked closely with the Egyptian Ministry of Antiquities for about fifteen years. He was well versed in Old Kingdom, Middle Kingdom, and New Kingdom writing.

But as he had mentioned the night before, Old Kingdom Egyptian hadn't been spoken in over a thousand years, so he was concerned about his ability to quickly grasp the sounds of Khufu's accent.

In addition, the ancient people of Kemet hadn't used vowels in their writing, and modern scholars had, thus, placed them randomly in attempts to speak the vernacular. Masud was reasonably confident they would be able to communicate via written hieroglyphics, though. And he was excited about the chance to work with the pharaoh. Heretofore, unimaginable answers to Ancient Egyptian script would likely be solved.

This would be an unprecedented opportunity, in just a few months, perhaps, to begin deciphering cryptic texts that Egyptologists had been attempting to understand for centuries. The most important—the renowned Pyramid Texts—had been construed to contain everything from proof of the ancient civilization of Atlantis, to the answers to the genetic code.

Meanwhile, the pharaoh was still sleeping while a white board and erasable markers were brought into his quarters so Masud could begin writing in the ancient script:

"HELLO PHARAOH KHUFU, WELCOME TO THE 21st CENTURY...."

He explained in hieroglyphics that the pharaoh had been asleep for a long time; and while it might have appeared that this was *Duat*, the Egyptian Heaven, he was not in *Duat*, yet.

Masud could not bring himself to explain to the pharaoh that he had been transposed some forty-five hundred years into the future. He'd reasoned, along with the psychologists, that it might be too much of a shock for Khufu. So he inserted the term "21st Century," deciding it was cryptic enough to forestall any sudden jar to the pharaoh's psyche. Proceed with caution was their modus operandi.

At the foot of Khufu's bed on a wooden chest was a fine-linen kilt made by modern Egyptians; probably not as silky like as the ancients had been able to make, though. And also, an intricately jeweled necklace found in the tomb was laid out on a nearby stand.

Sandals patterned after a pair they'd discovered in the pyramid were also placed at the foot of the bed. And a braided human-hair replica of one of his wigs was provided. A wooden hair pick that was with the pharaoh's ancient belongings was surprisingly like modern afro picks. It suggested that, perhaps, he didn't wear his hair in the shaved style that was common for the period, the staff reasoned. Due to the hot climate, many Ancient Egyptians shaved their heads bald and wore wigs for special occasions. On a table, about ten feet from the foot of the bed, they had placed a nemes headdress over a wooden wig mount. Its gold and blue stripes added to the regal character of the room.

Suddenly, the pharaoh stirred and turned over resolutely, apparently reminded that he was in *Duat*, or some precursor to *Duat*. Then, he sat up and slowly ran his hands along his face and arms and looked in wonder around the room at the people in the white lab coats.

He then swung both legs over the side of the bed like an athlete; wrapped the towel he had fallen asleep in around his waist and fell to his knees in a prostrate posture, as if to give obeisance to the gods.

Masud quickly sprang into action and said: "*Kawit asru yunet Duat*," you are not in Heaven yet, in Old Egyptian.

Khufu rose to a kneeling position, watching as Masud pointed to the board at the hieroglyphics script.

The pharaoh read the writing, but did not seem to clearly comprehend. It was obvious that he still thought the people in the room were the gods. His religious indoctrination had not prepared him for anything like this. He had been taught that one day he would die and stand before the gods in the Great Judgment Hall of Osiris.

This was going to take some doing, they all realized.

Dr. Layla Urbi, meanwhile, figuring that Khufu was likely hungry, remembered that there was a bowl of fruit in the central office. "How about I bring him some fruit?" she asked Masud.

"Good idea," he responded.

"I'll be right back," she said anxiously, turning rapidly to leave.

She met James coming toward her in the hallway and blew pass him like a fish in water. "He's awake. He's awake," she said in an excited whisper.

She quickly retrieved the fruit bowl of apples, grapes, dates and bananas, along with a bottle of water, and returned to see Pharaoh Khufu writing with Masud on the board. They were in some type of dialogue, but she couldn't make heads or tails of what was being communicated. After a few moments, she quietly asked one of the speech specialists, who had recently come in, about what was happening.

"Khufu keeps writing about Duat, and Dr. Masud is attempting to subtly inform him that he's in the twenty-first century A.D.," the guy mumbled.

Masud looked relieved when he spotted Urbi and beckoned her to bring the fruit over. And Khufu, who seemed rather frustrated, was noticeably pleased when he was presented the bowl.

It was evident he'd never seen such a well-proportioned yield. His eyebrows arched when he saw the large red apples, bananas, grapes and freshly picked dates.

The pharaoh sat on the edge of the bed and bit into an apple, before nodding his head affirmatively, eliciting a gasp from the onlookers. Looked like the head nod for yes had been around for a long time, they realized—Khufu, meanwhile, munched the apple ravenously.

Masud was just grateful there had been some basis for communication there in the initial periods of interfacing with the pharaoh. He figured that only about twenty percent of the information he was writing was getting across, however.

"It's difficult for me to be sure of the word order. That's the main thing hindering our written communication," he said out loud.

Doctors Mosi and Edwards, meanwhile, had wheeled medical devices into the room while Khufu was eating, and now began to conduct EKG tests on him. He was as healthy as an athlete, they reported. Their fears of possible ill effects resulting from his premature birth seemed unfounded.

James, noting that Nadat and President Hamadi were en route, along with two busloads of officials, reminded Masud of the impending engagement. The speech expert thus began to take on his unprecedented role as handler to the pharaoh. He proceeded to direct Khufu to the bathroom and shower, which were discreetly positioned behind the leopard-skin-patterned curtains.

Khufu looked puzzled as Masud pulled back the curtain to the shower and turned on the water. Finally, it dawned on him that he was expected to walk under the flowing water and allow it to run over his body. In Ancient Egypt, the servants had often poured large jugs of water over him when he wished for a quick bath, so the shower wasn't too much of a stretch.

After a short while, he finished showering and the crew showed him his wardrobe, now stretched out across the end of the bed. They then led the charismatic sovereign to an adjoining room to show him his closet, which had several changes available. He selected a well-starched tan-colored kilt, perhaps desiring it over the pleated white one in the adjoining room, and accepted a pair of modern-day cotton underwear, clearly realizing what they were—he simply slipped into them.

Next, Khufu walked summarily back into the adjoining room and retrieved his nemes headdress from the wig mount and put it on, while looking into a full-length mirror with a noticeably surprised look on his face. Perhaps it was the mirror, but also ten years had been shaved from his age due to being birthed from the gestation chamber early. The refreshed look on his countenance indicated that he was pleased with the outcome.

"A decade younger, and he's probably taller," Edwards chimed.

The Egyptians *had* made high-quality mirrors from polished metal, but he seemed bemused at the clarity of his reflection, also. He turned and looked around at the assembled staff and then perused the room, standing gracefully with his hands clasped behind his back; he really felt he was in *Duat.*

He then walked over to a chair and sat preparing to put on his sandals.

"Well, let me do the honors," Dr. Layla Urbi said.

She bowed in homage and placed his sandals on his feet, slipping them on effortlessly, while he nodded at her respectfully.

He was dressed, now, so the crew decided to take the pharaoh on a tour of the building, since Nadat and the president had not yet arrived. Masud gestured toward the open door, and Khufu arose, followed by the others, and headed out. The pharaoh stopped abruptly, however, when they entered the corridor. He was apparently startled at the air-conditioned atmosphere, which was much cooler than his room. Meanwhile, he looked up at the florescent lights in awe and seemed to wonder what they were made of. The staff accompanied him as he took his first hesitant steps into his new world. Understandably, he was unsure of what to make of his new surroundings. Again, he stopped. This time he just stared up at the wall.

"What is he staring at?" someone wondered out loud.

"The clock," James said speculatively, peering from beside Masud. After all, there wasn't anything else on the wall. Masud had his pad and pencil at the ready and wrote a hieroglyphics sentence that read: *"location of sun."* Khufu nodded his head affirmatively, and they sauntered on.

Nadat, President Hamadi and the officials had now arrived. And Nadat was looking at his watch a second time when Masud followed by Khufu, dressed in his regal finery, and James trailing, walked out of the lab building. Many of the other doctors and staff had dispersed to get some much-needed rest.

The officials on the buses, meanwhile, gasped in unison when they saw the stately ebony-colored monarch. He had the countenance of one accustomed to being a sovereign; yet a certain carefulness pervaded, likely because everything was so new to him.

The sudden, bright sun-light caused him to squint his eyes. And the feeling that he was among the gods was certainly no small matter. President Hamadi and Nadat summarily exited their limousine and walked over to greet the party with a diplomatically reserved enthusiasm. Then without warning, a military jet, traveling faster than the speed of sound, cut through the sky at about three hundred feet or so overhead, startling the group. Khufu involuntarily ducked, while the others looked up alarmed also, its reverberated sound trailing in a waning decrescendo. Khufu, of course, had no context for such an event. He remained crouched—awe struck—while the others looked on in chagrin.

James, acting in the role of protector stepped in: "Maybe we're moving Khufu too fast," he shouted above the fading noise. "Let's give him a few days before we bring him outside."

"We've done two EKG's on him. He'll be alright," Masud countered, gesturing Khufu toward the limo.

"Wait just a minute," James roared angrily.

"This man has been brought forty-five hundred years into the future? You can't just throw him out here without some preparation. Let's give him time to get acclimated before we push him into the outside world."

"*I make those decisions!*" Masud said—so icily James could feel the chill.

Attempting to contain himself, James looked over at the president and Nadat.

"Perhaps *we should* prep the pharaoh a little, Mr. Masud," Nadat intervened. "What do you think, Mr. President?"

"You guys are the experts," President Hamadi said dodging the controversy. "It's your call."

Masud backed down. "Whatever you say, Raheem; I'm here to simply salvage all we can from this important scientific breakthrough."

James pivoted, enraged now, and stormed back towards the building, incensed over the situation. He walked rapidly to his on-site quarters and began packing, seething at what he felt was Masud's impatience and apparent apathy for the well-being of the pharaoh. A knock on the door interrupted his thoughts, and he opened it to find Nadat standing in the hallway looking apologetic.

"Hey, what is life without a few disagreements, *huh*, my friend?" Raheem said extending his hand for a shake.

James ignored his hand, turned and retrieved an armload of shirts still on hangers and simply uttered "excuse me," as he brushed pass Raheem to continue packing.

"Have a seat, Mr. Nadat," he said finally, gesturing awkwardly to a chair as he began putting the shirts in a suitcase.

"No thanks, I just wanted to see how you were doing, James. I'm in agreement with you. We should not, and we must not, move the pharaoh along too quickly."

James blared out: "This is a matter of respecting human dignity, Raheem. The pharaoh is a real person like we are." He then pulled up a couple of chairs in the cluttered room and sat down. "The first thing is to spoon-feed Khufu with the information he'll need to survive in this era."

"Yes," Nadat said, thoughtfully, deciding to sit for a moment. "But, I've already promised Masud we'd take a drive out to the Pyramids later in the day *if* Khufu seemed up for it."

James leaned back with his feet firmly planted: surprised that they were at loggerheads.

"It's your call, Raheem. This is your research. But keep in mind that's a real individual you're dealing with out there, not just some experiment."

"Yes, yes. Your sensitivity to the pharaoh is laudable, James. But please be mindful that this is Egypt's pharaoh. This is *our* ancient king. And we would never do anything to harm him. We're talking about judgment calls, here. If I deem we're moving him too fast, we'll slow down, but right now everything is on course," he said rising abruptly.

James remained seated as Nadat walked to the door unescorted. They had both made themselves clear.

Nadat exited and almost immediately there was another knock.

"The door's open," James said agitatedly.

It was Brooks Edwards.

"What's up, Brooks," he said taken by surprise. He arose and clasped his friend's hand in a vigilant soul shake, looking into his eyes for needed support.

"What's up with you, James?" Brooks asked, foregoing James's greeting. "I thought you guys would be long gone by now?"

"They're using him, Brooks. They just want to use him for their inhumane scientific aims," James said turning his back to Edwards and walking further into the room. "We need to get him out of here," he continued, turning to face Brooks once again.

"Wait a minute. Slow down, James. What's caused you to take a three-sixty so quickly? A few moments ago everything was hokey dory. What happened when you went outside?"

"Khufu's not ready for this, Brooks. He was just birthed from that gestation chamber yesterday. They should not be parading him around this soon."

"Maybe you're right, James. But let's maintain cool heads here. You've always been the Teflon professor. Now's not the time to go south, brotha."

"You're right, Brooks," James said taking a chair. "Maybe I'm over reacting; but I really didn't consider deeply enough how this research would affect the pharaoh as an individual."

12

Masud and President Hamadi had retreated inside with the pharaoh, following the altercation with Hannibal, and were met by slack-jawed stares from the two security guards at the front desk, who still couldn't quite believe what had transpired in the lab over the past months. Khufu, meanwhile, looked and acted as if he had stepped from a time warp—he stared at the electric sockets and light switches, looked up at the vents, and peered at the telephone system on the security desk. Everything was so new to him.

Masud remembered that Nadat had suggested he show Khufu magazine pictures to prep the pharaoh for modern times. So he decided that, *that* might be the best way to begin the day, since Hannibal had so *abruptly* cut short the day's plans.

"I had not realized it, but he lived before the wheel was invented," President Hamadi said bringing Masud out of his thoughts.

"The pharaoh has a lot of catching up to do," Masud agreed.

Khufu, meanwhile, looked relieved that he was heading back towards the more familiar laboratory and his quarters.

"Are there magazines here in the offices?" Masud asked Nailah Ali as they met her heading down the hallway.

"Yes, I'll get them for you," she said with a sense of urgency matching his. She had just awoken from a long night's rest and was excited to see how events were shaping up surrounding the pharaoh. She retrieved copies of *Ebony*, *World Geographic*, *Good House Keeping*, and an English-language periodical on Cairo.

She returned to the pharaoh's quarters, handed Masud a copy of *Ebony* and pulled a chair up to the table where he and Khufu had sat down. Masud began to flip the pages, and then nodded to Ali, nonverbally asking her to join him in the task. She moved her chair around closer to the other side of Khufu and began flipping through the colorful pages of people and scenes. Masud, meanwhile, got up and began to write on the white board while Ali continued.

"Pictures," she said in English.

"Pix-chures," Khufu responded.

She pointed at various photographs and said the word picture several more times to ensure that he understood what the word meant. Surprisingly, he picked up her accent pretty well.

Masud, meanwhile, had written the hieroglyphic words for "new type scroll" on the board, but Khufu's countenance remained puzzled when he pointed it out. Ali continued to patiently turn the pages of the magazine, enunciating words for the pharaoh. "Car," she chimed, as she pointed to a car in an advertisement.

"Ca," Khufu responded, nodding affirmatively.

She finished the copy of *Ebony*, retrieved a copy of *Good House Keeping*, and resumed flipping pages.

Masud, meanwhile, left the room and headed down the hallway to what was to become his new office. Hannibal had removed most of his belongings already. But a few of his things remained cluttered here and there, along with ink pens, paper clips and other basic office utensils. In the file cabinets were Khufu's vital records. Also, on the wall was a striking copy of the Prince Kewab fresco, a likeness of Khufu's eldest son. His jet-black skin contrasted with the colors in the room, much like black and white TV in a color TV world.

Prince Kewab epitomized the reality of unfulfilled potential that often manifests despite man's best intentions. He had been Khufu's heir apparent, but had died mysteriously before ascending to the throne. Scholars still had not solved the puzzle of his demise.

Masud's hands trembled slightly as he thought about the profundity of the research. The answers to a lifetime of work were about to be breached. He had worked so many years among the elite of Egypt. With his expertise as a hieroglyphic's expert, he had gradually risen to a place of prominence, in academic terms. And he was esteemed by Egyptologists the world over. But he was tired of the endless search for research funding, and the paradox of living among the rich, while he sustained himself on a bureaucrat's budget.

Now, he could parlay his expertise to accrue financial resources beyond his wildest dreams.

He sat at the chair of the desk, and since the computer was already on, he decided to learn more about James Hannibal. Their paths would surely cross often in the foreseeable future. He clicked the plastic mouse and googled 'James Hannibal' in the search engine to find out more information about the African-American professor.

Hannibal was indeed brilliant. He embodied the spirit of Tuskegee University and its greatest scientist, George Washington Carver. And he exemplified the solid role model its founder, Booker T. Washington, represented.

Hannibal had perfected his cloning technique. And while he utilized the basic tenets of contemporary knowledge on cloning, he had implemented applications that were *uniquely his*, a newspaper article said. He had graduated near the top of his class at the Harvard School of Medicine, an online biography indicated; yet he had foregone higher salaries from prestigious Ivy League schools for a chance to spearhead a genetics department at Tuskegee, a historically black university in the Southern United States.

Masud was of Armenian Turkish heritage. He could trace his lineage back two hundred years to the Ottoman Empire. His family had immigrated to Egypt in 1898, following the Armenian massacres in Turkey. And, even today, he and his extended family were rigidly apolitical. They had purposely steered away from politics. They had immigrated to Egypt as literal gypsies with a collective memory of governmental harshness. His father, especially, had believed that such dealings only brought about trouble and enemies. And as a result, Masud had always sought to operate within the status quo. He simply wanted to live a good, long and prosperous life; that was not so bad, he thought, philosophically.

He noted, meanwhile, that Hannibal was part of the Pan African movement of the Diaspora, which placed Ancient Egypt at the center of black-classical thought. He understood it, but he was ambivalent about it.

Hannibal was an American, just as he, Masud, was an Egyptian. Bygones should be left as bygones, he felt. He realized, however, that Europeans had arisen under the shadow of an ancient world that had come of age long before their emergence on the world stage. Greece and Rome themselves were mere toddlers, and that—a generous stretch—to the Ethiopians, Egyptians and other black empires, long forgotten, that had populated Africa and the current Middle East to India.

The Johnny-come-lately societies had surgically divided the culture between classical blacks and sub-Saharan African societies, before literally turning high-achieving black cultures into white cultures. An effective strategy, notwithstanding its diabolical results—a hemorrhaging of the natural affinity and subsequent diffusion of ideas between the North and sub-Sahara Africa, contributing to the latter's underdevelopment.

A voice startled him. He looked up to see President Hamadi and Nadat approaching the open door. They entered without stopping.

"Mr. Masud, I gather your office is sufficient?" Nadat asked, his hands clasped graciously.

"Yes, perfectly functional," Masud replied, straightening his wire rimmed, oval eyeglasses and standing to meet the two men.

"We must keep in mind the public relations aspect of this unprecedented breakthrough," President Hamadi asserted, as the two leaders unconsciously crowded in on Masud at his desk. "The increase in tourism and prestige for Egypt will be enormous. We cannot let a flap like what occurred in the parking lot happen in public again. I'm sure we're on the same page, Mr. Masud," the president said. "A misstep could make us look like the bad guys, here."

"I understand," Masud said, disconcerted. He straightened his glasses out of habit; then pointed proudly to the Prince Kewab fresco. "Egypt will again be viewed as the leader she deserves to be. Don't worry, Mr. President, I love this nation as much as you do."

"Yes, a public fiasco with the African Americans would not be good for our image," Nadat agreed.

"Well, shall we look in on the pharaoh?" Masud asked, clasping his hands, now, in anticipation of perhaps some new development concerning Khufu.

They headed out and up the hallway nodding acknowledgements to a new security guard Nadat had ordered stationed outside Khufu's door. He had posted another inside at the door, also. They entered the quarters to see Dr. Ali and Khufu still flipping through magazine pages. The pharaoh was apparently at ease, and Ali seemed to be enjoying the experience as well.

The three crowded around the two as Ali continued to flip through the magazine pages, enunciating words and pointing out whatever she felt Khufu could understand.

Suddenly, Khufu got up, looked at Masud and articulated in rapid-fire Old Kingdom Egyptian a statement that neither Masud nor anyone else could begin to comprehend.

Khufu's intrepid brown eyes peered knowingly at Masud. Then the earth-colored monarch nodded directly toward the door. "Looks like he's ready to go," Masud deduced, gesturing toward the doorway.

President Hamadi, Nadat and Ali yielded the lead to Masud and Khufu as they exited the room and made their way towards the entrance where they were met by Brooks Edwards, who was en route to the pharaoh's room, himself.

"Looks like he's ready," Masud said gingerly, continuing down the hallway.

"Should I get Professor Hannibal?" Edwards asked, realizing he was in the midst of a potential powder keg.

"Please," Nadat interjected.

They were at the lobby doors now and heading into the reception area where the security guards were as perplexed as ever.

"Did the buses leave, yet?" Nadat asked.

"They shouldn't have, no one gave them clearance, did they?" President Hamadi responded.

They walked outside to see the buses still running patiently—it had been less than an hour—and they walked to the limousine prepared for the historic journey. Khufu would be visiting the Pyramids, at the Giza plateau. Hannibal, meanwhile, walked out with Edwards in tow and climbed into the limo with a nod to the rest of the occupants; while Edwards and Ali headed over to Ali's car which was parked on the opposite side of the doorway area. She started the engine, reversed from the parking lane and waited for the motorcade to get underway.

Almost immediately, the procession padded by security police, headed out and reached the gate to an onslaught of media trucks and camera crews camped outside. Thus, they began the drive toward Giza with a trail of followers that turned into an ever-elongated caravan.

Inside the limo, there was an element of tension made worse by the earlier exchanges between the men. Everyone realized, however, that the confrontation had occurred from Hannibal's need to protect the pharaoh; nothing spiteful had been intended.

"Soda, James?" Nadat asked, opening the mini-refrigerator of the luxury automobile.

"No thanks, but our pharaoh is probably thirsty," James answered, looking at Khufu, who was apparently keeping tabs on everything, including assessing the landscape outside.

"Hey, take my seat, Pharaoh, James said moving to the open area and gesturing for Khufu to move to the window.

The landscape was checkered with fields, palm trees, desert, and new, modern construction, together with roads and fast-moving cars. Men worked in fields, led by oxen, like they'd done thousands of years ago.

Nadat retrieved a can of orange soda pop and smiled as he offered it to Khufu who looked perplexed at the container before James offered to do the honors of popping the tap. Khufu then accepted it and slowly took a sip which caused him to cough and clear his throat. He smiled agreeably, though, and took a larger gulp—then nodded affirmatively several times as he looked around at the other men. They all laughed in an uproar, including Khufu in a bravado tone, at the novelty of the event.

James, meanwhile, had a copy of the *World Geographic* magazine that Dr. Ali had given him, which had a picture of the Giza Pyramids on the cover. Initially, he had expected to show the publication to Khufu during a series of formal briefings, but now he realized the pharaoh needed to see it before the possible shock of viewing the actual Pyramids came too suddenly. He sat with the publication on his lap but didn't quite know how to breach the matter; so he simply handed it to Masud and began to give his assessment of the situation.

"This might lessen the potential jar, to Khufu, upon seeing the Pyramids, Abasi. What do you think?"

"You're probably right, Doctor. The pharaoh likely thinks he's in some version of Duat."

"Good heads up James," Nadat said. Nadat and Masud were sitting on opposite sides of the refreshment bar where they faced Khufu, James and President Hamadi.

Masud nodded to James and summarily handed the magazine to Khufu who riveted his attention to the cover like a jeweler scrutinizing a gemstone. He seemed intrigued and puzzled at the same time, as if trying to place the structures and unfolding events in their proper perspective. In his day, his pyramid was covered in polished limestone with a gold-plated capstone at its peak. The images of the structures he saw there were ancient; literally rubble, compared to the sleek pyramids he knew.

"We're almost there," James said, a nervous edge to his voice as the Giza Pyramids appeared on the horizon.

Khufu looked up, and his facial expression said it all—he was stunned. Likely, not only by the ancient, time-worn Pyramids—but the modern city of Cairo arose in the background like a gigantic monolith—or perhaps a heavenly city, in Khufu's eyes.

Meanwhile, the limousine pulled up to the edge of the necropolis and stopped. Personnel at the gate had been instructed to let only the listed VIPs in. The complex had been closed to the public, and the commercial media, to short circuit the possibility of a circus environment—which, at-any-rate, was already beginning to occur.

Thus, only a few select vehicles were allowed to enter the world-renowned burial grounds. Khufu and the VIP entourage drove into the necropolis slowly, while others, including media people, haggled with security before resigning themselves to their fate; they would not be getting in.

Inside the limo, a surreal energy dominated as the passengers took in the reality of the moment...Khufu, so classic in his blue and gold nemes; and outside the windows, the ancient Pyramids majestic, despite the passing of the ages. To their right, now, was Khafre's noble structure, its aged limestone-marble crest still clinging at its cap; and farther out was the stately edifice of Menkaure. Menkaure's pyramid had been two-toned in color. The bottom half had been covered in Red Aswan granite, while the top half had been coated in white polished limestone. Meanwhile, the caravan edged past Khufu's grand forty-five hundred year old abode—the Great Pyramid—one of the Seven Wonders of the Ancient World.

Khufu's countenance was impenetrable now; only time would tell what this moment meant for him.

Finally, the chauffeur turned into the half-circle driveway in front of the Great Sphinx and stopped. From there, Khufu could take in a panoramic view of the necropolis. It had consisted of his lone gleaming Great Pyramid in his day, with its attendant temples and one queens' pyramid, his mothers', bereft of any rivaling structures. But now, the enduring remnants of his descendants' colossal constructions completed a triad. Whether he was aware that this was the graduated version of his masterpiece was not revealed in his expression, but the reality that the pharaoh was a reservoir of potential answers for historians was not lost on his entourage. Scholars had long debated whether the Giza pyramids were one planned project, or simply a randomly fostered enterprise of each successive ruler.

Masud's black beady eyes, meanwhile, peered from behind his wire-rimmed glasses and revealed the fervid look of a scholar handed a serendipitous discovery, overwhelming in its potential. The usually composed language expert could barely contain himself. Long dormant, even inconceivable possibilities awakened in his thoughts; and he exited the limo unabashedly like a fawning suitor, assisting Khufu in getting out. The remaining party, meanwhile, in the limousine and in the buses and cars exited rather officious like.

Before them was the heralded Great Sphinx. Though ancient, it still projected the strength and vitality of dynastic Egypt. Relaxed in its splendid outstretched position, the lion-man monument was at once strong and retiring—a poised celestial protector of the necropolis—its countenance weathered, but seemingly content that it would defeat time itself.

The slow walk, meanwhile, towards the edifice, evoked a mix between a reunion and a marriage; a fantastic, yet solemn pilgrimage. Khufu represented a new link between the ancient world and the new; an unprecedented doorway that was indelibly changing mankind's perception of reality.

The flashing camera lights from the government media crew, meanwhile, created a blitzkrieg of clicking illuminations inside and outside the circle of bodies surrounding the pharaoh, engendering a futuristic paradox to the moment.

Gradually, the pharaoh began to make out the facial features of the larger-than-life figure.

"*Khafre!*" he murmured in Old Egyptian, barely audible, as he stopped just short of the base of the structure along with the others. The hieroglyphic experts immediately translated.

"He said Khafre. He said Khafre," they echoed feverishly through the crowd.

It was apparent that Khufu was moved. He blinked several times as he attempted to maintain his composure—as he tried to make sense of this new altered reality.

Why was Khafre, his son who had held so much promise in life, connected to this strange celestial place? Was Khafre not still alive?

He summoned everything within himself to maintain his poise. He double blinked now and marshaled his faculties with the discipline of a soldier. It is the pride of pharaohs to keep their emotions in check, he mused, insulating himself further.

The Egyptian experts, meanwhile, continued to mumble to each other. "The face on the Sphinx is his son Khafre…."

It had been debated for centuries whether the Great Sphinx had been modeled after Prince Khafre or whether the features belonged to his brother Prince Dedefra. Already, a historical question had been put to rest.

Khufu now looked out across the plateau toward the Great Pyramid and began to walk in that direction, seemingly oblivious to those around him, as if drawn by some psychic magnet. So engrossed was he in his destination that he began to out distance his entourage. They trailed him in utter fascination. What might he be thinking? they wondered. It would likely be some months before they'd be able to communicate with him.

He reached the queens' pyramids first.

Despite his stoic expression, his mind was turning, asking questions, reasoning: *Perhaps this is the land of the Ka,* he said to himself. The Egyptians believed that the Ka or spirit-like twin of a person lived in a parallel universe.

That is why these structures look so old, he rationalized, trying to make sense of what was unfolding. *Could the ideas of Kemet be fostered from this place?* The photographic team was still busy shooting pictures and video. The cameras captured every angle of the historic moment.

Khufu found himself, now, at the foot of the pyramid of his mother, Queen Hetepheres. Did he know this was his mother's resting place? He reached out and touched the texture of the uncovered blocks. They felt so real, so worldly like. Meanwhile, the early pre-noon sun had begun to cause his ebony skin to glisten in perspiration.

Reflecting, he thought about the last thing he remembered when things were normal. He had just eaten a succulent meal of roasted duck, lentils, tomatoes and cucumbers. And as he had made his way to his terrace, to catch a breath of fresh air, he had felt himself losing consciousness and falling to the floor.

Turning, now, he looked out at the modern buildings of Cairo and the suburb of Mena, which were encroaching on the necropolis. He turned back and looked up at the large pyramid overlooking the smaller queens' structures. The edifice had the same dimensions as his Great Pyramid. Was this its Ka twin?

Inexplicably, the clanging sound of metal workers began ringing in his ears. His memories of his construction crew so vivid he now saw Ancient Egyptian men measuring dimensions and others moving huge blocks. He seemed to be in the midst of two worlds simultaneously.

Meanwhile, everything about his body told him he was alive. The sand pebbles between his toes; his chest rising rhythmically. And sweat beads turning into trickles down his mahogany physique. He placed his hand over his heart area and could feel his heartbeat.

Now, he looked at the pyramids of his wives Mereyites and Henutsen; he'd had plans for such an outlay of queens' tombs when his structure was designed. Meanwhile, he was fully aware of the curious onlookers studying him. *Were these people Ka beings or the heavenly hosts who were supposed to meet him?* he wondered.

Where was the jackal-god Anubis with the Scale of Maat to weigh his heart against the Feather of Truth? Where is Osiris, Horus, Isis? Where are my forefathers Snefru, Djoser? he asked himself. *Were they not supposed to meet me on the other side of death? Who are these beings in the strange clothes?*

He began to walk again, this time taking long strides toward the Great Pyramid. He reached its base and could literally smell the dust that had been stirring during its construction. But he didn't see an ancient, decrepit mausoleum. He saw a well-polished classic work of art, with work crews conscientiously tending to the finishing touches.

He looked up at its apex and there the gold-capped crest remained. Meanwhile, he slowly fixed his gaze at the entrance and saw his high priest, Ini-Herit, ordering it sealed with a final granite block.

Masud walked up to the pharaoh, bringing him out of his thoughts, and gently gestured toward the entrance. But Khufu had already decided not to enter. He pointed, instead, toward the limousine, which had just pulled up at the roadside.

13

T he limousine pulled back onto the open road, now. This was enough for the pharaoh's first day in the twenty-first century, the officials agreed. He was handling himself quite well, at-any-rate, in spite of the confusion he must have felt.

They decided they would have another EKG done on him immediately, however, when they reached the laboratory. The pharaoh looked healthy, but the obvious stress of encountering such a perplexing reality might weigh heavily on him, they figured.

While the limousine headed back towards the lab, Khufu had much to ponder. He wondered if perhaps his conception of Duat had been all wrong. Perhaps this *was* Duat. Or, perhaps this was indeed a visit to the land of the Ka, some pretest before he entered Duat.

One thing he was certain of, however, was that the ancient necropolis they had just visited was an exact replica of the one he and his vizier, his priests, and later his son's had designed. Why, the Sphinx had been merely a passing fancy Khafre had mentioned one day when they discussed possibilities for the future of the complex.

He'd had enough for one day. Perhaps he would awake from this bad dream and resume the duties of overseeing his kingdom. He reflected on an Egyptian proverb his uncle, Kemnebi, had once taught him.

"To destroy an undesirable rate of mental vibration, concentrate on the opposite vibration to the one to be suppressed."

He would assume this was a bad dream and ride it out in more relaxing thoughts.

President Hamadi, meanwhile, telephoned his favorite restaurant and ordered lunch to be catered to the lab—he was sure the pharaoh was famished by now. "Food," he said to Khufu, reaching into the limo's mini cabinet. He pulled out a small bag of Cheetos and reached into the refrigerator for another soda pop. This time he pulled out a grape-flavored one and handed it to Khufu. He proceeded to ask the others their preferences and retrieved a grape flavored one for himself.

"Food," Khufu nodded in acknowledgement, as the president handed him the plastic bag covered in strange script, with something orange inside. It contained something edible, Khufu deduced. He had enjoyed the bubbly sensation of the earlier drink and wondered what *this* orange-colored ration would taste like. President Hamadi generously opened the package for the puzzled pharaoh who liked the smell of the cheese-like spiraled food stuffs. Indeed, it tasted like crunchy cheese. Khufu was having a taste-bud sensation; he had always wondered how food in Duat might taste. He now decided to open his soda pop on his own; he looked at the others who mirrored his amusement, then pulled the tab which elicited a pop.

"Pop," Nadat said with a chuckle.

"Pop," Khufu pointed.

"Pop," James nodded.

"Pop," President Hamadi chimed, followed by Masud.

"Pop."

Khufu looked at the countenance of the human-like beings with the strange attire. They were all well disposed towards him. But this place certainly wasn't anything like he'd been taught to expect concerning the afterlife. Yet, when he had showered earlier, he was astonished to notice there were no scars on his body. He was like brand new. Not one of the scars or scratch marks he had accumulated in his entire lifetime was present. The cut he had received on his forearm during military training as a youth—vanished; another mark on his shin he had gotten from running into a grass-shrouded broken down fence as a boy, vanished; no scratches, no marks, no scars...all were gone.

He needed to be alone for awhile. He had never imagined visiting the land of the Ka. While he had read in folk tales that others had visited the land of the Ka, he had never been certain that a separate land for the Ka actually existed.

14

T he next morning Khufu awoke before dawn and found his room immersed in a strange blue light. He felt the unfamiliar but soft textures of his bed coverings and looked around the room at the TV, the mirror, lights and other strange objects in the room. No, the day before had not been a dream. He must indeed be in the land of the Ka. But if the man who wrote on the white board yesterday was a Ka, why could he not write understandable hieroglyphics—or even speak Egyptian well?

He eased out of bed quietly to look out the window and noted the fantastic automatic carriages and the strange buildings, like the one's he had seen the day before. And mounted atop tall black poles were the source of the blue light. And the humming continued. He always heard humming sounds in this world.

He reflected on the day before: After they had returned from the pyramids, he had been encircled by men in white robes who attached tiny wires to him that were connected to little black boxes with rapidly moving figures inside. It was a ritual they had done before, which apparently monitored his insides, he figured. Later, they gathered for a meal comprised of what was called falafel, which he acknowledged as very good. Then, he was led to his quarters where a big screen called a TV was turned on. He was given a small rectangular control device and shown what buttons to press in order to change from one vision to the next, or turn it on or off. The device was like magic, no stick or string was attached to it.

Left alone, he had continued to zap the vision screen from one interesting vision to another. He wondered how the Ka had gotten into the screen and vowed to one day open it and introduce himself to them. He wondered if in this world he could make himself small, somehow, and enter the screen also.

Khufu returned to his bed and bounced on it lightly to get a better feel for it. The springy feel was certainly different from anything he had slept on before. How did one explain this dimension of existence? And if he was in the land of the Ka, *Why* was he here? The faster he learned their celestial language, or whatever it was they spoke, the quicker he'd be able to get to the bottom of the puzzle, he figured.

Fortunately, it had been important, his father Snefru had believed, that his sons and daughters spoke several languages for trade and diplomatic purposes. Khufu had, subsequently, been quite proficient in languages; and had learned to speak four idioms, including several dialects. It was simple, he surmised—first you learn the major sounds of a language and then begin pronouncing words. He rattled off several words he'd already learned.

"Eat, food, ca, yes, no, hello, falafel." Not bad for my first day here, he mused.

A knock on the door brought him out of his thoughts and reminded him it was time to proceed with his language lessons. He wasn't sure what the day would bring, but he'd decided to learn as much as he could. Meanwhile, if these beings turned out to be the gods, they'd certainly expect him to be attentive to their goals and aims, he figured.

"Good morning." It was the short one who spoke poor Egyptian and the good-looking female who'd led him through the picture scrolls.

"Good morning," Khufu responded, in a resonant tone, matching Masud's accent as best he could. He had learned early in life that when one matched a foreigner's voice sound, the prerequisite for bonding and relationship building was initiated more quickly.

Masud and Ali, meanwhile, looked at each other in astonishment, jolted by Khufu's response and its clarity.

"Hotep sedemef," Masud said in Old Egyptian, peace be unto you.

"Haatep sudamef," Khufu responded in his basic accent, as he perceived that the Ka was attempting to talk Egyptian better.

Masud then handed Khufu a terry-cloth robe he had brought in with him and gestured in a swirling-washing motion as he headed toward the shower. Next, he took wash cloths out of the linen closet and gave them to the pharaoh. Khufu, meanwhile, followed him to the shower where Masud demonstrably turned on the hot-and cold-water knobs so Khufu could begin his shower.

President Hamadi was en route to pick them up for breakfast, so Masud acted as efficiently as possible, without rushing the pharaoh, who apparently realized they were about to go outside the facility again. He finished showering quickly.

Masud then showed him to the closet, as he had the day before, and Khufu picked out his attire without much ado. Soon, they headed out to meet the president and begin their day.

The limo had arrived promptly, and Ali, Masud, and Khufu climbed in ready for an eventful morning. James

Hannibal had spent the night at his house in the district of Zamalek. And Nadat was attending an early conference, but promised to meet the group later in the afternoon. Khufu, meanwhile, marveled at the accouterments of modern society. The sky blue leather seats in the metal encased transportation vehicle, called a *ca*, were shaped like the lair of a king's harem, and the softness and smell of the material was unlike any *earthen* fabric he had ever encountered. The windows could be raised or lowered with the push of a magic button; meanwhile, the carriage moved at lightning speed, almost without sound. The road rushed towards them like altered time. And a celestial music, too encompassing to compare, emerged out of thin air.

President Hamadi nodded, "Hoatep," bringing Khufu out of his thoughts, and presented the pharaoh with a pair of sunglasses to halt the glare from the morning sun. He then put on a similar pair himself, as they were heading east directly into the sunlight. Khufu was bemused by the total change in scenery the glasses provided; everything was brighter, more vivid, more fantastic. And the pretty honey-colored female was indeed the personification of Isis.

She had retrieved a pair of sunglasses from her bag, and a flirtatious glimmer peered from behind her dark lenses. Khufu was beginning to enjoy this land of the Ka. He challenged himself to learn this celestial language even faster; there was so much to know about this place. He would hone in on the conversations of the Ka for keys to the language sounds. He had already noticed that the riders with him spoke in a second idiom, sometimes, and that often Masud and the statesman looking Ka, who sat across from him, and *this goddess*, spoke in that idiom.

The black brother who looked like his cousin Horemheb and seemed to hold special sway with all of the Ka, was the one who consistently spoke in "English," the primary language used in the lab.

The limousine continued its trek eastward towards the sun, buffered by motorcycle police, presidential security, and media vehicles. Stray cars, meanwhile, joined the motorcade like magnets attracted to a lodestone. The rest of the traffic, however, gave way to the procession, heeding the flashing lights and intermittent sirens.

Just ahead, the Nile came into view. Feluccas, the single-sailed boats, common to the region, speckled the waterway, and bright sunlit waves sparkled like jewels. High above, they crossed on a modern steel-beamed bridge.

This must be the Ka of the mighty Nile, Khufu figured. It was like the river Khufu had played along as a child, but more tamed, more contained by the ubiquitous construction of the celestials. His Nile—its untamed breadth—could only be spanned by boats or barges. And the location of *this* city was northeast of the site of his capital, Memphis; a fact he deduced by its orientation to the Pyramids.

Tall buildings loomed high along its shores, and automobiles, including trucks and utility vehicles traveled along its banks and crisscrossed on other bridges farther up and down river.

Khufu beckoned to Masud for the writing utensil and pad that lay in his lap and jotted down a question in hieroglyphics:

"WHAT MEANT BY TERM 21st CENTURY?" he asked. Masud responded in a sentence that read: "MANY, MANY YEARS."

Khufu replied: "I MANY, MANY, YEARS AGO? NOW IS MANY, MANY YEARS FORWARD?"

"MANY *THOUSANDS* OF YEARS" was Masud's reply.

Khufu was dumfounded by the response. But that brought everything into perspective. That *was* his Great Pyramid. This *was* the mighty Nile. And these *were not gods or Ka*; they were men like him.

Outside the tinted-glass windows, the early morning mass of humanity crowded the pavement in Cairo's downtown area like ants on desert mounds stirred by sprinkles of rain. Khufu mused at the press of people and the varied clothing they wore. None wore loin cloths, he noted, while many of them wore sandals or foot coverings like the people in the car.

Mules, donkeys, bovine, goats and dogs were also to be seen. Indeed, he was in the future and still earthbound. He wondered about these people's relationship with the gods. Did they know the deities Amen Ra, Horus, Osiris, or Isis?

The varied colors of the cars also amused him, and he marveled at how they traveled effortlessly along the smoothly paved roads that seemed to go everywhere. If this is not Duat, it couldn't be much more fantastic than this, he mused in amazement.

The limo slowed and came to a stop in front of a row of tall buildings. The driver promptly got out, opened the doors, for the group, and they unloaded onto the sidewalk. Khufu, still in his sunglasses and dressed in a kilt and trademark blue-and gold-striped nemes, epitomized the look of a legendary pharaoh. Around his neck was a four-inch wide gold necklace embedded intermittently with blue topaz, emeralds and semi-precious stones that glistened in the sunshine.

Khufu looked up into the sky at the high-rises and marveled. What kind of kingdom could build such streamlined edifices as these? Meanwhile, crowds of people had gotten wind of his presence, in the area, and pressed to get near him and his entourage. But his majesty was quickly ushered into the building where he and his party were promptly led to an elevator.

"Elevator!" Ali smiled, noting Khufu's quizzical countenance while entering the small compartment. Too many of the entourage tried to squeeze into the little room before three agents backed out giving thumbs ups to the others as the doors closed.

"Elevator," Khufu replied returning the thumbs up, but unsure of what it meant.

Meanwhile, the floor shuttered slightly, and Khufu could tell they were moving, but how and where to, he knew not.

Moments later, the doors opened magically to the ring of a bell, revealing a large room where music played softly—like in the limousine—and no musicians were present. It was an exquisite restaurant, where a slightly balding maitre d' stood several feet away with a broad smile and an expectant gaze. He quickly ushered the group to a row of tables perched near windows, which provided a splendid view of the city skyline and the Nile. It was eight-thirty AM but only a few people were in the restaurant, as the management had agreed to limit entry to only select VIPs, to prevent overcrowding and help with security issues. In addition, they were separated from the pharaoh by agents who cordoned the perimeter.

The breakfast was hearty, and Khufu learned much from the group, during the meal. He'd had difficulty at the lab in using the eating utensils, but now he'd gotten the hang of it and poked certain foods with his fork and scooped other with his spoon, as the others did. He had eggs, lamb chops, bean cakes, pancakes, and nawahif; and drank orange juice and coffee. A photographer was on hand to take pictures of the group sitting around the table. And Khufu was stunned when he looked at the photographs the guy gave him from an instamatic cell phone printer.

Ali, meanwhile, enjoyed the incredible novelty of just sitting there with the renowned Pharaoh Khufu. Frankly, she could barely bring herself to believe it; one of the ancient forefathers of Kemet, as the ancients called themselves, sitting there alive and well in the twenty-first century.

Khufu, all-the-while, viewed this modern-day daughter of Kemet as the personification of Isis. She was as close to a goddess as he had ever come.

President Hamadi, after a time, realized that Professor Hannibal wasn't likely to show up, now, since he was generally a stickler for time; so he dialed Hannibal via his cell phone and reached him at home.

"Professor Hannibal!" President Hamadi said when James answered the phone. "I thought we'd see you here this morning at the restaurant?"

James had resigned himself to the reality that it was time to leave Egypt. So he had spent the morning packing. "I'm sorry, Mr. President. I'll be leaving soon, you know, so I've decided to finish the packing process."

"Yes. Yes, but we're here at breakfast having a wonderful time. And you would have enjoyed it."

"I'm sure I would have," James replied. "But this has been a long two years, Mr. President," he said, frankly. "I've got a wife and family matters to take care of back home," he explained. "Tell Khufu and the others goodbye for me. I'll be getting my plane ticket to the States—but I'll be available when you're ready to make a tour with the pharaoh."

"Thank you for your incredible work, Professor Hannibal," the president said. "And don't worry about a plane ticket, okay? When you're ready to go, let me know. The presidential jet is at your disposal."

"Why thanks, Mr. President," James replied, "I appreciate that."

"I'll have my secretary call you," Hamadi said. "We'll work out a schedule to shuttle you home."

"Great, Mr. President," Hannibal said as they hung up.

More people, despite the earlier arrangement, had begun to trickle into the restaurant, and the security agents were beginning to get edgy as more and more individuals asked if they might shake the pharaoh's hand or take a picture with him.

The restaurant catered to wealthy Egyptians and many European and American expatriates.

"Well, the regulars are arriving," Hamadi said. "We'd better wind down before it gets too crowded in here. The pharaoh's literally the hottest item in history, you know."

Meanwhile, a few people, whom the president knew personally, had already relayed messages to Hamadi about a photo opportunity or a handshake with Khufu before the group left. The security chief was skeptical, but Hamadi gave his okay that the admirers could simply stand along the exit route as Khufu was leaving. And he gave permission for them to take pictures while he and his entourage exited. So they left doing a literal right hand of fellowship amidst an incessant flashing of cell phone cameras. The guests and all of the employees, literally, shook Khufu's hand as the pharaoh and his entourage made their way out. Meanwhile, this was a nightmare for the security agents. The crush of people was too close, and the flashing lights literally blinded them as they tried to sturdy the crowd.

Once outside, they realized the people had expanded to thousands. The astute Egyptian police had cordoned off the entrance of the building to ease the pharaoh's exit, but the press of people was more than anyone had expected.

Suddenly, out of nowhere, a dagger zipped past Khufu, missing him by inches, lodging into a palm tree. Pandemonium broke out, meanwhile, as the crowd pointed towards a fleeing suspect who ran into oncoming traffic, dodging cars. Immediately, Khufu was covered by gun-wielding security agents before being quickly ushered into the waiting limousine along with the president and Dr. Ali.

Breathing heavily the president announced: "This, certainly, changes things"; as he, Khufu, Ali and two gun-wielding security agents looked out at the ruckus. "We'll have to adjust our schedule," he said in Arabic turning to the driver.

Hamadi directed the chauffeur to one of Egypt's several presidential palaces. He had decided that Khufu would move into the luxurious residence immediately. After all, the pharaoh was Egypt's de-facto king and needed the highest level of protection, now.

≈

The media and police publicly called the attempted knifing of the pharaoh an "unfortunate meeting of the sovereign with an extremist mad man." A TV camera panning the crowds and cell phones had inadvertently captured the man on video, and they suspected someone who knew him would contact authorities sooner or later. Meanwhile, the question remained…Were bigger elements behind the assassination attempt?

The days turned into weeks and slowly the episode lost some of its sting. Khufu took it all in stride: *there would always be "mad men" in the world,* he surmised upon hearing his handlers' assessments of the incident.

He'd used his time wisely, therefore, and continued to engage himself diligently in his language lessons. He'd already learned the names of many objects in his immediate surroundings. In addition to *ca*—his accented way of saying car—and a few greetings, he'd learned the names of many of the foods he liked. He'd even begun to name his various rooms in the palace—it had fifty-six of them; eight bedrooms, a laundry room, two kitchens, three sitting rooms, a library, nine bathrooms, a movie theater, and a weight room and gym, just to name some of them.

The weight room, with its connected gymnasium, was his favorite. He marveled at what the comrades of his youth would have thought of the facility.

It had padded mats, for starters, and a rectangular metal apparatus that had protruding limbs that contained weights at their base. With the insertion of a metal pin, he could change the poundage to any desired amount. He also liked the sport his handlers' called basketball. Out on the polished wooden floor, he had been taught to bounce a ball while walking toward a highly placed circular rim. The object was to arch the ball through the air and into the rim. He especially liked the swish sound of the net when the ball reached its goal.

The weeks passed quickly. By the third week he had even begun to grasp verbs. And now, one month later, he was speaking in simple sentences.

All Egypt was excited about their pharaoh. And the People's Assembly, Egypt's Parliament, voted unanimously to create a titular monarchy, similar to that of Great Britain. Khufu would retain his title as pharaoh of Egypt, but the day-to-day responsibilities of running the nation would be left to its elected chief of state and Parliament. He was awarded an undisclosed endowment, rumored in the tens of millions, in American dollars, plus expenses for servants, valets and housing. He was also provided an additional palace in Luxor, a third in an undisclosed location and use of the presidential jet until he was ready for one of his own.

Suitors vied for a moment with the pharaoh; from heads of state, to media moguls, to college and university professors. But he declined most public contact via a statement from his press secretary, Masud, that said he would not be available until he'd completed his language studies and learned more about this new world, he'd found himself in.

Meanwhile, the details of how he had been brought to the twenty-first century A.D. were becoming clearer to him the more he learned the new language. He was indeed, somehow, in the future. But had the god's made some mistake? The more he learned, the more befuddled he became.

He had seen Professor Hannibal's picture on the portal called the Internet, and he had seen visions of "himself" in the gestation chamber. Still, he could not read the text well enough, yet, which apparently explained the procedure that had brought him to this time. And since the technology was far beyond ancient standards, he devised a plan to follow an elementary time line of discoveries to bridge the gap between the past and the present.

Taking the initiative, he asked Masud to teach him about the modern calendar and how it corresponded with his Old Kingdom calendar. He wanted to clearly pinpoint where he was on the historical time line in relation to ancient Kemet. And finally—he got it. He realized clearly, now, that he was forty-five hundred years into the future. He was astounded. Amazingly, however, it seemed like he had been in the Old Kingdom just a few days ago.

15

A basi Masud could barely believe his good fortune. He was now the right-hand man to Pharaoh. History would record his name along with that of the Great Khufu. Meanwhile, he was glad that his majesty was learning English quickly and was excited about the prospect of deciphering hieroglyphic texts that had perplexed Egyptologists for centuries. Now, as he read correspondence, at his desk in his office at Khufu's sprawling Cairo palace, he realized that he held the reigns to an incredible cultural phenomenon.

Already, an international text-book publisher had contacted him concerning the writings on the tomb walls at Saqqara. He was flattered, in fact, that the president of the company, Johan Vogel, had flown to Egypt to have dinner with him and discuss the details. Vogel was head of Germany's fastest growing and most prolific text-book publisher, Grammatik Deutsch. When he personally came out to pitch an idea, one had better believe it amounted to something huge.

They'd met over dinner at the Mena Hotel and discussed the marketing strategy of showcasing Khufu explaining the text to the modern world. The idea expanded to include talks concerning a DVD documentary, to be sold along with the print story. And Masud would be paid two million in American dollars for giving Grammatik Deutsch first rights to accessing and marketing the arcane information. It would be an under the table deal, but who would it hurt? Masud rationalized.

He swiveled his chair and retrieved a stack of periodicals from the credenza behind him. The newspapers and magazines entailed Khufu's advent into modernity—some well written, others poor exposés. He could scarcely keep up, he admitted, things were unfolding so fast.

Along with the Egyptian Ministry of Information, he was responsible for sending out press releases to the mass media, which never seemed to get enough. In fact, he had been compelled to deal with broadcasters and the press on a constant basis, due to false and misleading information that arose whenever there was a dearth of official correspondence. It seemed the public hunger for details of the pharaoh's new life, in the twenty-first century, was insatiable; so intense that tabloid-type newspapers and TV shows took advantage of gaps in the flow of information and came up with sensational tales.

Dr. Nailah Ali had offered to help, and Masud had agreed to take her up on the offer. After all, he couldn't keep-up alone. And she wouldn't be intimidated by being in the presence of the pharaoh like some outsider would.

Already, one tabloid had misquoted Khufu as saying the Pyramid Texts contained the explanation for an earth-based star gate that connected extraterrestrial civilizations throughout the universe. Another stated that Khufu had specialized pharaonic knowledge that would unravel the reputed concealment place of lost scrolls from the legendary library at Alexandria. The latter failed to explain that Khufu had lived during the Old Kingdom, over two thousand years before the building of the library, which was constructed during the Ptolemaic era, sometime after 332 B.C.—by then, the black pharaohs had essentially receded into history. Furthermore, no historic record had ever been found that overturned the common belief that all of the holdings of the library had been burned and destroyed.

He returned the periodicals to their place on the credenza and looked to other matters. Masud enjoyed the multitasking his work entailed and now busied himself in arranging for a historic cruise, for Pharaoh, up the Nile. They would have their own private yacht, and Khufu would be able to see the historic temple remains of his descendants up close and personal. On Friday morning they would be leaving, so Masud perused the last-minute details. The menu would include the pharaoh's favorites: Roasted duck, lamb, fish, falafel, buttered pita bread, dates, and his newfound delights, soda pop and chocolate ice cream.

≈

Nailah Ali was quite smitten by her new assignment. Who would have imagined? she mused, as she walked to the front door of the presidential palace. She had telephoned when she drove up, and Masud was there to greet her as she reached the entrance.

"Good to see you, Dr. Ali," he said. "You're the perfect person for the job; you'll be my right hand," he added eagerly, while she nodded an acknowledgment to the door guards. He led her into the palace and into an open concourse that revealed an exquisite winding staircase and adjacent rooms connecting the concourse to other parts of the mansion.

"Let me show you your office," Masud said, veering to the left as she followed him across the expanse. "Actually, you can choose from one of several rooms, here," he gestured, spreading his arms out in either direction and then up. "This is my headquarters," he added, entering a nice but cluttered space. It was clear he was overworked.

"My, you *have* been busy," Ali said looking at piles of papers on his desk.

"That's not the half of it," he responded. "Well, at least you'll know where to find me," he nodded, before walking back out into the hallway. "I'll have to get us a secretary, also. My assistant at the university is overloaded from helping us."

He explained the various projects they would be working on and delineated her duties. She had retrieved a small pad from her purse and was taking notes.

"The cruise is set for Friday, two days from now," he explained. "You'll need to bring your laptop. We can catch up on correspondence and help Pharaoh learn post Fourth Dynasty history, as he views the sites along the river."

"This should be a very interesting experience," Ali beamed, writing quickly.

"It's amazing," Masud said, thrilled to have her working with him. "I understand you're from Aswan—you'll be a great help to us in those parts."

"I hope so," she said, graciously. "I don't get down there often enough, actually."

"Well, whatever help you can give will be appreciated," he said. "Khufu's up in the library, presently—you might begin by assisting with his vocabulary," he said heading in that direction. "He's learning fast. I think you'll be impressed."

They walked back out into the concourse, and Ali was surprised when Khufu appeared at the top of the stairs. He was dressed in his usual kilt but he had shaved his head. The shirtless, well-defined monarch looked mysterious, and affectionately vulnerable, she noted. He turned without acknowledging them and headed back towards what was likely the library, she assumed.

They climbed the stairs and arrived to find him clicking the channels on a wide flat-screen TV that had been ordered especially for him.

Physically, he was quite athletic, she realized—very masculine. He'd flung his brown leg across the recliner, nonchalantly, as if he had nothing better to do in the world. Meanwhile, a certain astuteness emanated from him that belied his youthful physical age—at least youthful to her. She was forty-five years old. And he looked thirty-one or thirty-two, at best.

Something else was unexpected; she noticed a certain arrogance in his manner. *Having been a godlike figure and an absolute monarch would certainly contribute to that*, she surmised.

"Pharaoh, remember Dr. Nailah Ali? She will be helping us to assist you in your knowledge attainment; get you ready for the world. Millions are waiting to make your acquaintance."

Khufu could not possibly have understood all that Masud said, but he nodded acknowledgement of Masud's remarks, then resumed channel surfing.

"Well, I'll leave you two alone. He's in your hands, Dr. Ali."

She nodded graciously, as Masud left, and turned to Khufu who seemed totally engrossed in the television. He's fully engaged in learning, she acceded. After all, he was one of the greatest men in history.

She didn't know what else to do, so she simply watched as the pharaoh clicked across the channels. He would stop for awhile and peruse a station, then flitter across several others.

Finally, Ali walked over to a large table in the middle of the room and beckoned Khufu. He summarily stopped and rose to join her. *As suave as a movie star*, she mused.

"Good to see you," she said at last.

"Good see you," he replied casually.

He still had an accent, of course, but it was amazing how well he came across.

Inside himself, he realized he was enamored with Nailah Ali. She really did look like a version of Isis. He worked to conceal his opinion of her, however.

She had caught him by surprise, actually. Masud hadn't mentioned that she was coming or that she'd help as his tutor—at least tutoring seemed to be her responsibility, based on his earlier encounters with her.

She retrieved a book on modern Egypt and immediately began to point out sights to Khufu. "Nile."

"Nile," he said.

"Building."

"Bill-ding," he responded.

"Need connecting words," he blurted suddenly, as clear as day.

Ali was flabbergasted. After such a short time and Khufu was already grasping English.

Well, if he was intelligent enough to seek out verbs and conjunctions, already, he would no doubt become proficient in English sooner than later, she thought.

She realized he was also prepared now for sentence constructions and word order. For the most part, he had already learned the names of things.

Unbelievable, she mused.

They studied for an hour or so, and both of them found themselves enjoying the session as the time passed quickly. A knock on the door, meanwhile, revealed it was lunch time, as a housekeeper called out that they could come down to the dining room. Ali remembered she had some last-minute shopping to do for the cruise, however, and said her goodbyes, leaving uneventfully.

≈

Yes, Khufu was smitten with Dr. Nailah Ali. But no one would know it looking at his countenance. He was also smitten with modern technology. TV, radio, telephones, the Internet, electric lights and cars all fascinated him. It was beyond his ability to conjecture how the many technological advancements worked, he admitted.

Nailah Ali was, in fact, rather enamored with the pharaoh, also. But she would never admit it even to herself. While shopping she had bought him several comfortable galabayyas to wear and modern sandals—rubber flip flops, actually. The attire was quite comfortable, he admitted; and he donned the garb as a pleasurable novelty.

They were boarding the boat, now, prepared for their trip up the Nile. And he wondered what had ever possessed them, back in Ancient Egypt, to try to preserve their boats for eternity. He had noted that a special modern museum had been set up next to the Great Pyramid, housing his royal craft. But compared to this innovation, his was no match. His boat had measured nearly 150 feet with an enclosed cabin. But his sleeping quarters, on this *yacht,* was as large as the bedrooms of some nobles' homes. And there were other rooms and quarters on the yacht. He could feel the subtle vibration of the motor as they left the dock and was tempted to pinch himself for a reality check, as the boat made way, magically parting the waters.

"How about some chocolate ice cream, Khufu?" Nailah asked, coming up on deck with two bowls of the icy treat. Masud was up front talking with the pilot, and the security agents were dispatched around the craft.

"Yes, thank you," he said taking the bowl and sitting on a padded lounge chair across from hers. She set her ice cream on the table between them and raised her canopy. "Want some shade?" she asked, "those sun rays will burn you to a crisp."

"How does work?" he responded.

"How does *it* work?" she said, correcting him, as she walked around to assist him in raising his canopy. He stood next to her and their hands touched, sending bristles of energy between them as they prepared to lift the canopy together.

"How does *it* work?" he responded putting his hand on top of hers and gazing deeply into her eyes.

She could feel her knees buckle, but managed to maintain her composure. "Well," she said, gathering herself. "Just push up like this."

She was dressed in a modest blue-colored, tie-dyed galabayya. She had worn it especially for modesty. Attracted to the pharaoh, *maybe*, she realized, but her professional standards would not be breeched, she told herself. Meanwhile, she and Masud had a lot of work to do. And taking on the pharaoh as a romantic tryst would have fall out she wasn't sure she could manage.

Ali returned to her lounge chair and adjusted the backrest so she could sit more erect. She then turned towards Khufu as she took a scoop of ice cream and said, "Tell me about Ancient Egypt, Pharaoh?"

Khufu savored a scoop of ice cream, his chin pointing slightly upward, noble like, as he decided on a choice of recollections.

"Are you two enjoying yourselves?" a voice interrupted. It was Masud approaching.

"Poised for a wonderful weekend," Nailah said looking up at Masud. She had put on her sunglasses.

Khufu, meanwhile, raised his backrest and turned to Masud with a smile. "Nice biig boat."

"Yes, we call it a yacht," Masud said. "You like?"

"Nice as me yact in Ancient Egypt," Khufu said tongue in cheek, his mispronunciation sounding charming in English.

Masud walked over to the railing and looked out over the river and the countryside. They were nearing the necropolis of Saqqara, an older burial ground than Giza. It was just outside Cairo to the south. The remains of the city of Memphis and Dashur, another necropolis, were just a few miles farther up river. Khufu had been tightlipped, despite subtle efforts from Masud, on the exact burial places of his father Snefru and the legendary genius Imhotep. Imhotep had been a physician, architect and statesman, the Hippocrates of his day. He had started a medical school that lasted for some two thousand years in the ancient world. Perhaps Khufu was reluctant to reveal their burial places because of some fear he had that they would be disturbed, Masud speculated.

Thus, Masud had decided to make those stops on the return trip. Khufu would have much time to think of them and would perhaps open up following the excitement of seeing the later sites. One thing was for sure, Khufu, without question, had the right to be the trustee over his father Snefru's burial site and would certainly impact all other digs from there on out.

They were just a mile or so from Memphis now—Egypt's capital during Khufu's reign. It wasn't much to look at anymore, after some forty-five hundred years, Masud observed. He wondered how Khufu would take to the reality that his great capital had diminished to a mere extant stop-off point for tourists.

Khufu looked out at farmers trailing their oxen, while children and families waved as the boat passed their small holdings and simple abodes.

Meanwhile, he leaned back in his lounge chair and thought about the Egypt of his day:

He noted how Ancient Egyptian society was structured like a huge extended family. *Pharaoh was the benevolent head, or father figure. The nobles were benign uncles and aunts; and the populace-at-large were the genial offspring of the dominion. Every Egyptian, including Pharaoh, was expected to abide by the cosmic principle of Maat—the rule of order, justice and goodness.*

Turning to Nailah, thoughtfully, he explained: "We were biig family. Protected by desert to east and west and provided for by *thiis* eternal Nile. We wove culture that became self-perpetuating. No matter what one's class...through work and dedication, could rise above birth status."

He elaborated on other black cultures of the period: "Our cousins, the people of Tyre from north, and Nubia from south; traded with us, and we maintained alliances. My reign was peaceful time, and we prospered greatly," he said in deep, longing reflection.

"Memphis," Masud shouted, pointing up ahead.

The place they were approaching was little more than a sandy junction. It belied its grand past. Memphis had boasted a large harbor in Khufu's day. Now, what he saw was a small sightseeing stop-off point for tourists. Khufu was taken aback, actually. It seemed as though he were in *his* bustling Memphis just a few weeks ago. Now, however, this pride of the ancient world was a stolid by-way.

Humbling. Humbling indeed, he thought, in Old Kingdom Egyptian.

16

Back in the U.S., James Hannibal was spending catch-up time with his wife, Marika. The house in Chicago's Pill Hill section was quaint and a good fit for the two of them. It was less than ten minutes away from Rainbow Beach, where they took early morning walks together. And only a few blocks from Stony Island Avenue and 87th Street, where they had easy access to restaurants and shops.

"This is such a nice area," Marika said cheerfully, while James steered the navy blue Mercedes sedan along Stony Island Avenue. She was glad he was home and happy they were in Chicago. It reminded her of their undergraduate years.

"Yeah, our modern-day 'Black Lands,'" James quipped.

They drove north and soon made their way onto Lake Shore Drive, where they could smell the freshwater breeze off Lake Michigan. Sailboats and motorized craft dotted the waterway, which stretched against the far-reaching horizon. The massive lake, a part of the Great Lakes chain, was Chicago's best-kept secret. And they, like other sun lovers, made good use of it during the hot July weather.

They'd decided to spend the afternoon at Navy Pier, where they would take in an arts and crafts show, followed by dinner on the *Windy City Cruiser*, a water-faring restaurant.

James and Marika clasped hands and strolled through the sparse Saturday afternoon crowd, immersed in each other's presence. They purchased an item here and there and gazed into each other's eyes, as they'd done as teenagers in love for the first time. It had been a long while since they'd spent quality time like this together, and they clung to the moments as if afraid they might slip away. They savored this reunion— soul mates whose ship had come to harbor. At last, it was anchored to port.

Over dinner, the captain of the *Windy City Cruiser* announced landmarks amidst Chicago's architecturally renowned skyline, via the intercom. He pointed out the famed *Ebony* magazine building, the John Hancock Center, and the one hundred ten story Willis Tower; meanwhile, the sharp tuxedo-clad waiters were quick to assess and fulfill the diners' every need.

Then James noticed a special report on the news scrolling across the television screen above the wet bar. An assassination attempt had been made on the life of Pharaoh Khufu, in Egypt.

17

It had happened so suddenly. Khufu replayed the events in his mind like a video recording. He and his entourage had reached the final destination of the cruise at Abu Simbel. And while listening to the tour guide at the base of the sculpture, assassins had appeared out of thin air, it seemed, unleashing a volley of machine-gun fire that tore into the group like the claws of an invisible panther.

The security detail, meanwhile, had astutely shoved Khufu to the ground and covered him, but most of them had lost their lives in the process. Masud had been hit in the chest and upper arm, but was alive and had been airlifted to the nearest hospital by helicopter. Fortunately, Nailah Ali had decided to remain in Aswan with her family. They were supposed to retrieve her on the return trip. The tour group of twelve, including two local guides, had been reduced to just five survivors. Seven people had been killed. Only Khufu, Masud, one of the guides, and two security agents had survived.

Now, it was just before dawn, and a lightning-bug-like chopper edged downward to airlift Khufu and the remaining survivors from a local hotel parking lot. They would be taken to the awaiting presidential jet in Aswan. While sullen over the earlier melee, Khufu paradoxically marveled at the advancement of modern technology—the bug-like apparatus floated in the air, despite its apparent heaviness—*but what a sad irony, even in this time period—so tremendously removed into the future—men still resolve issues through assassinations,* he realized.

Raheem Nadat climbed out of the helicopter, crouching instinctively beneath the swirling blades and took determined strides as he eyed the remaining retinue heading to the chopper. The two agents maintained their professional poise on opposite sides of Khufu, but it was evident they'd had enough for one weekend.

Raheem quickly ushered them into the chopper and scrambled in behind them as the pilot skipped the usual pleasantries and rose into the dark sky, before veering northward toward Aswan.

≈

Earlier in Cairo

Back in Cairo, President Fadil Hamadi sat at his desk with a look of disdain as he read the email printout. It was as he had speculated all along. Al Najja, a right-wing terrorist group, had claimed responsibility for the murders and the assassination attempt on the life of Pharaoh Khufu, at Abu Simbel. They had made their point loud and clear—they blatantly challenged Khufu's claim to the Egyptian crown—a position they had effectively reverberated via the media around the globe.

Hamadi pressed the intercom button at his desk.

"Aziza, could I see you for a moment, please?"

She entered, promptly, with the quiet calm executive secretaries learn to cultivate. "Yes, Mr. Hamadi?"

"Would you see to it that no one interrupts me within the next hour?" he asked tersely.

"Yes, Mr. President, no interruptions," she responded, repeating his instructions. She waited to see that he was finished and pivoted, closing the door quietly behind her.

Hamadi would have to personally call several of his military top command and did not want to be disturbed as he engaged in talks with them.

"General Gahiji, how are you? I'm sure you're surprised to hear from me, personally, but I wanted to get the ball rolling, as they say. As you are probably aware, Al Najja has claimed responsibility for the killings and the assassination attempt on the pharaoh, at Abu Simbel. This call is to issue a Code Six. Is that clear?"

"Yes, Mr. President, a Code Six."

"Thank you, General. Goodbye."

"Good-bye," Mr. President.

≈

Khufu had enjoyed the cruise up the Nile tremendously, leading up to the terrorist attack. They had literally traveled through four and a half millennia of Egypt's history on the five-day excursion, visiting ancient temples and ruins that, ironically, had not even been thought of yet in his day.

Now, he reflected on the terrorists again. In ancient Kemet, he would have quieted the malcontents before they breathed another breath on Amen's green earth. Meanwhile, he realized that he had been evolving into a kinder, gentler person as he had grown older. He could, at least, now understand why they might be suspect of his claim. What an incredible tale, a king from forty-five centuries ago, revived to see the light of day... younger body, wiser mind, what a trade off, he mused.

It was dark during the flight: Khufu was mesmerized by the instrument panel—the gauges, and the red, blue, green, yellow and orange buttons in the helicopter. All was quiet except the chopping of the overhead blades and the engine. The deaths of the others had left the passengers introspective, and sober. Down below, the occasional proliferation of lights on the ground made Khufu wonder again whether he really *was* among the gods, despite their potential for violent outbreaks. He reflected on the Egyptian story of the *Battle of the Gods,* in which Osiris was murdered by Seth, and the resulting confrontations between Horus and Seth, in Duat. They had fought for eighty years before Horus—Osiris's son—finally overcame Seth—his father's brother and archenemy—and banished him to the underworld to serve with Anubis.

Meanwhile, the chopper began to descend over a patch of lights that were streamlined like heavenly, blue-bordered roadways. The pilot spoke into a strange headpiece, which completed the bug-like motif. And while Khufu couldn't figure out who the pilot was communicating with, it was apparent that they were settling down in the midst of what was, indeed, a lighted city.

Nadat, meanwhile, was glad he had taken the flight to retrieve Pharaoh. The risk of another attack, perhaps aimed at the yacht, was too much of a possibility.

He thought about Abasi Masud, still in the southern Egyptian hospital. The scoundrel had sidestepped death. Nadat was decidedly disappointed with the hieroglyphic expert's undercutting tactics, which he'd been aware of. But he acknowledged the inherent opportunities that arose out of being handler to the pharaoh. Fortunately, they'd had a wire tap on the palace phones and spy ware on the Internet. You can never be sure about people in these types of situations, the security chief had cautioned.

Masud would have profited scot free. Now, any profits made from the pharaoh would go directly to the pharaoh, or to Egypt. Nadat would see to that, he promised himself.

Khufu, for-the-most-part, recognized in Masud the striving of an ambitious bureaucrat. He had seen men like him in the Old Kingdom in countless administrative positions. Men with talent but unfortunately shaped by their environment. For his part, he realized he had learned a lot from Masud. The language expert's attention to detail along with an eagerness to better grasp Old Egyptian had shortened the pharaoh's learning curve. Masud's efforts had brought Khufu to his present English-speaking proficiency and awareness level of the twenty-first century. He could now express himself in complete sentences in English. And he understood this time and place in history better than he would have ever expected.

This was a period that had been built on the accomplishments of all the civilizations before it, he realized. Like runners in a relay race, each culture had passed its legacy on to the next. And now, the culmination was this highly technological age.

≈

In his first day of the twenty-first century, Khufu had been astounded by the thundering supersonic jet that roared overhead at the research lab. It was unlike anything he had ever imagined—a rumbling, powerful, metal bird. He had assumed then that it must have been the result of some activity of the gods. And days later, from the windows of his palace, he had seen a long cloud-trail high in the sky—the wake of a bird-shaped airship zipping rapidly through the heavens. Now, in the morning sunshine, he prepared to board what was a big 727, the Egyptian presidential plane.

He shook hands with a tall confident man, whom he assumed was the pilot of the craft and was ushered by Nadat, along with several security agents, down a short aisle between four or five rows of seats. This opened into a larger seating quarters comprised of plush cushioned chairs along the windows and a central conference table with chairs that were apparently secured around it in the center of the compartment.

Nadat instructed the agents to sit wherever they'd like, in the general area, and led Khufu farther back to sets of swivel cushioned chairs, on both sides of the aisle, that faced small tables and companion chairs. They were hedged against a contoured wall, on each side of the aisle, which sectioned the area off from other rooms in the rear of the plane.

Nadat gestured for Khufu to sit at one table and sat across from him, apparently eager to talk with the pharaoh. Khufu had studied with Masud for three- and-a-half months, now, and Nadat wanted to sample the results up close and personal.

"Good to see you, Pharaoh," he said eagerly, wiping his brow with a handkerchief, as he slumped into his seat and began putting on his seatbelt.

"Good see you," Khufu replied in a resonant tone, as he followed suit with *his* seatbelt.

"Was a close call there at Abu Simbel," Nadat said beckoning for the flight attendant as he talked.

"Yes, opened eyes to realize this really no Heaven," Khufu responded.

His accent sounded Hamitic, but Nadat was amazed to hear how well he spoke English already.

"Yes, how might I help you, Raheem?" the flight attendant asked in English as she approached. They were on a first name basis since Nadat had often flown with the president on official business.

"I wanted to be the first to introduce you to Pharaoh Khufu, Halima. He will often have use of the presidential plane, now, and I want him to know that he'll be in good hands with you."

She nodded her head humbly towards the pharaoh, issuing a pleasant smile.

"May radiance of sun consume you," Khufu said, clasping each of her hands in his.

Suddenly the pilot announced over the intercom that he was ready to taxi to the runway for takeoff. The engines revved for a moment, and the aircraft slowly began to move from the hanger area. Halima headed to her duty station, and Khufu looked out the oval-shaped window next to him. He watched the grounds crew wave bright, orange utensils that apparently assisted the pilots up front.

He then felt his heartbeat increase rapidly as the metal bird hummed before coming to a halt as it faced a long runway ahead. Next, without warning, the jet began to accelerate down the pavement at an incredible speed, before rising into the air effortlessly, leaving the ground and the busy grounds-crew behind.

Everything was so small now, so incredibly small. Khufu could see canals and roads and the patched colors of fields. And the Nile, so colossal up close, meandered lazily through the landscape like a long serpent. Then wonderfully, he began to look down on fluffy clouds. Here a patch there a patch, like snow-covered oases of the gods. The urge, yet again, was to imagine that he was, indeed, among the gods. But this time he held the tendency in check. No, these were not gods. These were mere men like him, no different from the men of his day. It was just another time and another generation, but an amazing time and an amazing generation.

18

N adat had cleared James for immigration, and now the professor was en route to Egypt to retrieve the pharaoh for a temporary stay in the United States. It would be safer if Khufu resided incognito in America for awhile and perhaps return to the Republic of Egypt after the government got a better grip on the extremist group Al Najja.

The Gulfstream executive jet sped at near full velocity, rapidly approaching Western Europe at almost six-hundred miles per hour. James, meanwhile, sat amused in one of the private aircraft's plush leather seats, studying his potential chess moves, while his friend Robert Luster, the plane's owner, sat across from him and chimed "checkmate!" beaming cleverly.

"Castle," James retorted, as he leaned forward moving his king outside his rook.

"You can't castle when you're in check," Luster protested.

James sighed, and reconsidered his options. Luster had him on the run now. The president of Triad International, a corporation that consisted primarily of hotel holdings, was an old high school chum of James's from Mississippi. Luster had been shrewd even back then, James mused. Now his multi-million dollar success at Triad was pure poetic justice. James moved his king laterally now to buy more time.

Up front, the pilot and co-pilot made small talk as the plane sped along on autopilot. They were on-staff employees of Luster's and were called to fly at least two or three times a week as they shuttled the company's executives and hotel employees to diverse areas of the United States, Canada and the Caribbean.

This trip was a nice diversion for them. It was a chance to give the jet a major transcontinental tune up, and they would have a day off to see the sights of Cairo as well. But first, they would stopover for refueling at Paris's Charles de Gaulle Airport before continuing on to Egypt, where they'd pick up a friend of Hannibal's and Luster's.

≈

Back in Cairo, now, Khufu began to intensify his studies of the United States, on the Internet. He was pleased he could read and speak English better, and his knowledge base was increasing exponentially. He still sometimes left out the word "the" in sentences, since it was not used in Old Egyptian, but for the most part, he had become fluent in English.

Meanwhile, he had found that the U.S. was, in many ways, fascinated with Ancient Egypt. He sat in his easy chair shirtless, with only his kilt on, and surfed the Web on the flat-screen TV his Internet was attached to, gathering information like a sponge.

On the U.S.'s medium of exchange, its dollar bill featured a pyramid with the Eye of Horus as the capstone. And in its national capital, Washington, D.C., they had constructed a five hundred and fifty-five foot obelisk—now the tallest in the world. They had also carved a monument of several of their presidents into the side of a mountain, much like the Rameses sculptures carved into the rock at Abu Simbel. It seemed the U.S. sculptor had lost favor with the American president of the time, however, and funding had been cut, forcing him to truncate *his* monument at the shoulders rather than the mid-body length he had initially proposed.

Khufu also read up on the Masons and Eastern Stars; secret societies for males and females, respectively, that held the ancient teachings of Egypt as the foundations of their beliefs.

But then it hit him like a ton of bricks. Most of the leaders in this era were not black-skinned people. He had already noted that in Egypt the people had become mixed. But it appeared that the black man, as a collective group, had been usurped as the dominant innovators in the world. In his era, black people dominated the world from Africa across what is known as the Middle East, today, through southern Asia. He researched the Dravidians of India, Polynesians, Melanesians and Fiji Islanders—and Nubians, Ethiopians and the people of Punt, along with Egypt, who had anchored a block that set the trends of the ancient world. But somehow, black-pigmented people had experienced a great socio-political demise, he realized, utilizing a term he had read recently, and he was interested in finding out why.

He saw gross errors in the modern world's conception of history and laughed at what were often hilarious mix ups and misnomers.

For example, Egyptian surgeons were no strangers to textbook medicine, and the mathematicians of his day had reached conclusions about the so-called Pythagorean theory over fifteen-hundred years before Pythagoras was born. Meanwhile, the shipbuilders of Tyre, who later became known as the Phoenicians, had circumvented the coasts of Africa, set up colonies and navigated the Mediterranean for eons before the emergence of the Greeks and Romans.

It was clear, to those who really wanted to know, that the people of Tyre, and many other so-called Middle Eastern nations were descended from blacks. It could even be traced through their modern Bible, when one studied the descendants of Ham. Modern historians had everything mixed up. It was so egregious that he thought he'd need stitches from laughing at times; while at other times he was saddened.

Meanwhile, he was pleased at the modern world's mapping of the entire earth and lauded their efforts to protect the environment and the planet's eco-systems.

Khufu had now followed Egyptian history up to modern times and recognized that the Hyksos, Greek, Roman, Persian, Turkish and Arab conquests of the Black Lands had left it a culture of trans-racial people. Studies had shown, meanwhile, that the blood of the pharaohs still flowed in the veins of modern Egyptians; and he was pleased with their general efforts to maintain the integrity of the ancient world.

A knock on the door brought him out of his research.

"Come in," he said, as one of the housekeepers poked his head into the door opening.

"Lunch time, Pharaoh...Khufu," the man said, timidly entering the room.

"Yes, thank you," Khufu said to the dark-skinned man at the door.

"Speak English well?" he asked the man, suddenly curious about him.

Khufu had seen this black middle-aged servant but had barely taken note of him before; this man who had often tucked him in and turned his lights off, as Khufu went to bed.

"Yes, speak *some* English," the servant responded humbly.

"Come, have seat please," Khufu suggested, as he stood and gestured towards a chair. "Speak to me," Khufu said frankly. "What you think about reality that Black Lands are now comprised of mostly mixed people?"

"I never thought about it, sir," the man responded shyly.

"I explain," Khufu said soberly. "In my era, we called this Black Lands because of its population of black people—our soil is red, not black," he said in reference to the Eurocentric assertion that Ancient Egypt was called the Black Lands due to the color of its soil. "But today, appears that most of the people in Egypt are of mixed heritage."

The man shifted in his seat before speaking, as if to measure his response to the pharaoh. "Well, we are different skin-tones, from very light to very dark, like me. That is why to us Egyptians, color is not so much big issue. Was issue in your time, Pharaoh Khufu?"

"No, but dominant color of Egypt was dark-brown people, like you and me, what you call black race today."

"There *are some* minor problems, Pharaoh," the man said decidedly, shifting in his seat again. "Let me speak my mind while have light of day with such a personage as you. Is often assumed by white foreigners that I am Nubian and not Egyptian. So yes, there is perception issue from outsiders that if one is black, in Egypt, he or she is foreigner. Also, the Americans and other Westerners often portray Ancient Egypt as white civilization in history books and in movies. Rameses the Great, for example, whom you recently became aware of at Abu Simbel, often portrayed as white guy in movies. Resulting confusion is result of Greek and Roman conquests. In admiration of our culture, they imported our ways to their lands. During those periods they adapted our dress and borrowed our gods."

"I see," Khufu nodded thoughtfully. "Thank you very much friend," he said getting up. "Perhaps we discuss this further, in future. Now, what's for lunch?" he asked, shaking hands with him. "And didn't get you name?"

"Am Omari, thank you. And have special Egyptian meal for you, Pharaoh Khufu. Beef dolmas, rice, tomatoes and baba ghanoush with pita bread and feta cheese. Come, we serve you in the dining area."

≈

Khufu would be leaving for the United States the next morning, so after lunch he resumed his research on the country. He knew it was best to get a good understanding of the society he was about to enter. So, back in the sitting room, he stretched his legs to their full length, crossed them at the ankles and perched them on an octagon-shaped marble coffee table. He was learning that America was perceived as a melting pot of people from all over the world; and was considered the superpower, much like Egypt had been during his day. It was the world's leader in technology; the birthplace of electric lights, television, telephones and the Internet. In fact, a large number of technological breakthroughs and achievements had occurred in the United States.

After tiring of the Internet, Khufu set his attentions on the video that Masud had recorded of Professor James Hannibal in an interview he had held with the BBC, in Britain, not long after he'd left Egypt. He slipped the DVD into the player, and there was Hannibal talking about the cloning process and what it meant to have an Ancient Egyptian pharaoh in the twenty-first century.

"Khufu is a bona fide historical treasure. The builder of one of the Seven Wonders of the Ancient World among us. It's phenomenal. But not just a testament to what my team and

I have done, but a testament to the exciting age in which we live today."

Nodding his head slowly, the interviewer asked: "How is he doing? And, how long do you think it'll be before he can communicate with the public?"

"The pharaoh is doing well. He could be a poster child for good health. Chronologically, he's about thirty-two-years old and seems to be in good spirits. He appears to be a focused, sober individual personality wise. I have no idea how long it'll take for him to communicate with us, but given the culture he lived in, in the ancient world, I wouldn't be surprised if he has a natural affinity for languages.

"You know, there were more disparate tongues in those times than there are now. He was already using some basic English nouns when I left Egypt, by the way."

The interviewer continued: "We've been told that initially the pharaoh thought that he was in Heaven—or Duat is what he called it—that he thought you and your staffers were the gods. How did you overcome that hurdle and get him to realize that he was in the future?"

"Well, fortunately, we had a hieroglyphics expert, Mr. Abasi Masud, working with us who made things much easier initially. He was immediately able to communicate, in a rudimentary way, with Pharaoh Khufu through basic hieroglyphics on a white board. Professor Masud's first written words to the pharaoh were, 'Welcome to the twenty-first century.'"

"Here is footage of the scene that stunned the world, Professor Hannibal:"

Khufu looked incredulously as he saw himself being birthed from the gestation chamber. He was amazed by the DVD, its ability to capture moments in time.

"Tell me: How was it that you were so confident that Pharaoh Khufu would survive the long-term gestation in the gestation chamber?" the interviewer continued.

"Well, there are certain things in life, which I feel are divinely inspired," Hannibal answered. "Initially, when I was asked to take the DNA sample—the Egyptian government had never allowed this before, mind you—I had an uncanny belief that we could bring him back, and we did. It was Albert Einstein, I believe, who once said that: 'When you find a simple answer to a very complex problem, God has spoken.' Well, I feel, God spoke in this research."

Khufu pressed the pause button. He needed answers. Why was he here in this age? And if Hannibal felt God's hand was on the project, what did God want from him—a forty-five hundred year old pharaoh?

The sound of Beethoven's Symphony No. 5 turned his attention to his cell phone, which he kept tucked in his sash. It was likely Raheem Nadat on the other end. He had given Khufu the phone prior to the cruise in order to have a ready link with the pharaoh.

"How are you, Pharaoh? We've gotten you identification papers for the American State Department. But you'll also need some Western clothes to help you avoid detection when you get over there," Nadat said. "The limousine is ready to drive you over to the al Khalili, district in a couple of hours for some shopping, Ok?"

"No problem, but those Western pants seem so uncomfortable," Khufu said, reticent about wearing the garb.

"I agree, Pharaoh," Nadat said. "It takes awhile to get used to them, but you'll also need them when it gets cold over there. Ever see snow?"

"No, but have heard of it."

"Well, you'll need pants and a coat too." Nadat chuckled in a guardian-like tone that surprised him *and* Khufu.

He had conceived the idea to bring a pharaoh back to modern times, and the responsibility he found himself feeling for Khufu was like nothing he had ever expected. He had not reared a family, but this was akin to that feeling, he realized.

"What do you think about that cell phone?" he asked, changing the subject.

"Seems miracle," Khufu confessed. "I hear you voice in this little box, but there no ropes, no strings—nothing's attached, voice travels through air."

"Yes, it's pretty amazing to me too," Nadat said. "This cell phone is one way we'll be able to communicate with you once you reach the United States. I'll have my line on twenty-four hours a day. All you'll need to do is press the number one and I'm here," he reminded Khufu. "Any questions about anything?" He paused..."Well, maybe you'll think of some pressing issue this evening when I pick you up—or remember, you can simply press the number one."

"Ok," Khufu responded, rather proud of himself. He was getting better each day at speaking English.

≈

Robert Luster's private jet was given access to a government hanger at Cairo International Airport. James, meanwhile, had called Nadat's office where instructions had been left to meet Raheem Nadat and Khufu down at a coffee shop in the Khan al Khalili marketplace.

They made their way through the narrow alleys of the al Khalili, subsumed in the Arabic motif of the busy bazaar. "How tall is Khufu?" Robert Luster asked bemused amidst the activity.

"He's about your height, man; about five feet nine and about a hundred and seventy pounds."

"Really?" Luster was obviously captivated by the thought.

"Yeah, he's average sized and touts a highly honed intellect, brother. From what I understand, he's already speaking English well."

The al Khalili was the Arab world's largest outdoor marketplace. People pressed from far and wide to visit the veritable institution. It would be a great place for Khufu to get a feel for the Egyptian people, James realized, as he and Luster made their way through the crowds.

"After only a few months, and he's already speaking English well?" Luster asked amazed.

"Oh yeah. But speaking several dialects was normal in his day. Language hadn't become as standard as it is now. Today, we've made everything so uniform, with dictionaries and such. They started from scratch, you know. No Mr. Webster to catalog things."

James had often frequented the coffee shop, but did not know the exact address—he simply knew where it was. Nadat had likely decided to meet there because he knew James was familiar with the establishment.

The street scene, meanwhile, was lively. And though it was dusk, deals were still being negotiated like it was high noon. James, however, walked with a frosty veneer that told any sensible vendor with any awareness of body language to stay away. And no one dared, unbelievably, to infringe on his stalwart, well crafted, nonverbal communication. It was a posture Hannibal had gleaned from many months of walking the streets of Cairo. And Luster, also a veteran international traveler, prudently mirrored the posture of his long-time friend.

A belly dancer cast a probing glance at the two as they passed an open-air pavilion crowded with onlookers, but they kept walking until James reached the coffee house. They entered to animated chatter and the sweet-smelling smoke from shisha pipes and took a seat near a wide window that allowed them to look on the stream of humanity flowing outside. James actually admired the tug and fervor of the high-strung entrepreneurs, but besides not being in the market to buy anything, he knew he needed to maintain a quiet presence in Cairo on this trip. He had appeared on Egyptian television before, and since he didn't know much about the underground group, Al Najja, decided that lying low was the only thing to do. So the two people-watched and drank rich Egyptian coffee, as they waited for the incognito pharaoh and Nadat to arrive.

19

K hufu had enjoyed the shopping trip. It represented an interesting change of pace, mingling with the commoners of modern-day Egypt. The array of goods and services were beyond anything he could have ever imagined. And while he had worn one of the galabayyas Nailah had brought for him, he was still uptight about wearing the Western pants that James and Nadat had insisted he acquire for the U.S. trip. The shoes felt odd, also. It was hard for him to believe anyone could make it through the day comfortably in the attire. But there it was; tomorrow's clothes hanging on the haberdasher rack in his bedroom.

He had seen people on television with pants on. And many Egyptians wore the tube-legged wear on the streets every day. But to think *he'd* be expected to wear them was absurd, he mused in annoyance.

He thought about Al Najja. He did not fear terrorists. He had faced death before. To go underground—to avoid them—was to admit defeat, he thought, not quite resigned to the idea.

He rolled over on his bed and zapped the control of the television to a channel that featured a Spaghetti Western with a lone horse rider and two Native Americans in pursuit. The Native-Americans chased the rider shooting arrows at him, while remaining poised on their steeds at full gallop. Then the rider turned and let loose several shots in their direction with his pistol, toppling them from their mounts. Next, he topped a hill and pulled the reigns of his horse in panic, his animal's front hooves rising and pawing at the air, fervently. Before him was a band of over a hundred mounted braves. He aimed his weapon pulling the trigger, but it only clicked. Then the inevitable occurred as the warriors surrounded him and closed in for the finale.

That was all Khufu remembered. His phone alarm went off, and he was awakened to the light of another twenty-first century day. It was time to head to America.

≈

The Gulfstream hop scotched from Egypt, to France, and now it approached Washington International Airport. Out to the right, maybe a mile away, was the towering obelisk, the Washington Monument; its pinnacle-light blinking like a surreal beacon that linked Kemet with its modern-day superpower counterpart, the United States.

James, in an exuberance that was difficult for him to conceal, even in the darkened cabin, marveled at Khufu's impenetrable countenance from across the aisle. This was an unimaginable odyssey they were experiencing. But no one was being impacted as amazingly as the pharaoh, he realized.

Khufu was dressed in modern Western clothes for the first time. He donned a smoke-gray European business suit and wore a pair of hand-made black alligator shoes, his own selection. And his new growth of hair had been cut in the latest style; all to help him blend-in easily with the population and avoid detection.

While they were set to visit the White House the next morning, no mention of his arrival in America had been made known publicly. Khufu would continue the informal education process he had begun in Egypt. And then, when he felt ready, he would introduce himself formally to the twenty-first century.

He looked quite contemporary, indeed, James thought, relieved. He would blend in as just another African American.

From up front in the cockpit, the senior pilot urged the passengers—which included four security agents, Khufu, James and Robert Luster—to fasten their seatbelts as they might experience turbulence on the descent. And as expected, the plane rode roughly at times as it edged downward toward the ground. Blue lights marked the taxiing lanes, and the aircraft touched down on the landing strip with a minimal thud and ground-bound rattle. Then it slowed and edged towards its designated hanger. They had arrived in Washington, D.C., the nation's capital.

That morning, preparing for their White House visit, Khufu insisted on wearing his sovereign's state regalia. He donned the blue crown, which was generally slated for state visits and formal diplomacy; a fantastic neck piece of gold and precious stones and a white pleated kilt. Lastly, he wore a white linen robe, as a covering.

He carried with him a flail and scepter, which represented dominion and authority. And as long as the news media didn't get wind that Khufu was in town, all would bode well, James conceded. After all, in America it wasn't news until it reached the media.

The White House sent a limousine to pick up the pharaoh and his entourage. And while James and Luster rode with Khufu, the security agents trailed the stretch limo in a rented car. The ride to the executive mansion was one of quiet introspection; they drove west down Constitution Avenue, where they saw the Capitol Dome poised majestically behind a stand of trees, and up ahead the Washington Monument pierced the breezy sky. Finally, they reached Pennsylvania Avenue, which led them directly to the White House—the world renowned *1600* Pennsylvania Avenue.

Khufu, meanwhile, was *perfectly* in his element. His mannerism and posture reflected the bearing of one long familiar with diplomatic meetings. The historical monarch, in regal splendor, sat among them.

The limo arrived at the east gate of the White House, and the guards did a customary perusal of the occupants before letting them onto the grounds of the executive mansion. They parked and made their way to the South Portico, where they were greeted by two men who escorted the pharaoh and his party to the Diplomatic Reception Room. There, the president and first lady met them with warm and hearty handshakes. They took their seats in a semi-circle around a splendid cherry-wood table that looked to be from the days of John Adams, the first occupant of the White House.

Obviously amazed at being in the presence of the pharaoh, the president seemed tentative in his thoughts before beginning to speak. "Good to see you, Pharaoh Khufu," he said. "We're delighted to have you here in the United States, and I want to let you know, personally, that the doors to this nation are open to you for however long you would like to remain. I have a hotline number I want to present to you, which gives you direct access to me whenever you feel the need arises."

He reached into his inside suit-jacket pocket and retrieved a small rectangular-shaped box that contained a gold Rolex wrist watch and presented it to Khufu. It had his cell phone number engraved in code on the back of it. He explained the coding and mentioned, apologetically, that the wrist watch was a basic diplomatic gift, in line with current traditions exercised by dignitaries and heads of state.

Khufu accepted the gift with an affirmative nod and remarked that it was a very old diplomatic tradition, indeed, since gift-giving amongst dignitaries was also common in his day.

"You've probably learned a lot about our country through the Internet and such," the president continued. "But I can only speculate that what we've been told about Ancient Egypt and the Fourth Dynasty is accurate. What could you tell us that might benefit posterity, Pharaoh Khufu?"

Khufu remained gracious, nodding his head pensively in recognition of what the president asked. Then, he answered in a measured but straightforward response.

"The pyramids were conceived as a unifying element to strengthen the linkage between Upper and Lower Egypt. Contrary to a major misconception in modern history books that the pyramids were built by slave labor—nothing could be further from the truth. The projects encouraged a common mission among the average citizens that was larger than the day-to-day 'bread and butter' routine that many were exposed to in their lives. This focused the workers on a national agenda. And, in our case, the national agenda was the agenda of our creator god, Amen-Ra."

"Yes," the president said enthused. "Our traditions in America are built on the foundations of religion too."

"Yes," Khufu continued. "I've studied your Christian Bible closely and noted that many of the proverbs and anecdotes it contains were wisdom truths of Ancient Egypt. In fact, the God Amen is highly esteemed in your Bible texts. His name often ends statements and prayers in your scriptures."

Obviously amused, the president grinned at the first lady, and said to Khufu, "Go on, you don't have to stop there. We've allotted a lot of time for you, Pharaoh Khufu."

Khufu protested mildly and insisted that the hallmark of an honorable man is that he must listen as much as he talks.

So, he asked a question, instead: "How long has there been air flight?" Mr. President.

"It began via hot-air balloons in 1783 in France, a country on the European continent," the American potentate explained. Then he hesitated...looked at his wife, and continued. "There are new, revised accounts, however, which indicate that there was some type of smoke balloon down in South America, I believe, created by the Nazcas Indian Tribe in Peru. It seems to have stayed in the air for awhile with a lone passenger." He went on to elaborate that balloons were used more as observatories than for travel, initially, though. And that it was not until the early twentieth century that the Wright brothers developed the air plane in the United States, which prompted wide-spread air travel to emerge.

"Balloons and air planes refined surveying techniques, and a better understanding of the lay of the land helped to build more efficient roads, which were a boon to the automobile industry, which had already begun, by the way, in the late nineteenth century."

"Fascinating," Khufu said with all the regal bearing of a sophisticated twenty-first century politician.

The president enjoyed talking and was on a roll now. "The interesting thing about the automobile," he continued, "is that it prompted the U.S. government to get involved in building roads. The better roads we built; the more cars people wanted—and the more cars people bought; the better roads we needed to build. This was an unplanned growth industry that created untold numbers of jobs and security for American families. But you can learn all about that via TV, the Internet, or in general talk. Please tell us more about your era, Pharaoh Khufu?"

Khufu nodded affirmatively: "Our building projects were much like your public works initiatives today, Mr. President," he said. "During the flooding season of the Nile, there wasn't much to keep many of the young men busy; so the pyramids, and our canal construction kept them occupied, and it also rationalized our reason for providing food and provisions to families in slow seasons. They became engrossed and enthused about nation-building which, subsequently, contributed to the relative peace of my era. I have read that today the Great Pyramid is known as the last remaining Seven Wonders of the Ancient World. That makes me proud," he said, revealing a sense of triumph in his countenance.

He continued: "Pharaoh Menes, who is often known in your literature as Narmer, united Upper and Lower Egypt in around thirty-one hundred B.C., in terms of your calendar. And by the Fourth Dynasty we had blended the names Amen, the creator god of Upper Egypt, and Ra the sun and supreme god of Lower Egypt, into what you often see today as A-m-e-n Ra or A-m-o-n Re, or A-m-u-n Ra, he said spelling out the various English spellings."

"Now that's hearing it from the horse's mouth," the president said, laughing loudly. "Professor Hannibal, may I say congratulations to you on your research. This is one for the ages. Anything else you'd like to share is our privilege," he said turning back to Khufu enthusiastically.

"I don't want to overstay my welcome," Mr. President, Khufu said with the savoir-faire of someone born in this century.

"No, please continue, I insist," the president urged.

"Well, one thing I might note in assessing this age is that man has not changed very much, fundamentally, from the people of my day. The technology your generation has advanced is great and exciting. But wars still exist. Poverty is still evident on the streets of your great cities. And the vast percentage of the wealth still resides in the hands of a limited few people. Although the middle class—if I might share your modern-day term—seems to have expanded.

"In my kingdom, I came to my senses very late in regards to inequities. In fact, I had just begun sweeping changes at my unexpected passing."

The gravity of the moment flittered across the room, as they all recognized that they were experiencing an unparalleled nexus in history. The superpower leader of arguably history's most fascinating land was face to face with the superpower head of today's most heralded nation.

It was obvious the two leaders had connected, and they rose at the end of the meeting promising to talk in the not-too-distant future. They were men of like minds—despite their forty-five hundred year differences in birth dates. They recognized in themselves the traits of statesmen—men whose innate preoccupation was nation building.

≈

The limousine driver had been instructed to chauffeur the president's guests to wherever they desired while they were in Washington. And since Khufu and his entourage hadn't eaten, they decided to stop somewhere for lunch.

Along Constitution Avenue they noticed a couple of cafes that had outdoor seating and decided to eat at whichever had the shortest waiting time. And to ensure they didn't attract too much attention, James suggested that the security personnel and the limousine be available outside the restaurant within an hour.

James, Luster and the pharaoh then went inside and approached the maitre de who responded, "Whoa, whoa....What's up here with this costume? Is this Egyptian day, or something? Tell me you're an actor from the Smithsonian Institute, and this isn't the newest fad? Never mind," he said, taking a three hundred and sixty-degree change of mind.

"Gentlemen, we don't normally let a person in without a shirt," Khufu had left his robe in the limo. "But how many for lunch?" he asked, taking short, delicate steps toward seating. "It's no shirt, no service here, but you look so authentic, what the heck, you'll add to the ambience."

They were led through the restaurant to café sidewalk seating. The mild breeze made for a comfortable sit-down experience. Khufu ordered a Caesars salad to start, at James's suggestion, and then dug into the main course that included a steak, baked potato, grilled vegetables and rice. He had enjoyed rice in Ancient Egypt and seemed to appreciate the modern long-grain variety. He also enjoyed the A-1 sauce on his steak and indicated that the condiment made his meat taste better than any he had ever eaten. The pharaoh wanted to take the bottle of brown sauce with him until James convinced him he could purchase it in any city in America.

"Let me get the check," Robert Luster offered when they had finished.

"Well, if you insist, Robert," James chuckled.

Luster gave the waiter his credit card and signed the receipt when he returned, penning a twenty-percent tip.

"Generous are you?" James nodded, peering over at the check. "You're finally a big tipper, huh?"

"I try to spread the wealth, man," Luster said graciously. "The waiter was good to us; we should be good to him."

"What's a *tipper*?" Khufu asked genuinely interested.

"Well, it's extra money you give the 'food server' for taking care of you well," James explained. "It's a custom that has caught on all over the modern world."

"Interesting practice," Khufu said. "An incentive to ensure good service?"

"That's exactly right," Luster chimed.

"Well, in my day, the incentive was they'd keep their heads for another day," Khufu said laughing in an uproar. "I'm only being facetious, brothers..." he said, settling down. "We were biig family in Kemet."

Other guests never seemed to realize they were in the presence of the great Khufu, which was all the better, because Pharaoh was suddenly beginning to realize he'd have the opportunity for the first time in his life, or lives, to be incognito and have a good time as a private person.

"Incognito. I like that word," he said resolutely, as they made their way out of the restaurant. It was still noon time, so they decided to cross Constitution Avenue, which bordered the long green parkway, the Washington Mall. Hannibal often referred to it as America's version of Ancient Egypt's Karnak, an outdoor museum of temples built in ancient times. On the Washington Mall they could visit the Capitol Building, the Lincoln Memorial, the Vietnam Memorial, the Washington Monument and many others of the capital's premier museums, including the Smithsonian Institute.

Towering due west on the mall, the giant obelisk Khufu had seen from the air plane the night before, jutted upward about a half-mile away. They naturally decided to make their way towards it. Occasionally, a child would point at Khufu as the three strolled down the mall, but overall people just seemed to think he was a guy out for laughs, or a part of a theater production, at best. The three stopped here and there to read the information guides outside the various museums, and when they met an ice-cream vendor, James insisted that Khufu have a banana split, which the pharaoh enjoyed immensely.

Suddenly, Khufu noticed an apparent homeless black man lying sprawled against a fence, off the walkway, with his belongings strewn in disarray. His body language told the story of a man who had given up on life.

Khufu walked compassionately over to get a closer look at the man and leaned over him earnestly in an effort to help. "What's up, my friend?" he asked.

The man did not look Khufu in the eyes; he continued to look downward. "Hard times, hard times," he responded quietly.

"Why are you here?" Khufu asked, as Luster and James walked up behind him.

"Never got a break," the man said. "Never got a break," he repeated in a somber tone.

The mall was peopled by individuals, couples, families and groups from around the world. However, Khufu could see that black people represented a minuscule number of tourists on the mall. Turning to James and Luster, Khufu asked fierily: "My brothers, Why is it that so few blacks are enjoying the amenities of this park? And the one I see here has been defeated by life it seems. Something is drastically wrong here."

"Africans the world over," Luster said, quietly measuring his words, "are suffering the residuals of hundreds of years of colonialism and enslavement. Economically, educationally and socially blacks are playing catch up in all categories of modern life, Pharaoh."

"I'll pay back whatever you guys can do to help this man," Khufu said ardently.

Luster whipped out his wallet and gave Khufu two hundred dollar bills. "Make sure the guy's not mental now, or he'll lose that money," he cautioned. "I try to help as many people as I can, Pharaoh, but many of them are on drugs, or have a mental condition."

After ascertaining that the man was of sound mind, they gave him the money and wished him well and made their way nearer to the obelisk.

"Everything is upside down in this world," Khufu said critically, still brimming over the incident. "That guy had high-caliber countenance. Maybe he be scribe, in Old Kingdom."

He vented some more: "Even geographically—we traveled *up* the Nile to Nubia, to Punt, to major centers of world. In this generation, you...*map* has been reversed."

"Interesting," James nodded. "Is that because the Nile River flows north, Pharaoh?"

"Yes, that's right, James. We traveled upriver to great kingdoms of Africa. To Nubia, to Punt," he said, his hands behind his back, seriously pondering what he was seeing firsthand about modern life for far too many black people. Khufu explained that the Ancient Egyptians were aware of the pull of the magnetic poles, in his day, and believed that the pull in what is now called north represented the pull of what we call gravity today, which pulls things downward. "Where those in North once looked up to us, they now look down on us," he said soberly.

"Fascinating," Robert Luster chimed in. "Your perspective on history will open the eyes of many folk who are asleep, Pharaoh."

A certain bonding was taking place among the three. The modest, focused Luster seemed energized by the pharaoh. And James understood, without question, that he had a veritable intellectual on his hands.

Khufu, meanwhile, was appreciating that he had a second chance to live a life of substance. He had lived the first twenty of his twenty-three year reign, in Kemet, as a self absorbed, egotistical despot. Not this time around, he said to himself. Then, inexplicably, he stopped walking.

"What's up Pharaoh?" Luster asked, while he and James slowed and stopped also.

"The last time stopped in front of a great monument, was nearly blown to smithereens," Khufu reminded them. "That area around the obelisk is too open; I've got a pretty close-up view of the edifice from here. Maybe I do full tour another time."

"Well, I don't blame you," James said, laughing. "You can always say you once stood fifty yards or so away from the Washington Monument, you know."

≈

Back at the hotel, Khufu was in surf mode again. He realized he would eventually speak before world audiences, possibly the UN General Assembly, and other international bodies. So he continued to immerse himself in information, this time getting as much from the television as his laptop. Now, all of the TV channels were in English, with the exception of a couple of Spanish stations. He was like a two-year-old, soaking in every stimulus encountered. Often he would stop at a television channel, ascertain what was happening and promptly go on to something more challenging. If it wasn't on television, it would certainly be on the Internet, he figured.

20

Abasi Masud could not believe his ears as he sat holding the telephone in his hospital bed.

"Pharaoh Khufu is in hiding?" he asked, flabbergasted.

"Yes, I'm afraid so," Raheem Nadat said on the other end.

"But what about our research? What about our studies?" the small-statured intellectual asked.

"It will carry on as long as the pharaoh is alive. We will learn a little here, a little there," Nadat said soberly.

"What do you mean, a little here, a little there? Don't you see, Raheem? We could have lost everything at Abu Simbel. Everything..." Masud said in an unraveled voice.

"That's why we've had to keep him out of the mainstream, Abasi. As his protectors, we cannot allow him to be taken advantage of, *or* taken out."

"And where *is* Khufu?" Masud asked, pensively.

"That is confidential, my friend. We can't risk an information leak on this one."

"What do you mean, information leak?" Masud asked, in the same unraveled tone that had emerged earlier. "What do you mean by information leak?" he yelled, as he looked over at some family members who stood at his bedside. He sat the phone down on the receiver slowly and stared into the distance. It didn't take a rocket scientist to figure out Masud had been conveniently eased out of the inner circle. And he knew why. Nadat had gotten wind of the Grammatik Deutsch deal. It had been a calculated risk, not telling his superiors. He had known that from the beginning. But the windfall would have been enormous had he succeeded.

Alas, he was alive…Praise be to Allah for that.

21

"Chicago, *the City that Works....*

"And boy does it ever," James remarked, as he maneuvered the Mercedes sedan onto the Kennedy Expressway. He'd just read aloud the sign posted near the 'Welcome to Chicago' greeting, where travelers emerge from O'Hare International Airport en route to the city. It was 10:00 AM in the morning. The bumper-to-bumper rush-hour traffic was over, but the city's streets were as busy as ever.

Marika had picked James and Khufu up, but gladly turned the driving duties over to her husband. Whenever she'd make the long trek to O'Hare to pick him up, she was left frazzled. Although she was a good driver, she admitted the Kennedy was testy. Luster had planned to have his pilots fly into Midway Airport, which was in the heart of the city, but delays over Midway forced them to accede to landing at the larger O'Hare Field.

Outside the quiet luxury auto, the El rapid transit train matched their speed before slowing for one of its many stops along the expressway median. Marika, meanwhile, had to admit it *was* fascinating to have the *real live* ancient Khufu there in the car with them—and to see him adapting so quickly to modern ways.

Ironically, she wore her hair in her usual Egyptian-styled weave and marveled that black women, throughout the

Diaspora, including her, were still intrinsically attracted to such an ancient coiffure. And while she hadn't agreed with James concerning the aims of his research, she acknowledged that he had pulled off one for the ages.

"And those are called?" Khufu asked, pointing to one of the many advertising billboards along the highway, on top of buildings, sides of buses or wherever there was open space.

"Billboards," James responded with a sigh, trying to figure out how to explain the question where Khufu could understand easily. "Advertisers, people, or businesses that want to sell something or make the public aware of a matter use those."

"Lots of people drive by and see them?" Khufu nodded.

"Yes, it's a great way to get ideas out to the populace, but it's rather expensive," James pointed out.

"Everything costs these days," Marika added, joining in on the conversation. She didn't know where women fit-in, in normal everyday conversations in Ancient Egypt, but she certainly wasn't going to acquiesce to being less than she was for the pharaoh. He seemed a pretty liberal sort, though, she mused.

"Nothing's ever free," Khufu agreed in the savoir-faire James had become accustomed to.

The guy is pretty normal, Marika had to admit, except for the accent. And certainly, no one would ever believe he was from the twenty-sixth century B.C. *And he is handsome,* she mused. Maybe Lorna will think about returning to the U.S., from Ghana, when she hears who we've brought home.

James zoomed through the tunnel that burrowed through the west side of downtown and edged farther south, leaving the towering buildings of the central business district behind. Meanwhile, a few remaining high-rise public housing apartments rose from the landscape ahead; they were being demolished for redevelopment in the area. In a few years, those Chicago landmarks would be erased from memory, he noted to himself.

They exited to south Lake Shore Drive and matched the cruising speed of the more leisurely water-side traffic. Sailboats speckled the horizon, and the cool breeze off the lake smelled of musky fish. Finally, they passed the lagoon near 67th Street and entered the South Side neighborhoods. Khufu noted for the first time an area populated by black folks and beamed when he saw a blue glass pyramid-inspired bank building at Stony Island Avenue.

"Black people are everywhere. At last, I must be in the Black Lands," the pharaoh declared vociferously.

"James and Marika laughed merrily and chimed in unison, "Yes the Black Lands, Khufu. This is the Black Lands."

Marika had prepared the guest house for Khufu until his condominium in the South Loop downtown area was finished. The Egyptian government had purchased and combined two adjoining suites on the thirtieth floor of a luxury building, with a stunning view of the lake, the south and west downtown skyline, and the South Side.

The guest house was certainly modest compared to what he was used to, but it had all the modern amenities, and Marika had already hired someone to cook and clean for him. There was also the swimming pool, which separated the guest house from the rest of the property. He could lounge under the canopy at the pool just outside his door and surf on his laptop to his heart's content, she figured.

"We're here," James said triumphantly, relieved that the long travel was over, but cognizant that the work of moving the pharaoh in was just beginning. He would have to take Khufu shopping for additional clothes and the incidentals he'd need. And he'd have to make arrangements for Pharaoh's move-in to his new condominium soon.

James had been given carte blanche to hire his own security detail for the pharaoh. The Egyptian agents had returned to Cairo, since they would have attracted too much attention trailing a black man in the Windy City. Meanwhile, James planned to use several street toughs in the new detail. They were young, smart and knew when to get rough if necessary. They also knew the terrain well.

The garage door closed behind them, and James decided he'd return and get the suitcases later. They went into the main house first and showed Khufu around the ground level before exiting through the patio door that opened to the pool and revealed the guest house cattycorner in the rear. James then gave Khufu the key to open the door and upon entering turned on the lights to show him around. Marika remained in the main house while James took Khufu on a tour that revealed a spiral staircase to the upstairs sleeping quarters and matching carpet throughout the cozy abode.

"Okay, I'm going to see about getting the rest of your things, Pharaoh. And you can start getting settled. Raheem might be glad to know you're in the Windy City."

"I thought this was called Chicago?" Khufu replied startled.

James laughed a belly laugh, as he left. "Ever heard of a nickname, Khufu…? That is the city's nickname," he roared, closing the door behind him.

≈

The day before had been settling-in day. James had taken the time to explain the rudiments of daily life in Chicago to the pharaoh. He had underscored the ever-present threat of being mugged in the streets. And he tried as best he could to explain the legendary racial divide in the city.

Now, as they cruised up Martin Luther King Jr. Drive, in James's Jaguar convertible, he took time to elaborate. "Every group has its own area in this town. The Hispanics are in Humboldt Park, the whites are on the North and Southwest Sides, and the blacks are on the South and West Sides. Also, there's Chinatown in the near southwest corridor and other ethnic pockets I can't quite put my finger on right now."

"Why a racial divide?" Khufu asked.

"Old prejudices die hard," James began. "It's the residuals of earlier periods here. Before the blacks came in the 1940's, the city was stratified against the Irish and the Jews. Seems all the way up to the 1960's, there were certain places Jews weren't welcomed. So they either hid their Jewishness or faced discrimination. Of course, blacks never had the option of denying who *we* were. We carry our flag wherever we go— skin color is a distinctive identifier in this culture."

"I've heard of the Jews. Interesting people," Khufu said suavely.

"Yes, they have the unique advantage of being a highly educated populace with substantial wealth, by the way," James said. "I'm told one Jewish guy in the early 1970s, after having been insulted while dining in a restaurant, went out and bought the whole franchise just to fire the fellow responsible for the incident." Stopping at a red light, he changed the subject abruptly: "I want you to check out the teaching on Egypt by the Afrocentrists, Pharaoh, at the South Side Center for Urban Studies. We're only about ten minutes away now. They work along with other groups around the country to properly position Kemet in its rightful place as an early classical culture of black folks."

"Classical culture?" Khufu asked.

"Classical, Khufu, meaning of the highest order. The top of the classification system."

"I see."

"The aim of the oppressor has been to prevent diffusion of anything redeeming in the black social construct."

"Social construct?"

"Yes, the way a social order is constructed. For so long, the black origin of Egyptian civilization was hidden from us," James explained. "Eurocentric Egyptologists concealed it, and when confronted with the truth they tried to gloss over the issue. In fact, they're still trying that ruse today. General-market publications, even encyclopedias, have for-the-most part never printed pictures of black Egyptians like you, Ku. In fact, in the eyes of the world prior to your re-birth, you've been depicted as a Caucasian guy, Pharaoh."

They stopped at another red light as two young black women in layered shoulder-length braids crossed the street. James pointed: "You see those hairstyles they're wearing? Black women in this country had to challenge corporations *in court* to overturn policies forbidding them to wear their hairstyles to work. We've had to fight for black culture every step of the way," he said passionately. "They've been trifling in their attempts to keep us down. The left wing liberals in America have generally been progressive, but the right wing conservatives have been blatantly against us."

Ironically, Khufu understood well the nature of the conqueror towards the conquered. The ages-old tactic was to make the vanquished a people without a history and only laud their accomplishments in relation to their falling under the canopy of the conqueror's domain.

They reached the South Side Center and made their way into the building amidst groups of African-garb wearing activists-types huddled in animated talks that invariably centered on the African condition in the U.S., Africa and the diaspora.

"Hotep, brothers," an intellectual guy who was apparently a staffer greeted them. "I'm Brother D'Ron Asante. Welcome to the South Side Center."

"Hotep, my brother," James responded, clasping Asante's hand in a soul shake. "I'm Brother J., and this is Brother Ku," James said suavely. James was dressed down in jeans and wearing a cap with the bill over his eyes. He hoped he wouldn't be noticed, but this was a pretty aware crowd, he realized. "Who's speaking today, Brotha?" he asked Asante.

"Brotha Yusef Jamil. He'll be analyzing the media 'blackout' of the King Tut exhibit that came through the city, recently. Hope you enjoy it, brothas," he added, as he moved over to greet others who were arriving.

Khufu, meanwhile, still felt strange in his new Western clothes, but he admired the West African attire, many of the people were wearing, which consisted of flowing outerwear *and* pants.

He and James then walked into a modest-sized lecture room and took a seat near a middle aisle as the room filled quickly. A few minutes later, the lecturer for the session entered from a side door and the animated chatter quelled as Asante walked to the podium to introduce him.

Khufu, meanwhile, scanned the room and couldn't help but note that these modern people looked very much like his beloved Ancient Egyptian contemporaries. They ranged from jet black to cream-colored and everything in between. The speaker was a rather large man with light skin and almost

Caucasian hair. In fact, one might not have realized he was black but for his accent and cultural mannerisms.

"My brothas and sistahs. All men get knocked down, but great men and women get up. It doesn't matter what happens to you. It's how you respond to what happens to you."

The audience went wild. People stood to their feet clapping and cheering him on...and he was just beginning.

"We are the original man. The usurpers, over the centuries managed to turn the tables. But *this* is a *new* day...."

Up on their feet again...it was evident this wasn't going to be a standard lecture.

"Look at this!" Jamil said adamantly, raising an artist's picture of a white person identified as King Tut. "This is an example of their tactics," he said ardently. "But look at this!" He lifted a copy of the authentic picture of the ebony-skinned King Tut and his wife Ankhesenamen, taken from the back rest of the throne found in Tut's tomb in 1922.

"This is the kind of blatant and malicious misrepresentation that is still heaved on black folks today," he said simmering. "Suppose we took liberties and colored Romans and Greeks to look black? Generation after generation, heaving that lie upon the public—never putting a white Roman in a school text book, except to present him as a slave. We'd appear to be a very sophisticated people, wouldn't we?" he said sarcastically.

"I come to you, today, to expose a very real and damaging campaign designed by the oppressor to keep your offspring, my brothas and sistahs, in the dark about the positive achievements of black folks...."

The enthusiasm exhibited at the lecture was rubbing off on Khufu. He was beginning to feel the verve of the brothers at the South Side Center. He realized, more certainly than anything he'd ever imagined, that he could indeed help reconnect the black man with his vaunted past. He did not know where he would begin, or how, but he knew that he was in the right place at the right time to get started.

≈

They left rather stealth like, because James didn't want anyone to recognize Khufu or himself. "That's *Ebony* magazine," James said pointing to a neatly designed high-rise building with an Afrocentric élan, as they drove up Michigan Avenue now. "We showed you a copy of that publication back in Egypt," he reminded Khufu.

"Yes. I remember," Khufu said looking skyward, as they passed the impressive building. "It was the only magazine that showed black people," he remarked irascibly.

James turned right on Balboa Street and made another right onto Columbus Drive as he headed toward the Field Museum of Natural History. Once inside, he led Khufu to the Egyptian display and commenced to explain the Ptolemaic era of Egypt, when the Greeks and later Romans took control of Kemet, which led to the start of the modern conception of white pharaohs.

The museum had upgraded from earlier years, and now displayed a mixture of black-skinned and light-skinned Egyptians in its illustrations, but Khufu seemed distraught in a way that James hadn't expected.

"What's up, Ku? Why so downcast, brother?" James asked.

"My people's remains seem to be scattered all over the earth in these museums. Does this generation display the remains of all the deceased in such a way? Or is this another example of the *double standards* in this culture?"

Khufu was exhibiting a simmering indignation, much like Jamil had displayed during his lecture. His vocal cords had tightened, and his fists were unconsciously clenched.

"I'm not sure if these mummies are real," James said hoping to lessen the tension. "But, yes, in some cases bodies have been warehoused like artifacts for tourists to look at."

"I've had enough," Khufu said suddenly. They immediately pivoted and made their way out of the building without further talk on the matter. Both men were sorting out their thoughts and any additional conversation would be redundant. Out on the south steps of the building, the marble columns rose majestically in honor of some Roman ideal; so did those across the street at Soldier Field, the city's football stadium. Little did most passersby know that those edifices to Western glory were mere copies of grand designs engineered by black Kemetians long ago.

≈

"Game for some soul food, Khufu?" James asked as he sped the drop-top Jaguar onto Lake Shore Drive and headed south.

"Soul food?"

"Yeah. That's what we call black-American cuisine. Soul food."

"Well, I can certainly use some soul food about now, my friend, James. What does it comprise of?"

"Turnip greens, corn bread, black-eyed peas, sweet potatoes and *fried chicken*. We're going to *Gordon's*, my man. This guy Gordon is a genius in the kitchen. He's taken our basic soul food fare and removed the fat calories."

"Fat calories?" Khufu asked flabbergasted.

"Yeah, fat calories. We modern scientists have learned that high-fat foods clog the blood vessels and they also cause people to become over weight resulting in diabetes and other diseases."

"I notice lots of people overweight here in the America," Khufu said. "In my day not so many people fat," he said chuckling.

"Well, folks don't do physical labor as much as they once did," James said.

"That's possibly what took you out, brother, that high-fat food."

"Took me out? What you mean?" Khufu asked earnestly.

"Well, you said you'd just eaten when you passed out back in Ancient Egypt. That points to a possible cardiovascular obstruction. Let me explain. If one of the blood vessels which carry the blood to and from the heart is clogged by too much fatty residue, the result is a faulty artery or vein. And when arteries and veins don't pump the required amount of blood to and from our heart, we can pass out or even die."

He exited Lake Shore Drive and took the Dan Ryan Expressway south before getting off at 87th Street. As usual, the parking lot was packed, but there was plenty of seating, and the hostess took them to a booth where a framed painting of Frederick Douglass, the great abolitionist, orator and U.S. ambassador was on the wall. The establishment was tastefully done in an African-American motif of paintings and Afrocentric sculptures in marble, basalt, granite and other rock.

The clientele, meanwhile, was a smorgasbord of Chicago's black community. Men in business suits talked deals. Cheerful couples laughed at each others gags. Parents and grandparents chided children around the family meal. And here and there street toughs, some sporting sunglasses, gold teeth and baseball caps posed as if for a music video.

"Is this a modern king?" Khufu asked looking at the Douglas portrait.

"No, that's King," James said jokingly, pointing to a picture of Dr. Martin Luther King, Jr. across the room. "This is Frederick Douglas. He was an abolitionist during the period of black enslavement here in America."

"So, he was enslaved?" Khufu asked earnestly.

"Yes, he had been enslaved," James explained. "But he escaped and began to advocate for the abolition of the institution and was very effective."

They ordered their meal and continued to talk about the black experience in the Western world and about the institution of slavery, historically and internationally, and its relationship to the modern economic system.

"That's why we must tell your story," James said adamantly. "The full range of the black experience has never been told. The West has worked to bog us down in spiritually debilitating images of the slave era and not much else. We need you before the media painting the picture as it really was."

"So do I get to get into that box?" Khufu said in jest, pointing to one of several overhead televisions in the establishment.

"You've already been in that box," James chuckled. "Remember when you first saw yourself on DVD and thought your Ka was trapped inside there."

"Yes indeed," Khufu said. "But I understand now that television is only light waves that capture the image."

The waiter brought steaming plates of fried chicken, turnip greens, black-eyed peas, sweet potatoes and cornbread. A special blend of soybean oil, butter milk, and secret ingredients had been mixed to create a no-fat margarine, and the sweet potatoes were cooked with a no-fat sweetener. The chicken, meanwhile, was fried in special non-trans fatty oil, while the black-eyed peas had a ham-hock flavor added, but without pork.

Giving a thumbs-up to the waiter, James said: "My type of cookin', my man."

"Not bad," Khufu nodded, taking a bite out of his fried chicken.

James poured Louisiana hot sauce on his golden-fried breast and cut a nice-sized piece for consumption when his eyes met someone familiar a few tables over. It was Felicia Maxwell smiling broadly, as if nothing had ever happened, and getting up to come their way.

James could feel his blood-pressure rise but tried to calm himself as she came nearer.

"Dr. Hannibal. You're in Chicago...I would never have known," she said in an immature affectedly proper voice. She reached the table and futilely attempted to shake his hand, which he let hang like a limp rag.

After all the trouble she'd caused in Egypt, the nerve of her, he thought steaming.

She squealed excitedly, "And this is Khufu? May I have your autograph?" she asked with pen and paper already in hand.

"It's a modern tradition," James explained apologetically, noticing Khufu's state of perplexity over the request. "When one is famous, or celebrated, we take their personal signature in this culture as a souvenir."

Over at Maxie's table, there were two other young women just as bright eyed and bushy tailed as she was. This is not good, James thought to himself. There was no telling how much she had already told them.

Khufu signed the slip of paper in hieroglyphics, which apparently pleased her the more, as she squealed loudly..."It's in hieroglyphics," looking back at her companions at the other table. "Here's my card," she said handing them both a business card.

As if I would care, James thought irascibly. "Maxie," he said under his breath. "You need to keep this quiet—no ones supposed to know Ku is in the States."

"Oh!" she said stunned.

"We're keeping his presence in this country discreet...do you follow me," James snarled under his breath.

"I understand, Dr. Hannibal," she replied, curtsying like a wounded twelve-year-old.

"His name is Ku, got it?" James whispered.

"Got it," she said sullenly, as she turned around and headed to her table like a wounded puppy.

22

K hufu reluctantly agreed that it would be educational to visit a large university lecture where he could get the mainline spiel on Egypt—after James's incessant bantering about it. Frankly, he'd have plenty of time for that later, he realized; besides, he'd already seen much of their teachings on the Internet.

For now, he wanted to know more about the local black community and its culture. He felt he needed to understand the complexities of the culture if he was going to help fix it. He was aware that many African-Americans lived well, as was evident by the upper-middle-class neighborhood in which James and Marika resided. But he had been in Chicago for over a week, now, and his every move had been orchestrated by James. He wanted to go out and learn on his own for a change.

Here he was at home doing nothing, while James was who knows where. He looked at the business card again. What the heck, he thought at last, what's a bored man to do, twiddle his fingers?

"*The Chic Boutique*. I'll simply need to dial these numbers and Felicia Maxwell will show me the other side of Chicago life," he said quietly, as he began dialing the numbers on the card.

"Chic Boutique, may I help you, please?"

"Yes, may I please speak with Felicia Maxwell?"

"Oh. You mean Maxie," hold-on, please. "Maxie...telephone sweetheart."

After a pause, Maxie came to the phone. "Hello, this is Maxie."

"Maxie, this is Ku." There was a long silence on the line. Khufu wondered if she'd hung up. "Hello, are you there? Hello?"

"Yeah, I'm here. Just surprised to hear from you," she managed to say.

"Well, I'm new here and haven't had an opportunity to see the everyday side of the city. Could you drive me around?"

"Why sure," Maxie said with a giggle. "I'll be off work at four PM. Where do you live?"

He gave her the address and his phone number, and they hung up—he would begin his tour in a couple of hours.

≈

Maxie called Khufu on her cell phone as she neared his address and was all smiles as he met her in front of the house. He wore knee-length khakis, sandals and a sleeveless sweatshirt. He was geared up for everyday South Side.

"Take me to Rainbow Beach," he asked in his Hamitic accent, as he hopped into the open Jeep Wrangler.

"Great," she said, and pertly accelerated the yellow military-style vehicle down the street.

They drove over to Jeffery Boulevard; made their way to 79th Street, which was the direct artery to the beach, and headed towards Lake Michigan. Minutes later, Khufu could smell the fishy beach scent, and he could see seagulls gliding on the winds over the water.

They stopped at a red light, and a subtle rumble suddenly shook the jeep startling Khufu, which caused Maxie to laugh deliriously.

"Oh, that's jus a hip hopper's boom box," she explained. "Some kids think it's cool to blast music wherever they go."

The music became louder, and Khufu could see it was from the car behind them. As they neared the beach, they heard more rumbles. And as they turned into the parking lot, a myriad of rumbling music systems seemed to compete for dominance.

Maxie trailed several other cars driving along the parking lot border, while parties of people congregated at the park's edge to have easy access to their automobiles. Finally they found a parking space in an open area where Maxie could see the jeep from whichever direction they walked. Although the park expanse was beautiful, she was street-wise enough to know that crime was always a possibility in Chicago—especially break-ins and petty thefts.

"Got that Bo," a baritone voice rang out, as a heavy-set brother passed them while they headed towards a bench under a stand of trees.

"No thanks," Maxie smiled back.

"What is Bo?" Khufu asked.

"Oh, that's marijuana, a weed people smoke to get high off of."

"To get high? Like in a beer high?" Khufu asked.

"Yep, plenty of drugs all over this town. No jobs. People sell drugs because it's the easiest way to make quick money," she said.

A few people swam and frolicked in the water at the nearby beach. And a canopy here and there shaded others from the sun's direct rays. Bikers, some in skin tights and helmets, and others dressed in street clothes, pedaled along the lake's bike path. And hundreds of people lay on blankets in the grass or walked along the walkway enjoying the bright summer day.

Khufu felt his phone vibrating in his pocket and knew immediately it was James.

"Hello, James."

"Hello? *Where the hell are you*, Khufu?"

"Wait a minute—wait just a minute, you're not talking with a child, here, *Dr. Hannibal*," Khufu said irascibly.

"Well, I apologize, Pharaoh. I was just surprised to see that you weren't around. No harm intended, Ok? The reason I'm really calling is that I've put you a security detail together," James said, "and would like you to meet them. You're a VIP, you know, so I have to look out for you."

"You want to look out for me? Maybe I should just disappear; then you can look out for me. How about that?" Khufu said sarcastically.

"Come on, Ku. Where're you hiding yourself?" James asked concerned.

"My little secret, James. You can't know everything about a person. You have to give an individual some space. Know what I mean?"

"It's just the security issue, Khufu. Once I can get these six guys around you 24/7—"

"Six guards? Why, I'm enjoying my anonymity for the first time, and you want to surround me with six body guards?"

"Come on, Ku. Don't be difficult here. I'm looking out for your best interests, man."

"I'll tell you what, Professor. Until I begin the TV appearances and the like, I don't want any security men around. I've had armed soldiers buffering me all of my life, and now here I am with a second chance at really living, And you want to impose that on me again?"

"Okay, Pharaoh, deal. No guards until ya begin to make public appearances. By the way, when do you wanna get started on media engagements?"

"I'm still studying how this modern world ticks, James. One cannot be effective unless one really understands a matter."

"I like your thoroughness, Pharaoh. But we need to get you on the road now that you speak English so fluently. Too many people think this whole thing is a farce anyway, you know," James said, frankly.

"Yes, there are always the skeptics," Khufu responded. "But our focus must not be on them—our focus must be on our mission."

"Ok, okay," James said assured now that Khufu wasn't really about to disappear into the American landscape. "One thing I'm concerned about is that girl Maxie, Khufu. The one we saw at the restaurant the other night. She's pretty immature. I wouldn't be surprised if she goes to the media and reveals you're here in the States. Remember, she's the one who leaked the information about you in Cairo that generated the media foray. She could cause us a lot of problems, brotha."

"I understand, James. I'll see you later," Khufu said hanging up and preempting further talk.

"That was my daddy," Khufu said facetiously.

"Your daddy? You're calling Dr. Hannibal your daddy now, Khufu?" Maxie said amidst laughter.

"Well, in many ways he *is* my daddy. He brought me to the twenty-first century, and now he's showing me the ropes."

"Well then, I'm your mama," Khufu, Maxie chuckled. "Now come along with me so I can show you another beach area." She playfully walked ahead of him in a motherly fashion, dressed in her colorful sun dress, sandals and white summer hat.

They stopped to buy ice cream from a vendor, but Khufu hadn't brought any money. "See, I'm your mother, I'm buying little Sugar Pooh *his* ice cream."

They then hopped back into the jeep and headed farther north to the 63rd Street Beach. Maxie asked Khufu if he could drive and offered him the wheel, but he declined and explained that the technology was still far too new for him to attempt to steer an automobile. He told her about his first day in the twenty-first century and his encounter with the jet airplane. He admitted that he wasn't sure then whether the jet was a carriage of the gods or what. Then he commented that the wheel hadn't even been invented in his day and that he was awed by the things that could have been done in his kingdom with simple wheels, not to mention the motorized versions.

They reached the 63rd Street Beach to the sound of a different kind of music than that at Rainbow. This beach featured live music—that of African drums and musical instruments. Many of the people were dressed differently too. Dread-lock hairstyles and African clothes were apparent throughout the quaint park, amidst sizzling barbeques and fishing along the lake's shore. The sandy beach itself was not crowded, but for a few children splashing in the water here and there.

Meanwhile, the park was a reflection of the curvature of Lake Michigan, and having positioned themselves at a cove on the northwest edge of the landscape, the musicians kept it live with good sound, which attracted curious onlookers.

"They're out here every week," Maxie told Khufu as they strolled over to join the rest of the crowd. A man with a full beard and shirtless, beat congos with the energy and verve of one possessed; another played a ridged instrument of wood where he scrawled-out sounds treading up and down its length. A third guy played a guitar-like stringed apparatus called a kora, while a fourth musician played a wooden flute-like instrument.

"Music is to the Ka what food is to the body," Khufu observed.

"The Ka, what's that?" Maxie asked, as she rocked her head to the groove.

"The Ka parallels what you call the spirit," Khufu explained.

"Well, my spirit's eatin' good," Maxie said jamming to the beat.

After listening to a few tunes, they headed back to the jeep and drove north up Lake Shore Drive towards the Hyde Park area. Khufu noticed a difference in people's beach habits as they passed the 55th Street Beach. The sands were swarming with people lying out in the sun. White-skinned people were engaged in the summer ritual of sunbathing.

"Seems they want to get as dark as possible," Khufu mused.

"People are never satisfied," Maxie replied. "I'm somewhere in the middle, I guess. Sometimes I wish I were darker, and sometimes I wish I were lighter."

"Why you're the color those folks are trying to attain, Maxie."

"Yeah, I know. But it seems sometimes that it would be easier to be white," she said, pensively. "Black folks face psychological violence in this culture. If I were white, I wouldn't have to deal with that, you know?"

"Psychological violence?" Khufu asked.

"Yeah. It's in a book I'm reading…Societal manipulation—subtle manipulation. It makes me want to run far, far away, Khufu."

"But why would you want to be like those doing the oppressing, Maxie?"

"Oh, I don't know. I'm not a leader, Khufu. I've never been a leader. I'm just a regular girl trying to make my way in life." She began to cry.

There was a certain vulnerability about Maxie now. Khufu never liked teary, emotional scenes. But there he was trapped in the confines of the jeep.

"You've got a lot going for you, Maxie," he said, trying to console her. "Like my father used to say, 'When you know who you are and why you know it, you don't have to worry about what anyone says or thinks.'"

There was silence in the jeep, now, for a couple of minutes that seemed like an eternity.

"Hey, I'm hungry," Khufu said at last.

"Good, I know just the place for catfish," Maxie said, dabbing her eyes with a tissue as they exited Lake Shore Drive. She knew of a locally owned carry-out seafood restaurant on the fringe of Hyde Park and decided to stop in for a quick take-out meal. The establishment was efficient and well run; customers simply stood in line, placed their orders and went on about their daily endeavors. The staff, however, stood behind what Khufu learned was bullet-proof glass.

"The crime rate is very high in this city," Maxie explained as they stood in line. "Robberies are a common occurrence. As soon as you let your guard down, some deprived maniac might take advantage of the situation," she told him.

"The prey has become the hunter," Khufu said philosophically. "It's a strange twist of fate."

"You sound like a philosopher, my brotha," an unfamiliar voice rang out.

Khufu turned to see a medium height, brown-skinned man, who looked to be in his fifties, sitting in a seat along the wall just a few feet away.

"We need brothas like you to join us in the movement, man," the guy said earnestly. "Why don't you come down to the lodge on next Saturday and check us out?" He walked over and gave Khufu his card just as his number was called to claim his order.

"Hotep, my brotha," he said quickly, as he walked to the counter and retrieved his order. Maxie and Khufu were next in line to order, so the man waved a kindly goodbye as they walked up to the window.

≈

They ate as they drove and approached a row of high-rises that Maxie pointed out as "the Projects." It was getting late now but still daylight, since it was midsummer.

"This is where some of the high crime rates derive," she said. "My mom grew up in that building right there," she pointed.

Standing randomly, here and there, were young men in groups of twos and threes, talking about who knows what, with some of them drinking wine, beer or puffing on cigarettes. Scrawled across the entrance walls to the building was graffiti accompanied by grime, which underscored the extreme neglect of the high-rise.

Maxie pulled in front of the building, and a guy with his cap turned to the side, wearing a light blue sweat suit too hot for the weather, jogged out coolly to the jeep and sauntered around to Maxie's side issuing a loud greeting.

"What up, Cuz! What blew you over here? I heard you been over seas and doin' good fa yourself."

He looked over at Khufu and reached out his hand, clasping Khufu's in a soul handshake. "What up, man...? Len," he said greeting Khufu.

"This is Ku, Len. He's from Egypt," Maxie said.

"From Egypt? He looks just like one of us black Americans. Welcome to America, bro. Whatever you need come see me. I got reefers, cocaine, crack. If it's dope, I can get it fa you."

"He don't do no dope," Len. "I'm jus showin' him around. He jus wants to learn about how we live in the United States."

"He got some money? I'll show him how we live. How much he payin'?"

"How much you need?" Khufu responded, his head reclined on the headrest suavely.

"You cool, man. I won't charge you much," Len said gleeful that he might have a chance to make some money legally.

"One thousand dollars enough?" Khufu asked.

"One thousand dollars?" Len shot back quickly. "Hell yesss. Where you need to go, man? You da boss. Where you need to go?"

"A thousand dollars?" Maxie said startled. "You don't have to give him no thou..." Khufu shot her a look that said *cool it*.

"He can afford it, Len," she smiled smitten, looking appraisingly at Khufu.

"You ain't kidin', man?" Len asked quizzically.

"No, kidin'," Khufu said nodding suavely.

"Well, let the evenin' begin," Len clapped cheerfully, hopping into the back of the jeep. "There's this house party over on 53rd Street. They real people, ya'll."

Suddenly, Len changed the flow of the conversation; he wanted assurance that he'd get his money. "Give me somethin' for goodwill, man. My time is money and money is time." He reached his hand out, but Khufu left him hanging.

"I don't carry much cash around, my friend."

"To Pill Hill first," Khufu directed Maxie, his hand out thrust as if prepared to lead the Egyptian army into battle.

The jeep jerked forward forcing them all back into their seats. Meanwhile, Len shouted, "Ya'll bett'n not be wastin' my time, I'm warnin' ya'll, now."

"Cool out, Len. You really don't know who you messin' wit, here," Maxie said with the ghetto edge she'd grown up with, but sometimes managed to leave behind.

They reached Pill Hill, and Maxie and Len remained in the jeep as Khufu walked to the guest house via the side driveway. Once inside, he retrieved a wad of hundreds that Nadat had packed into a travel bag. He returned to the jeep and counted out ten one hundreds to Len and gave Maxie two one hundred dollar bills for gas.

"Let the evening begin," Khufu said, echoing Len's earlier remarks. Satisfied that all was in order, he leaned back for the ride across town.

Fifteen minutes later, they exited the Dan Ryan Expressway and began cruising down 55th Street west into the Englewood section. They turned over to 53rd Street and pulled in front of a small bungalow where a guy stood on the porch taking an admissions fee.

It was nighttime now, and Khufu was about to get a taste of the inner-city ghetto life he'd heard so much about.

23

"**W**hat up, dawg?" the young man asked, as he leaned against the wall next to Khufu, a beer in hand.

"Dog?" Khufu responded, looking around for the house pet.

"Get hip Ku," Maxie said, coming to the rescue. "He's not from the States, brotha," she said apologetically, while extending her hand to the guy for a handshake.

"Awe...you cain't tell. Where's he from?" the guy asked.

"He's from Egypt," Maxie proclaimed with a broad smile.

"Egypt? Hotep, my brotha. Moses is my name and Rappin' is my game," the twenty-something-year-old said, shaking hands with Khufu, revealing gold teeth as he smiled. He nodded his head to the ongoing beat and began spitting out lyrics to the song that he apparently knew word for word.

Already, Len had caught the affections of a female partygoer and was engaged in a smooth groove that Khufu found interesting. He couldn't help but tap his feet to the beat, as he looked on.

"Wanna dance, Khufu?" Maxie asked eagerly.

Why...sure, he was about to say as she pulled him onto the dance floor before he could answer.

Khufu flowed right into the groove and began making swirls and twirls with his hands and arms that the other dancers began to emulate.

Maxie also improvised and initiated some 'swirly-twirly' moves of her own. They danced until the music changed, and Maxie was propositioned by another guy, leaving Khufu to return to the area where Moses was still standing.

"Hey, good moves, Homey-o," Moses said, lauding Khufu on his dance steps.

"Dancing is a celebration of life, my friend," Khufu said graciously.

"I like that, a celebration of life," Moses echoed, taking a swig from his bottled beer.

"That could be a new song, dawg. I'm gon' hold on to that: *A Celebration of Life*. How 'bout a *Par-teh Called Life*? Yohhhh..." he chimed, as he clasped an approaching girl's hand and flowed onto the dance floor with her, not missing a beat, his brew held suavely to his side.

"Having a good time, Ku?" It was Maxie, dancing towards him, subtly. She had allowed another woman to cut in with the guy she had been dancing with.

"Great fun," Khufu yelled over the noise, which had gone up a few octaves as more people had arrived. The dance floor was now full.

Maxie clasped Khufu's hands and they began to follow the beat of the music. He suddenly became energized as he realized how young he was physically, in relation to his forty-seven years in Kemet.

In fact, he flashed back to the last large gathering they'd had at the Great House in his day. He'd sat calmly on his throne, actually wishing he could let loose like the rest of the party goers, but he was the pharaoh. His duties as the kingdom's sovereign required that he maintain a certain decorum. The revelers in Kemet weren't much different from these partiers, though. He could see them like it was yesterday. "Eat drink and be merry," Wati heckled, "for tomorrow you die."

Khufu was a good dancer—he just hadn't often had an opportunity to groove in public. His youthful frame still had it, he reckoned, as he engineered new moves that incorporated Old Kingdom dancing with what he saw around him. He twirled his hands like a black bird dispelling turbulence and was pleased as he saw others copying his groove. Yes, he liked this anonymity.

"We'd like to turn ya'll on to Moses." The D.J. was now turning the music down to get the crowd's attention. "The newest, completest, far reachinest, Rapper in the Midwest. Ya'll show ya love, for MO-SES...," the DJ said, as the dancers began to disperse, making room for the Rapper to begin.

"Yohhhhh...I say, yohhhhh...," he began, walking like a gangster before the mesmerized crowd, which was primed to see what might be a new sensation.

"How 'bout a party, ya'll...? How 'bout a parrrr-*teh*?" he yelled out to the crowd, which responded in adulation.

I wanna talk to you today 'bout a par-teh called life. It's down. It's profound, em-a-nating from my o-ration, these is words to the na-tion, 'bout the par-teh called life. Though you may be 'bout it, I don't doubt it. Raise yoh hands in the air—Yehh, you're goin' somewhere. You'll win in the end, yehh, just don't give in—It's a par-teh...ya'll. Yehhh, I'm talkin' 'bout a par-teh called life....

Moses had the crowd on his side, already, as they waved their hands in the air, moving to the beat that he had choreographed to amazing effect.

Pow...a firecracker sound rang out, followed by successive pops that apparently came from...guns. Everyone in the house sprang for cover while the pops continued into the next room and out the front door. A gun fight had erupted leaving several victims on the floor. And as quickly as it had started, it stopped. Khufu and Maxie scrambled along with others through the nearby kitchen and out the back door amidst a press where the door was, causing people to bounce off one another like arcade balls seeking the path of least resistance. Khufu held Maxie's hand and crouched as they reached the back yard before heading to the streets towards their automobile.

They spotted Len as he hopped in one of several cars which squealed off in pursuit of the shooters.

Apparently, a feud between two local gangs had reached a head, and the shooting was one gang's answer.

"I should have known," Maxie said as they bounded quickly for the jeep. "Whenever there's a cover charge for a house party, too many gangsters are on hand. That wasn't a bad crowd overall," she said breathing rapidly. "It's the bad apples that spoil the bunch."

"There's one of em," a voice rang out as three toughs rushed towards Khufu and Maxie. Khufu shoved Maxie ahead; she stumbled, clicking the remote door opener on her keys. Khufu managed to get one foot into the jeep but realized Maxie wouldn't get in quick enough. Just within reach on the floor was an umbrella that he retrieved quickly. Like a sword, it met the first guy, pin point under the Adam's apple.

Khufu then pivoted, as if doing a reverse lay up, and jerked the curved handle of the umbrella around the ankle area of a second guy, whose feet came from under him, causing a hard thud with the asphalt street. The youthful pharaoh followed up with a Kung Fu style kick into the guy's solar plexus, knocking the wind out of him.

He sensed movement from the third guy, but it was too late, a metal rod clanged...Moses met the oncoming metal rod, of the guy, with his own version, a companion rod that each of them had foraged from the ground. The guy's momentum had forced him into Moses who instinctively shoved him away, causing the guy to stumble backward. Then Moses stood on guard—he was a swordsman—he knew the art of fencing. He moved swiftly, did a double feign and slashed against his opponent's rod, dislodging it with little effort.

Startled, and looking at the demise of his fellow gang members, the guy turned and high tailed it into the night.

By now, the sirens of police cars could be heard approaching. Maxie, meanwhile, had started the jeep and was moving out before Khufu, and now Moses, was fully in. They hung on for dear life, though, and climbed in, as she stayed on the side streets putting distance between them and the sound of the sirens.

24

K hufu awoke the next morning to the incessant ringing of the door bell. After last night's fiasco, he didn't know what to expect. Maybe it was the police.

He'd nearly forgotten that he'd given Moses the couch as a bed, while Maxie had sped to her home nearby in the area.

He arose warily and imagined police officers at the door, like on television, questioning him about the previous evening's escapades. And Moses, with his gold teeth gleaming, would be all the evidence they'd need. He sighed; he was not in a mood for interrogation. Putting on his robe, Khufu sauntered down the winding stairs prepared for the inevitable.

He looked out the door peephole to see James, however, standing imperviously. Even before he could open the door completely, James began to rant: "If something happens to you, Khufu, the whole world is going to be asking *me* why *I* didn't take better care of you."

"I understand," Khufu answered pensively, letting him in, more relieved than James could possibly imagine.

"Who the hell is that?" James asked startled, eyeing Moses who was sitting in a chair combing his hair with an afro pick and wearing a sheepish grin on his face.

"Moses is the name and—"

Khufu's outfaced palms told Moses to quiet it. He cut the young man's customary intro in mid sentence.

"This is Moses; he's a Rap-pur. We met last night at a parteh. Is there anything else you'd like to know?" Khufu said his ire with James rising.

"Yeah, who the hell are we?"

"Okay, let me get this straight," Khufu retorted now clearly perturbed. "You're my Lord and my maker, and you dictate how I'm supposed to live here in *dis* twenty-first century? Is that what I'm gathering here?"

Moses' eyes became as big as silver dollars..."Now, I know...You're...that...nutty professor out of Tuskegee. And you're that, uhh, cloned pharaoh. Yehhh, you *are* from Egypt," Moses said, smiling inquisitively, apparently satisfied that he had just struck gold.

"Well, now you know," James said, stretching his hand toward Moses for a handshake.

Moses clasped the professor's outstretched hand in a soul shake accompanied by an African fingers tug. Khufu looked at the two oddly before Moses stepped over to him and proceeded to shake with Khufu in the same fashion.

"See: this clasp represents our togetherness as brothas; a bond that cannot be broken by colonialism. The final pull there, with the fingers, shows that blacks were torn from each other and that we understand our collective struggle."

James blinked a double blink of the eyes. "Why, I never knew that."

"Lots of things brothas out here don't know," Moses said taking a seat on the couch again. He then reached into his mouth and pulled the gold grill off of his front teeth. "Just part of my décor," he quipped, scanning the faces of the two incredulous onlookers.

"I got a bachelor's degree in bizness brothas, but Rappin' brings in the butter, so without a stutter, I flutter, spittin' the game, makin' it plain...bizness is bizness, so I play the role goin' for the gold; I'm gettin' there, yeah, I'm gettin' there, yeah," he said, nodding his head.

James and Khufu looked at each other, not sure what to say.

But James, feeling the need for some detective work began: "Well, how 'bout you two tell me how you managed to become fast friends at the party last night?"

Khufu looked at Moses with a solid nonverbal, *Do not tell him about the shootout* look.

Moses began: "Well, there was heat in the party," he said, wondering how he was going to re-frame what was on the tip of his tongue.

"Heat?" James asked with a quizzical frown on his face.

"Well, these girls—young ladies—I should say, kept asking us to dance. I mean, I like to dance, but a lot of people were in there—right Khufu?"

Khufu nodded in agreement, taking over. "They wan-ted to dance," he began, drawing on his story-telling abilities. "I danced. Let me tell you, I danced up a stormmm..." Khufu said with a reminiscent relish in his voice. "Do you dance James? We used to have a dance called the birrrd," Khufu said flapping his arms like wings, not waiting for an answer. "Whenever I'd flap—"

"Last night?" James asked, trying to keep up.

"Yes, James. Whenever I'd flap my wings the other dancers would begin to flap also. It was an exciting revelry, let me tell you. And my friend Moses, here, his repertoire of lyrics brought the house down."

"But it was too hot in there," James joined in.

"Too hot," Khufu nodded, "So Maxie—"

"Maxie! You got hooked up with Maxie, Pharaoh?"

"Well, I wan-ted to learn more a-bout this inner-ci-ty life I've heard so much a-bout and—"

"Don't tell me, Khufu, I don't want to hear it. She's trouble, let me tell you *now*, she's trouble—"

Hannibal bolted towards the kitchen. "What's to eat around this shanty of a bachelor pad you have here," he said smiling at Khufu, knowingly. "Pharaoh you smooth...Maxie, huh?"

Khufu winked at Moses. Their story had worked.

"Khufu, you wanna learn about the inner-city? Let me school you," James said thoughtfully. He was in one of his one of the boys moods, now. He clanged pots and pans as he began to prepare breakfast for the three—they gave the housekeeper Saturdays off. "Where're you from Moses?"

"Ida B. Wells, Homeboy. Bred and fed in the Ida B. Wells housing projects, right here in the Windy City."

"Interesting," James said thoughtfully as he retrieved bacon and eggs from the refrigerator. "Do you know who Ida B. Wells was?"

"She was this black lady, a journalist. She fought for the black cause."

James responded: "She was one of the most advocacy-minded journalists of her day." He was pleased that Moses was aware of the housing project's namesake. "You've got a college education, Moses, that's progressive. But what's up with the sistah's and brotha's in the hood nowadays? Maybe you can enlighten the pharaoh and me."

"Hey, it's 'bout the dollar, man. Everybody is 'bout the dollar."

Khufu, meanwhile, had, had time to do some serious thinking since the party the previous night. The bullet riddled bodies made little sense to him. Why should potentially bright youths ruin their lives and the lives of others for no rhyme or reason, he wondered?

"I'm all ears for finding out what's up with the young bloods?" Khufu interjected, earnestly, settling down in a cluster of large pillows comfortably arranged on the living room carpet. "Why aren't they striving to take advantage of this exciting world out here?"

"Let me give you some background, Khufu," James began solemnly: "Our condition in this society is the result of being under colonialism for centuries."

"Colonialism?"

"Colonialism, Pharaoh," he reiterated as the bacon began crackling; "that's when the powers-that-be drain you for your labor force but don't re-invest for your benefit.

"Following the slave era, blacks lived in a literal concentration camp without walls, here in America. Life for the black man was extremely harsh, and policies were initiated to demean, insult and relegate us to second-class citizenship— primarily to maintain an entrenched work force.

"Even from the nomenclature—that's a big English word, or Indo-European word, meaning how things are named—to describe us; we were not called Africans or African Americans, initially, for that would have linked us to the continent of our origin and would have provided fuel to the liberation consciousness of the masses. Instead, we were labeled as Negroes—a Spanish/Portuguese word for black, which was obscure enough to sever, in many ways, the linkage we had with the mother continent.

"Are you following my line, brotha's?"

"I hear yah," Moses nodded, while Khufu nodded pensively as well.

"We called that period Jim Crow," James continued, now beginning to scramble eggs in another skillet. "During that era—which ended relatively recently—access to economic resources and the better things in life were blatantly cut off from most of us. And if we created businesses and became too big, the Ku Klux Klan, or some other supremacist group, would find ways to run us out of business, burn us out of business, or run us out of town. In fact, many of the terrorists were police and local government officials."

James fixed their plates as he talked, while they sat down and began eating.

He explained how for two hundred years it had been against the law, in the United States, for blacks to learn to read; and lamented that even in the first half of the twentieth century public libraries were off limits to most black people.

The geneticist-turned griot talked for over half an hour, just laying out the framework of black life in America. Moses, meanwhile, was as engrossed in the history lesson as Khufu was. James told of how following the Civil War, poverty and lack of structural support from within the society further worked to keep African Americans from books. He outlined how share-croppers cheated the former slaves and then forced them to pay off contrived debts, often requiring all the members of a household to work in the fields just to survive. He explained that there often weren't any school buildings in rural areas. And in cases where there were schools, the

Negroes were relegated to such substandard facilities and materials that it could *barely* be called a place of learning.

"If it were up to many Americans, Pharaoh, the black man would never see a positive image of himself—we had never and have never, heretofore, gotten to see black faces like you in our literature. This culture, we find ourselves in, portrays history as if one group has done everything and others haven't done anything in the building of world civilization."

"A-men," Moses said nodding agreeably.

James savored a sip of coffee and leaned towards Khufu to ensure he made his point. "Khufu, even today when black pharaohs are paraded through the world's museums, color inexplicably loses its importance, and in the worst-case scenarios our children are still told that you were white."

Khufu was visibly stirred by the history lesson and interjected with a simmering question: "So it would seem James that these young people, today, would know this narrative you tell and collectively strike to shake off the shackles of oppression?"

"Well, Khufu, the reality is that the covert tactics of colonialism are being played out via neo-colonialism, a clever term which means new colonialism. All the actions that have been used in the past are being played out on other levels. Have you yet heard of the name Nicolo Machiavelli?"

"No, not yet," Khufu said eager to hear more.

"Well, the European countries bought into this guy's philosophy over five hundred years ago. Machiavelli, an Italian from Venice, taught, in a nutshell, that covert operations against your enemy are necessary to offset his inevitable covert operations against you. So the Western nations today have spy and counter-intelligence apparatuses to keep an upper hand on each other, as well as on non-

Westerners. Propaganda is used to defame certain groups, while it is used to prop up sometimes ruthless regimes, so they appear legitimate to the public-at-large."

Khufu admitted to James that he was familiar with tactics similar to those of the Machiavellian doctrine. He explained that his experience had been that the dominant power had always strived to maintain its position at the expense of the oppressed. "What we did, over time, was allow the conquered peoples to blend into our system, James. You can not always live at odds."

"And your solution might be, Pharaoh?" James asked pensively.

"This must be a time of cultural rebirth for blacks, Professor. Things that are self perpetuating and contribute to the upward momentum of the people must be embraced. Those things that hinder the collective good must be cast off."

"Cast off?" James asked.

"Yes, Professor, individuals must be cultivated to take ownership of our destiny as a people and recognize that their actions impact us as a collective whole. If it is not good for the whole, it must be cast off. We called this system—I'm introducing to you—Maat."

"Our folk culture, which consisted of our songs, literature and ways of doing things reinforced the collective values of our kingdom-at-large. I have observed, James, less than desired culturally affirming folk literature all-too-often in modern black life. Too many of the people today are inordinately impacted by the society's commercially-influenced culture.

"It appears credible to them, James; but subsequently, it instills in them materialistic values that are contrary to the inner needs of the Ka. The result is the cultural chaos we see in the ghettoes of your great cities," he surmised.

"My job, as Pharaoh, in my day, was to ensure that the tenets of Maat were in place. Maat, in your terms, means order. It embraces righteousness, justice, truth and moderation—with the ultimate aim of producing purity of heart. For if the heart of the individual is pure, so is the heart of the nation.

"One of our proverbs, James, goes like this: 'As the world is illumined by the sun, so is the human mind illumined by the light of the Amen—even in fuller measure. And once the divine sense has been commingled with the human soul, there is a oneness from the happy blending, so that minds that were lost are never held fast in errors of darkness, again.'"

"Why that's powerful, Pharaoh," James said. "Yes, as a people we need to realign our spirits with the illumined measures you speak of. Folks, all too often, want to go along with the status quo rather than overcoming the errors of darkness, however those errors arise."

They both turned to Moses who simply shrugged. "I'm listening, dawgs."

"You've said a mouthful," James responded, amazed at Khufu's veracity and pinpoint analyzation of the black struggle. "So you're saying we need positive, wholesome black culture that will affirm our up-and-coming young minds, rather than the market-based stuff they're getting all too often."

"That's exactly it, James. Another proverb I grew up with says: 'When opulence and extravagance are a necessity, instead of righteousness and truth, society will be governed by greed and injustice.'"

James was pleased with the exchange of ideas and said elatedly: "Something you must do, Khufu, is write a book comprised of Ancient Egyptian maxims. What you've shared today is what needs to become a part of our daily culture. You...and Kemet...*are essentially* a part of our classical folk literature, Pharaoh."

Khufu had already been approached in Egypt with the idea of doing a book about himself and Kemet, but now considered it a priority.

"James I'm going to look into that. I can see where maxims and the stories of our culture can be handed down to the modern world in a more Afrocentric perspective than has been done, heretofore. I have seen some collections of our wisdom teachings on the Internet—perhaps we can turn some of them into songs."

"Yo, Gee. I'm up for flippin' some lyrics," Moses said, nodding in fascination.

James, too, was overflowing with creative energy now. He was raring to go and realized the time had come for the pharaoh's mission to begin. He determined to wait until Khufu, himself, asserted that he was ready, however.

"James, black America's liberation is very recent. From what I've been able to deduce, the civil rights movement helped to break the binds that tied us in this current era," Khufu said. "At the current trajectory—by advancing what we've discussed into the equation—the next generation's prospects can be brighter."

James knew that Khufu's assessment and suggestions were feasible. It was simply a matter of application; finding ways to create a positively affirming culture in the midst of a commercially influenced society?

"What's up for the day, James?" Khufu asked, satisfied that they had exhausted the discussion for the time being.

"Well, I was considering taking you to one of the state universities to see if we could get a look at its history materials on Ancient Egypt."

"Don't worry about that, James," Khufu interjected. "I've already gotten a good sense of things from the Internet."

"Oh!" James responded, surprised.

"That World Wide Web is outa sight," Khufu chuckled.

"Well, your security detail is something we need to look into. The applicants are ready. Want to meet them today?" James asked. "We need to go over some particulars to see if they match your needs, Pharaoh."

"Excellent," Khufu echoed, as he rose putting his hands on his belly indicating that he was finished. "As long as they can escort me *discreetly*, I'm sure they'll work out adequately enough," Khufu said. "I'm enjoying my anonymity, James, so discretion is what I'd like most in my security apparatus."

"I understand, Pharaoh," James said. "It's kind of nice to walk down the street unnoticed. I'm recognized occasionally myself, and it *can* be distracting when I'm not looking to be seen by anyone."

"Security? Ya'll hiring?" Moses asked. "I'll be yo right-hand man, Pharaoh."

"What kind of skills you got?" James asked genuinely interested.

Khufu winked at Moses. "You're hired, young blood."

James looked rather puzzled but reluctantly resigned himself to Khufu's wish. The pharaoh was indeed his own man, James realized.

"I would like to do some talks over at the South Side Center. Think you could arrange it?" Khufu asked.

"Well, if you want to lecture at South Side, why not lecture in schools throughout the nation and around the globe?" James asked pointedly, relishing that the time was ripe to enlist the pharaoh on a media tour. "I can certainly get you some time over there and practically anywhere else you'd like to speak, in fact."

"I'm ready when you are, James," Khufu said with an eager edge to his voice and not as much accent as might be expected. "Around the globe, huh?"

"Yes, we'd better start off with an introduction from the White House," James opined, already laying out the strategy. "Anything less than that will bring the naysayers out of the woodwork."

Moses agreed, "Might as well be sanctioned from the top," Professor.

Nodding, James said, "Thank God we've got an open-minded administration in office. With the president's endorsement, we'll have to fight the media off with a stick. Get a look at this, Khufu," James said cynically. He had gotten up, walked over to the door and pulled a new magazine from the mail slot. "*News Leak* magazine speculates that the great *Khufu* is somewhere in Brazil incognito," he said flipping the pages.

"Let me get a look at that?" Khufu asked mesmerized by the picture he saw on the publication cover.

"Where do they get this stuff?" James asked not expecting an answer, as he handed the periodical to the pharaoh. Inside, it showed Khufu just moments after being birthed from the gestation chamber. "The stuff these publications come up with."

"Amazing," Khufu agreed, looking up from the pages. "I've been keeping up with the gossip on the World Wide Web. Accuracy doesn't seem to matter these days," he added, now passing the magazine over to an eager Moses who sat back down at the table and began to read.

"Yeah, that's for sure," James echoed as he began to clear the table.

≈

Back in Egypt, Raheem Nadat received an e-mail from James notifying him that Khufu was ready for the media blitz that the world had been anticipating for almost a year now.

Pharaoh had much to share with the modern world about his era. And Egyptologists, history departments, linguists, religious leaders, Afrocentrists and scientists all scurried to have an audience with him.

Nadat pulled away from his computer and prepared himself for an afternoon meeting with President Hamadi and his cabinet, along with governmental security chiefs and committee leaders of the People's Assembly. He would have liked to have driven his private car over to the People's Assembly building, but had accepted a ride in the presidential limousine for safety purposes. Al Najja hadn't struck in a while, but the government was on red alert, the highest warning for a terrorist attack.

Khufu, meanwhile, Nadat gathered, had grown in confidence and was now comfortable with the trappings of modern life. He carried a cell phone; he'd traveled by aircraft; and he surfed the Internet frequently. And now, he was even eager to learn to drive, Nadat had heard. What could the pharaoh possibly do for an encore, he chuckled.

The seasoned scientist's goal now was to see that Egypt's newest national treasure, the pharaoh, remained safe as he journeyed on his promotional tours. He called them promotional tours because he recognized that the more Khufu was touted, the more the tourism industry would increase in Egypt. Already, within the past year, since the cloning of Khufu, tourism had increased a whopping ten-fold, even with the relative slowing following the Al Najja assassination attempt. Furthermore, he was certain it would climb even more once Khufu began his talks.

He walked out to the waiting limousine and settled back into his comfortable seat for the fifteen-minute ride to the People's Assembly building—he never knew what hit him. It must have been a computer-guided missile, because the impact on the limousine was absolute and total. It flipped and rolled several times before coming to a crunched standstill and going up in an inferno.

25

"I talked with Raheem on yesterday, right before the attack," the president said to the men sitting around the glossy hardwood conference table. On hand were the president's cabinet, the head of national security, and a few senior members of the People's Assembly. "He didn't deserve this. His love for Egypt and the people of this nation was unsurpassed. We will hunt those fanatics down until the last one is brought to justice," he said vehemently.

Looking blankly at Nadat's final report on Pharaoh Khufu, he continued: "The pharaoh's ready to begin lecture tours to the English-speaking world. My major concern right now is Al Najja. What else have our intelligence sources found out about them?" he asked, swerving his chair in the direction of the security chief.

A sixtyish-year-old man with thinning gray hair, and the countenance of a leader, quietly shuffled papers and then began a report. "Al Najja is comprised of extremists who seem to feel that the presence of a black pharaoh will steer the religious sentiments of the nation in the direction of Ancient Egyptian spiritual leanings. The group essentially includes many of the same people who make up other Egyptian far-right groups. As you're aware, President Sadat was assassinated, and there have been attempted murders of some of our cabinet members by literally the same people.

"We've identified Muhammad Adou, a local baker here in Cairo, as the head of this cell. We simply need a solid case against him so we can round him up. Take off the head and you kill the body, as they say."

"Sounds good, but these terrorist organizations are becoming more sophisticated," President Hamadi interjected. "Once you take off the head, several heads come back in its place."

"Yes, the many heads keep us sharp on such matters," the security chief replied.

President Hamadi elaborated: "We have been effective in quelling terrorism in Egypt up to a point, in the past, and have been resigned to confronting a new threat ever-so-often. But this new jihad movement reflects a fresh menace that has wasted no time in proving its ability to be lethal. I want twenty-four-hour surveillance on Muhammad Adou," he said emphatically. "He'll make a mistake eventually, and we'll be there to get him."

"What's this ancient religious nonsense all about?" one of the parliamentary officials asked. "These zealots are the one's who give Egypt a bad name."

The security chief explained: "There seems to be some scroll that Khufu or one of his priests allegedly wrote before his death that was found in the tomb, near his sarcophagus. It came up missing in the days following the discovery of the pharaoh, and apparently Al Najja has gotten wind of what was written on it. According to hieroglyphic experts, it seems to mention the pyramids as being some kind of holding chambers, until the end times—some obscure point in the future—when man and the god Amen will be reunited on planet earth."

"A holding chamber?" the president asked.

"Yes, some kind of holding chamber. That's reputedly why the pyramids were built so foolproof; so they could withstand the test of time and protect the pharaohs' remains until the appointed hour."

"Well, they did a darn good job at making it foolproof," the president said as he shuffled some papers.

"Everything's always over religious matters," a second parliamentary official said.

The security chief agreed: "More men have been killed over religious conflicts than any other wars." He then turned to the president for further instructions.

"I've notified the generals that this is a Code Six," Hamadi said. "We'll need to send a couple of sleeper agents over to America with Khufu's regular agents. I want thorough reports on the backgrounds of each of the agents you choose. Given Al Najja's religious motives, their roots may reach deeper within our society than we realize," the president reckoned.

≈

James and Khufu promised Moses a slot on the pharaoh's security detail in the coming days and weeks. And they aimed to keep their promise. But the sudden loss of Raheem Nadat had unsettled things. It was a major blow they could not have anticipated. Their sense of safety was now compromised more than they had ever imagined. The TV news footage of the smoldering remains of Nadat's limousine had made the reality of his passing immediate and resounding.

Nadat's exit from life opened a gapping hole in Khufu's and James's plans, extinguishing the sense of continuity his presence provided. Indeed, he was the cornerstone in their alliance. He was the one who had conceived the research project from day one. And now, for all intents and purposes, it was just Khufu and James left to map out the strategy for the future. Nadat's gentlemanly ways and infectious smile had brought out the best in people. He would be sorely missed.

Nadat's family, meanwhile, decided on a quiet, closed memorial service. No use having a full-fledged public funeral when the attendees could not view the remains—the missile had obliterated Nadat's body.

≈

"The president has agreed to a 10:00 AM press conference in the Rose Garden on Tuesday," James said to Khufu as they made their way through Chicago's Midway Airport to their gate. Despite James's objections, Khufu had decided to wear his native clothes again. And incredulous stares, finger pointing and bemused chatter were the order of the day. Some people realized who he was, while others must have thought he was an actor, or something. There had even been a couple of autograph seekers, something Khufu hadn't bargained for. His handwriting in English was okay, but not up to his standards so he continued to sign his name in hieroglyphics.

"Let's keep in mind that you'll be a walking target for Al Najja now that you're coming out in the open here," James said as they sat down near windows that allowed them to see incoming and outgoing flights. James had access to the VIP section of the airport, but Khufu eschewed it; so they sat there amidst the busy fray of common folk.

"A scared man dies a thousand deaths, James," Khufu said, resolutely, with a staunch look in his eyes that suggested he was ready to take on whatever lay ahead. "By the way, is Moses with the security detail?"

"Yes, but you said you didn't want them surrounding us."

"Could I have your autograph, sir?" a woman smiled nervously, looking down at Khufu and handing him the flip side of a business card.

"Why yes," Khufu said, more surprised than anything that so many people recognized him.

"I saw you on television and YouTube, and I never forget a face," she said with a smug look. "And you wear that kilt well," she said with a wink. She turned to James: "And how about you, sir, could I have your autograph, please?" she asked.

"Why certainly," James smiled with an enthusiasm that belied his thoughts on the matter. He wondered what he'd gotten himself into, in relation to celebrity.

Over the intercom, the announcer called for first-class passengers to line up for boarding. And James hastily grabbed his briefcase while Khufu was in tow. There, they stood in line with Khufu in his favorite clothing: a beige kilt, his nemes headdress and a thick-cotton shirt; the shirt because James had warned him of the likelihood of a cool air-conditioning system on the plane.

Khufu had earlier attempted to do away with his Chicago security detail, with the exception of Moses. But James had convinced him to bring on an experienced Chicago-area guy whom he instructed, along with Moses, to tail him and Khufu incognito wherever they went. Once they arrived in D.C., four new Cairo-based agents were set to join them and work as part of Khufu's security apparatus.

They passed their boarding passes to the gate agent who while awestruck still managed to ask Khufu for his autograph, which the pharaoh proceeded to scribble across the face of his ticket stub. A collector's edition, James thought, facetiously. She'd probably disobeyed airport protocol concerning celebrities, but who could blame her.

The ensuing moments consisted of normal boarding procedures. Then after Khufu and James had taken their seats, an incessant curtsying by other passengers who boarded the plane began, as word had spread that the pharaoh was on the flight. Khufu simply nodded to each and every curtsy, while James buried his face in the stock-market pages.

As the crew prepared for flight instructions, the captain, a Southerner, blared out: "We have a special guest on our airline today by the name of Pharaoh Khufu, or Cheops...in case any of ya never heard of hem. He's the one who built the Great Pyramid. We jest wont to welcome you on our plane, Pharaoh Khufu. And jest know you're in good hands with me, Captain John Rainy, at the helm."

Applause and cheers ensued throughout the aircraft, which seemed to sit just fine with Khufu. And James, well, he was just along for the ride. It was Khufu's time to shine.

≈

The press conference the next day at the White House went well. And media outlets from around the globe picked up on the U.S. media reports and rebroadcast them in their local languages. Khufu's speech was electrifying, chilling, thought provoking and pragmatic, all in one.

He began by underscoring the fascinating progression that man has made from pre-recorded history until postmodern times. He declared that change and progress had been possible because of the ability and willingness of men to communicate and cooperate. He cited the invention of the wheel as a critical turning point that allowed communication between peoples of distant lands to become more widely accessible; and he pinpointed how diffusion took place whenever those varying peoples met—causing assimilation of the best each culture had to offer. He summoned the people of today to have the courage to capture the opportunities of the hour. And lastly, he challenged Islamic terrorists, Western colonialists and indigenous peoples to sit around the table of brotherhood and usher in an era of lasting peace.

James returned to his hotel without Khufu. He knew the fanfare would be intense from there on out and frankly wanted a personal break to recharge his mental batteries. Besides, Khufu would be interviewed that night for a TV news magazine show and probably needed some time alone to rehash his thoughts. Thus, he suggested that the pharaoh have the security detail escort him to lunch or wherever else he might require that evening.

Khufu, meanwhile, was already formulating his next moves, in his head. He planned to do lectures and speeches not only on college campuses but before governmental bodies, like the UN. He had decided to take his story to the leaders of the modern world. He would speak out for the modern black man and address the modern dereliction of his history.

≈

The drive to the television station was quiet and calm. Khufu sat in the back of the pine green Jaguar limousine alone and realized that it was the first time he had engaged in anything of significance in this era without his tutors Masud, Nadat or Professor James Hannibal. One of the advertising sponsors of the television network had supplied the automobile, and Khufu relaxed thankful that all was going well. He was buffered by his new security detail, the two Chicagoans and the Egyptians together, whose cars were in the front and rear of his vehicle. And since he hadn't heard of any reports on Al Najja activities in America, he rested secure that there were no safety issues to concern himself with.

He simply focused on how he might present himself to the public and tried to seek Amen for guidance in his endeavor. For his entire early life he had been taught to call on the god's of Egypt for his guidance and provision, but now he had begun to wonder if they had abandoned him, or if they existed at all. Ironically, he prayed anyway, if only out of habit. But nothing was like he had expected. Where had Osiris, Horus, and the myriad of other gods evaporated to? And did this era know something about the afterlife that he needed to learn?

The limo came to a stop outside the television station, and the driver opened the door for the pharaoh to get out. The security detail, meanwhile, surrounded him to block out possible interlopers.

Khufu had ventured out without the familiar nemes headdress. Instead, he wore his braided wig to celebrate the festive occasion of his new start. He had noticed that braids were the rave among Africans throughout the diaspora, and even more so, he was told, since his emergence nearly a year ago. He didn't feel out of place at all wearing the wig in America. In fact, his studies on the Internet had revealed that during the Renaissance era in Europe, wigs had been a part of every gentleman's wardrobe. And America's founding fathers all wore wigs, a tradition borrowed from Egypt, by way of Europe.

Inside the studio, the hostess of the show, Anna Lang, from the state of Mississippi, escorted Khufu to her powder person to ensure his skin didn't glisten too much when they went on air. The hot lights had a way of making guests perspire, she said. The powder could also be used to cover any blemishes that might draw undue attention, she explained.

Next, they went over last-minute details of what might be talked about—and before he knew it, they were on: Anna Lang looked directly into the camera to a global viewing audience. "This is the moment we have been waiting for America and the world. We have with us a very special guest who represents a new nexus with the past and, subsequently, the future. We were amazed when we first saw video footage of him being birthed from the gestation chamber in Egypt nearly a year ago. We wondered how he would act, how he would sound and what new insights he might provide concerning our ancient heritage. And so, without anymore buildup, I present to some and introduce to others Khnum-Khufwy—Pharaoh Khufu." The studio crowd rose for a standing ovation....

It took awhile to quiet the audience, but finally she was able to begin:

"What was it like, Pharaoh, to find yourself in modern times?"

"Well, first, let me explain by saying that I did not realize I was in modern times, initially. We had been taught, in my culture, that when one dies, his or her Ka—or spirit in your terms—is met at the Great Judgment Hall of Osiris; that the god Anubis weighs one's heart against the Feather of Truth and ascertains whether one merits entrance into Duat, or is expelled to the underworld. Upon opening my eyes outside the birth chamber, however, I encountered the flashing lights of cameras, which were certainly beyond my ability to comprehend as anything less than some kind of heavenly apparition of the gods."

"So were you frightened?"

"No, not frightened. I had done my best to live by the dictates of the gods in my latter years, so I was cautiously optimistic that my good deeds would outweigh my bad deeds, and I would gain entrance into Duat—our word for Heaven. That *is* how you pronounce it, Hea-ven?"

"Yes, you speak English well," Lang said. "Was English very difficult?"

"Difficult? Yes, Anna. But, I thought it was the heavenly language. So I put myself on an accelerated track to learn it," Khufu chuckled—as did the studio audience.

"But you are the pharaoh, you were perceived as a god-king. Didn't you feel you had a *right* as a god-king to enter Heaven?"

"I was *perceived* as a god-king, Anna. But after a lifetime of confronting all of my shortcomings, I well knew I was *not* a god." Khufu *and* the audience erupted in laughter, which was only eclipsed by incessant clapping that only subsided after stage managers began to give the palms down sign due to on-air time restrictions.

"So, what were you doing for the forty-five hundred years since your death, just sleeping?"

"That's what was so fascinating. It was like I closed my eyes one moment and awoke outside the birth chamber the next."

"Now, *that is* fascinating," Lang remarked. "What have you learned? What do you *think* about the twenty-first century, Pharaoh Khufu?"

"A wonderful time-period, a wonderful place; America did not exist in my day, and yet you have devised tel-e-phones without cords, tel-e-vision, air-planes, space-craft, micro-wave ovens. You know, in my times it took forever just to cook a meal. Your society has reached great heights...But on the other hand, you haven't changed very much. People are still concerned with their individual needs, their families, their futures, their careers."

"Careers, Pharaoh, how'd one embark upon a career in your day?"

"In much the same ways as you do today. Our middle class was not so large as yours is now, but those who felt they had an aptitude for a discipline generally gravitated toward that area. We had medical doctors, architects, military officers, scribes, artisans, and *women's rights*, believe it or not."

"Women's rights?" Lang asked.

Khufu smiled: "From what I've been able to deduce, thus far, Kemet seems to have been far more advanced than any of the societies that arose prior to the twentieth century, in the area of women's rights, Anna. Their ability to own land and become engaged in the broader areas of society was un-paralleled prior to the current era. In fact, we did have a few female pharaohs. Now, let me ask *you* a question: Why hasn't America ever had a woman president?"

Holding a hand up, Lang excitedly said..."Wait, wait. I'm doing the questions here, Pharaoh...how about I answer that at another time," the audience chuckled loudly, as did Khufu. "Who were the women pharaohs, how'd that come about?" Lang asked.

"Well, that was *after* my time, Anna...." The crowd roared.

"We've heard of Cleopatra..." Lang said playfully, as if helping to prod the pharaoh's memory. The crowd became tense. "Cleopatra. The Egyptians had turned Greek by that period," Lang chuckled.

The crowd roared again.

"That was *after* my time, Anna...." The audience went hysterical....

The show went on to be a raving success. Although Anna Lang had planned on the interview being a serious hour for the audiences around the world to look at the issue of race and the pharaohs, class and gender issues, and cloning; it never got as serious as she and the television producers had envisioned.

But unquestionably, the pharaoh had won the hearts of the people. He was quite literally modern, except for his accent.

≈

Robert Luster jetted in to Washington, D.C. to ferry Khufu and James back to Chicago on his Gulfstream, and thus renewed his acquaintance with the pharaoh, giving him a thumb's up for his performance on the Anna Lang Show. Upon dropping them off at Chicago's Midway Airport, he had them promise to call him whenever they wanted a trip to the Caribbean, or elsewhere. With that, he was off to his businesses, and they were back in the Windy City prepared for the wave of press that would follow. Already, Khufu was accepting bookings for a year in advance.

And James pondered the future of his own research career in academia. How would he ever be able to continue to do hands on genetic studies if he accepted all of the speaking engagements he was being asked to fulfill.

Meanwhile, Tuskegee University kept him on staff with an open clause that allowed him to teach and research at his leisure.

On the following week, Khufu was scheduled to speak to students at the University of Memphis. James, thus, telephoned Brooks Edwards to inform him that the pharaoh would be in the Southeast and asked if Edwards could possibly help on such short notice. Edwards resided in Nashville, Tennessee and gladly agreed to help. He volunteered to meet them in Memphis.

26

Memphis. Khufu could see the thirty-two story stainless steel pyramid built by modern Memphians down below, as the commercial jet approached Memphis International for landing. The city, on the banks of the Mississippi River, with the namesake of Egypt's ancient capital, was situated in the delta region of the great waterway, much like ancient Memphis's proximity on the Nile River.

Khufu, noting the similarities with the Nile and Egypt had mixed emotions about this city, however. The great civil rights leader Dr. Martin Luther King, Jr. had been assassinated there less than half a century ago. And much of the wealth was still in the hands of the descendants of the former slave owners. Had they named their city after Egypt due to the misconception that the pyramids were built by slaves?

The tires of the jet screeched on contact, and the one hundred plus ton aircraft grabbed the tarmac like the talons of an eagle. Inside the terminal, the pace was quiet and leisurely and no one seemed to recognize who he was, perhaps, because he was dressed in Western clothes.

Khufu, meanwhile, had gotten used to his ever-present body guards. There were three on each side of him—just like old times, in Ancient Egypt. Two of the agents were the African Americans, from Chicago—one of them being young Moses. James had worked to bring on the more experienced agent, Craig Kertis, because he understood the U.S. intimately and would navigate American cities well. Kertis and Moses would also accelerate Khufu's emersion into the subtleties of U.S. culture.

His cell phone rang..."Yes, we're here, James. No problems, whatsoever. Yes, we'll be looking for Dr. Edwards here at the airport...goodbye."

Khufu hated to be so perfunctory with Hannibal, but he knew the umbilical cord would have to be severed soon. James meant well, and his directives had been laudable, for the most part. But he could be like a smothering parent sometimes, Khufu mused rather agitated. *My father, Snefru, is long gone*, he thought with a sigh.

Kertis, the new security chief, moved ahead of the crew so he could meet Edwards who would be waiting outside with a university supplied limousine. Meanwhile, the rental-car agency had been instructed to post two rental cars out front for the agents.

To Kertis' surprise the limousine was out front but the rental cars and Dr. Edwards had not yet arrived. He called the rental-car company which apologized and said airport police had forced their drivers to move the cars due to traffic congestion.

Kertis, thus, retrieved one of the Egyptian agents who along with him took a shuttle to the rental facility to pick up the cars themselves. With six agents in tow, they'd decided to rent at least two cars even when travel accommodations were supplied by the host.

Meanwhile, the rest of the group had continued to baggage claims to retrieve their luggage.

"Who said travel was easy," Moses quipped, as they headed towards baggage claims.

Khufu heard the remark and chimed-in quickly: "This *really is marvelous,* my brotha. A five hundred mile trip in ancient Kemet would have taken eight or nine days up the Nile on high waters and weeks over land. The additional effort in provisions and manpower would have been enormous. Trust me, earlier generations would have given their right arm for this kind of ease in travel."

"Well, I guess you're right," Moses said enlightened— considering the fresh perspective.

They retrieved their bags and since neither Kertis nor Dr. Edwards had arrived, they took the time to people watch and relax.

After awhile, Khufu started reading a new book he'd purchased called *Scientific Trajectory.* The book underscored advances in technology and science and explored how the dissemination of scientific ideas was increasing exponentially due to modern research and the Internet. It highlighted self-driving cars and interstellar travel as inevitabilities of the future.

Kertis and the Egyptian agent returned with the rental cars, but Dr. Brooks Edwards still hadn't arrived; so they loaded into the automobiles and alerted Hannibal of the situation.

They had plenty of free time, so they had the limousine driver escort them to the university to assess the premises for parking and access for the next day's 10:00 AM session. After that, they headed to the hotel where Khufu took a nap first and then took a swim. Later that evening, he treated the agents to a steak dinner in the posh hotel's restaurant.

The next morning, Dr. Brooks Edwards still hadn't made contact, so Khufu decided to leave early for the college to allow time to meet the hostess, Akoswa Bindeli, the director of the university's activities association. The student liaison had contacted the pharaoh the prior evening by telephone, but the security detail wanted a lay of the premises before Khufu began his speaking session.

"Pharaoh Khufu, I'm honored to meet you," Bindeli said, as the monarch and Kertis reached her office's open door— "Come in, please." Bindeli, who also served as a drama instructor at the school, had been perusing what appeared to be a flyer promoting the event.

"I didn't expect you so early, but it's good that you're here," she said, getting up quickly to shake hands. "Your clothing is absolutely stunning. Is it original?" she asked Khufu.

"They're made on modern machines, but considering they don't have original patterns and techniques to work with, I think they do a pretty good job," Khufu said in almost flawless English.

"I'd say," she retorted, shooting Khufu an admiring glance. "Have a seat, gentlemen. Coffee?"

"Yes. Black, please," Khufu answered.

"Thanks, but I'll be attending to security matters," Kertis said, humbly, as he turned to head down the hallway.

Moses and another agent were posted outside Bindeli's door, while Kertis and a second agent worked with the university security to ensure the building was properly secured. The two other agents stayed at the automobiles.

Since her office was off to the side of the auditorium, Bindeli took Khufu across the hallway to show him his seat near the lectern and explained that Egyptologists and other professors, along with dignitaries, including the mayor, had also been invited to attend as special guests.

The forum would consist of a friendly chat with the audience, and he would be given the key to the city, since he was in the Ancient Egyptian capital's namesake.

People were now beginning to trickle in and Khufu took Bindeli up on an offer for a bagel, since he hadn't eaten earlier and was beginning to feel hungry.

Bindeli and Khufu settled down for small talk and chatted until the intensity of voices outside the office began to overtake theirs.

"It's probably the mayor with his entourage," Bindeli said, rising quickly to open the door. Outside, a tall black man who also had a security team with him stood smiling graciously. "Mayor, good to see you," Bindeli said animatedly with outstretched hands clasping his.

"Pharaoh, this is the mayor of Memphis," she said to Khufu, who rose and did a humble nod before his hand met the mayor's outstretched reach.

"Honored to meet you, Pharaoh Khufu, I assume your stay has been pleasant here in Memphis?"

"Yes, very. I'm very much interested in visiting your Pyramid Center before I leave. It made for an interesting view from the aircraft."

"My pleasure, Pharaoh. What is your schedule like, today?"

"After this speaking session, we're open," Khufu said matter-of-factly.

"Well, I'd be delighted to take you on a tour of the Pyramid Sports and Entertainment Center, myself," the mayor said heartily.

"Ready, gentlemen?" Bindeli asked. "It's show time. Mayor, you're seated next to Pharaoh Khufu. I'll be introducing you when it's time to present him the key to the city."

The two men nodded affirmatively, while she led them across the hallway to the doors of the backstage area of the auditorium. She opened it and continued walking onto the stage where they emerged before a couple of thousand, or so, chattering attendees who went into an uproar when the three came forth.

Bindeli sat them at their seats beside the other officials and walked over to the podium as the crowd quickly quieted.

"Ladies and gentlemen: It is with honor that we've been able to bring to our university one of the greatest figures of the ancient world. The namesake of our city bespeaks our admiration and respect for his nation and the capital in ancient Kemet where he lived.

"We have assembled with us on the podium, today, dignitaries from this area who need no introduction; a couple of them are authorities on Ancient Egypt. So first, before we get into our session, I'd like to present to you the university's very own resident Egyptologist, Dr. Lloyd Whitehall of the Department of Middle Eastern Studies. Please give him a handclap as he comes, would you."

After Whitehall's remarks, a couple of the other officials spoke for a few moments...this followed by the mayor's presentation of the key to the city.

Khufu accepted the key and began a lucid talk of his newfound mission. He explained how just a few months ago, it seemed, he had been the standing pharaoh of Egypt, the greatest power in the known world. And then he had awakened one day to see that the gods had placed him in another time under the sun.

He discussed how even this century's directions on the map had been strange to him at first; for in his era Nubia and Punt had been up the Nile, from Egypt, and literally north in his conception; and, subsequently, how today's Middle East had been considered down, below Kemet, like our designation of the south today.

"Egypt was the Black Lands, the gods' glory to the world. We were the sun, the moon, the stars; the provider of art, literature, science, religion and reason. All of the nations were our satellites, captured in the gravitational pull of our renown." His vocabulary reflected his modern education since being in the twenty-first century.

Then he explained how he had been perplexed, upon entering this time period, to see people like him, black men and women; no longer the standard bearers, but the bearers of burdens. Thereafter, he laid out a challenge for the modern-day Memphis of the West.

"Culture is a derivative of the word cultivate," he proclaimed. "In Kemet, our farmers would first plow the land, in planting season, and harrow the dirt in order to level the ground; then seed would be planted. From what I see here in America, the land was plowed during your Civil War, and later again during your civil rights movement, but it was never harrowed. Thus, there have been left uneven, un-harrowed fields, where some of your seed has not had an equal opportunity to grow properly.

"Your civil rights leader Dr. Martin Luther King, Jr. died in this city, Memphis, because he wanted to ensure that the poor, blacks, and the disenfranchised got better opportunities. So, I ask you: If I were to come to your city, without my pharaonic garb; without all of the fanfare? Would I be provided a fair shake? Will the land yet have been leveled?"

Khufu had planned to engage in a simple question and answer session, but felt compelled to underscore how the Memphis namesake represented a special opportunity and responsibility to the heritage of its legacy. He told how he had accepted the speaking engagement, in Memphis, over others that had previously contacted him for a simple reason, its namesake.

The pharaoh then reflected on how he had begun to learn of the history of the region and how the black fertile soils of the Mississippi Delta had been cultivated by black men who, invariably, had held second-class citizenship or no citizenship at all. He lauded the voting population for having elected an African-American mayor—and challenged them to work with the magistrate for greater opportunity for all of the citizens of the city.

In closing, he underscored that in his day names were given with the expectation that the person or place would live up to that designation. Thus, he challenged Memphians to give those who looked like him an equal chance.

The audience, divided by clusters of blacks and whites with a splattering of other groups, here and there, clapped vociferously capturing all of the energy of the moment.

The pharaoh then opened the floor for questions. A young white woman, in her early twenties, with a pronounced Southern accent, rose to ask the first question.

"Phayrow Khufu, have you personally been discriminated against, yourself, since you've been in the twenty-first century, and how?"

"That's a very good question," he said before beginning his answer. "Personally, the discrimination has not come directly from anyone, let me say. But it has come indirectly from the social framework. When I see illustrations of me and people of my era who were categorically black people depicted as white, I'm being discriminated against. When I look in your encyclopedias and note a gradual change, over the years, in terminology towards the black man based on the amount of pressure he has put on white society to change it, I'm reminded that I'm being discriminated against."

This time there was loud clapping amongst half of the audience, and a tense clutter of hand claps in the other.

The next question came from a young black man of about nineteen or twenty. "Phayrow Khufu, what do you thank would be the bess thang for young black men to do to git the oppressa offa our backs? You prolly heard already thet sayin': 'We the last hired and the first fired.'" With that question came another roar of hand claps from the black sections of the audience, and tense clutters from other sections of the room.

"I will begin my response, young blood, by utilizing a quote myself. And that is that: 'All knowledge is knowable.' The oppressor cannot oppress a strong man unless the strong man is bound. And to become unbound—in this day and age—you must attain knowledge. Knowledge is a compound word meaning 'to know'—to have information—and 'ledge'—meaning to extend out over. If you will seek to become one who is know-ledge-able," he said with emphasis, "the oppressor's hand on you and your generation will be broken." A burst of applause now rang out throughout the audience.

"Too often, oppressed people ignore the knowledge that is readily available," the pharaoh continued, talking over the applause—"thinking it is the domain of the empowered few. Young bloods, your generation must learn the words of the English language intimately. For words are the tools you use to construct your ideas and your future reality. Knowledge encompasses the fundamentals that any group must have to compete effectively in today's information-based society."

Other questions ranged from the more personal, such as: what was his first day in the twenty-first century like? to, what did he think of the new technology of today's world? to, his feelings about the science of cloning?

Concerning cloning, Khufu evoked an Ancient Egyptian proverb: "All develops upward, and anything that opposes the upward momentum of the universe is ultimately left in its wake." He explained that plants had been cloned and cultivated for centuries and charged the audience that while scientists must be god fearing and patient about the aims of science, they must not oppose the upward motion of nature.

The crowd gave the pharaoh a standing ovation; and he nodded and waved humbly in the hope that he had said something that would benefit the lives of those present. Bindeli announced that there would be no autographs or personal talks with the pharaoh, following the session, but said that he had agreed to return to Memphis later in the year.

"Great talk, Pharaoh," the mayor said as he walked out with Khufu, Bindeli, and the other dignitaries in tow. "Thank you very much," Khufu said, as they made their way across to Bindeli's office.

"Bindeli, that's not an English name, is it?" Khufu asked the hostess as she poured him a cup of punch from a spread of refreshments that had been prepared for the guests.

"No. It isn't," she said. "My parents are from Somalia, and my husband's from West Africa, but I'm born and reared here in the good ole USA."

"Seems like her ancestry's from the area that was called Punt in your day," Lloyd Whitehall said, stretching his hand out for a shake with the pharaoh.

Whitehall was tall and big. He stood about six-four and weighed at least three hundred pounds. He had blue eyes and red sun-burned skin. He enjoyed the outdoors, one could tell. "I admit, Pharaoh, our culture has literally turned Ancient Egypt white. It is a crime, I tell you. I was born in this society ya know, but I didn't create it," he said, in what was a South African accent.

The mayor turned from talking with another guest: "Well, if you'd like, Pharaoh, you can ride with me in my limousine and your security personnel can follow us. Is that okay with you?"

"Certainly, whatever's the most efficient is fine with me," Khufu said graciously.

"Oh, the press is biting at the chafe," Bindeli said, noting the pressing, near mob, outside her office door. "They want to get a few quotes from you Pharaoh Khufu, before you go. Do you mind?"

"Of course not, let them in if you'd like, or they could meet the mayor and me over at the Pyramid Center."

"Well, they'll probably want to do both, knowing the Memphis press," she said. Bindeli waved an Ok at Moses and the other agent, who opened the door, and a wave of press people flocked into her office with notepads, cameras and bright lights.

"Mr. Khufu, Pharaoh Khufu, Phayrow..." they all talked at once....

Khufu did his best to answer as many questions as possible, but after awhile he sensed the mayor probably had other things he needed to do, so he mentioned that they could finish the press conference at the Pyramid Center.

With that, they began to leave and almost as if by magic, the room was cleared.

"Why you're the hottest thing since Elvis in this town," Bindeli said.

"That's for sure," Whitehall said biting into another bagel.

≈

"The media in this country is all about ratings, Pharaoh," the mayor explained as they made their way up Poplar Avenue towards downtown and the Pyramid Sports and Recreation Center. "Television and radio, for example, encourage short, one-line quotes so they can compress them into their news stories."

"But wouldn't they prefer detailed explanations?" Khufu asked.

"Oh no, man. I mean, Pharaoh. Never. They're, unfortunately, really not interested in detailed information. Their aim is ratings numbers. How many people can they draw to the television, or the radio, at the same time. Sometimes it's almost wise to do something outlandish so all of the media outlets will carry an idea you want to get out to the public."

"And the newspapers are the same?" Khufu asked.

"Newspapers actually like a lot of detail so they'll have enough information to fill the pages; but no worry—they have research libraries where they access loads of information to complement whatever they're writing about. So, if it happens that you don't have enough to say when you're talking with them—they'll fill in what they need to make the story complete. They simply want to fill the space so they can sell newspapers for profit."

"So the media is connected with the economic system, and it's not just about informing the people?" Khufu asked, to make sure he understood the mayor.

"That's right, Pharaoh. You're a fast study, brotha."

"Fascinating society, Mayor," Khufu chimed. "I would never have thought in a million years that the world could be so different, yet so efficient," he said thoughtfully, leaning back in his plush leather seat.

They were pulling up in front of the Pyramid Center now, and Khufu noted the size of the stainless-steel structure; at least ten-stories shorter than his pyramid but large non-theless. It had an efficiency of workmanship that was apparently designed to help keep the costs down, and yet it appeared to be highly functional. A good union for their ubiquitous economic system, Khufu mused. He doubted the structure could last forty-five hundred years and counting—like the limestone coated pyramids of his day—but they weren't built for the same reasons anyway, he admitted.

Out front, in the plaza of the building, was a statue of Rameses the Great, also known as Rameses II. It was about twenty feet tall, placed for effect in front of the Pyramid Center. Khufu had seen many likenesses of this Nineteenth Dynasty pharaoh. Rameses II had built more statues of himself, during his reign, than any other ruler. He was almost as omnipresent as the US economic system, Khufu thought humorously. *Now there's one I'd like to meet*, he thought. *Wonder if he was as illustrious as his press.*

They finished the tour with the mayor suggesting that Khufu come along with him to a speaking engagement he'd scheduled at a local high school. Khufu agreed under the provision that they first direct the motorcade through a fast food drive-through restaurant, where his security detail could grab a quick bite.

They soon saw a McDonald's, and the cavalcade wound through the fast-food franchise with little effort and little loss of time.

251

Khufu was still curious about the West's prolific economic system. "This ubiquitous economic network of the modern world, how did it come about?" Khufu asked, amazed by how quickly they'd gotten their sandwiches from the restaurant.

"Well, bartering simply became inconvenient, Pharaoh. And invariably, men began to create coinage. Later, the Christian church expanded in Europe, and because of its large holdings, banking systems were created to centralize, protect and distribute the wealth that had accumulated over the centuries. The Church of the Knights Templar, in England, still holds huge tracts of property in central London, I'm told. These banks continued to invest their resources and over time the transactions snowballed, exponentially. Today, the World Bank and the International Monetary Fund are two primary arms of our economic system that have direct links to the Church of the Knights Templar."

"The World Bank?" Khufu asked, intrigued.

"Yes. The World Bank is essentially the central banking institution in the West, today. It has investments all over the globe. Currently, the thrust has been to invest in Third World countries."

"Third World countries?"

"Well, that's a term I really shouldn't use. It's, unfortunately, an expression that is bandied around by the Machiavellian forces, of this world, to disparage the poor countries. Via the media, it has gotten into everyday language."

Khufu leaned his head back against the seat in thought, "Yes, Machiavelli. I've heard mention of his doctrine."

"Well, we're here," the mayor said as the limousine pulled in front of the high school. The school was a well maintained, refurbished structure that looked like it had been a classic in the 1930s. "This is one of our magnet schools, Pharaoh—it's an old building, but we call it efficient use of assets. Are they going to be in for a surprise. Ya know, they hear from me all the time via TV, radio and newspapers. If you would, I want you to talk in my place today."

"No problem, What's the format?" Khufu asked academically.

Inside, the crowd in the auditorium rose to its feet as Khufu and the mayor walked to the stage to take their seats. News TV cameras caught their every move. Still photo cameras flashed, and newspaper reporters penciled every nuance they could capture in words.

The facilitator remained standing at the podium until the crowd of several hundred students and teachers finally eased their applause. "This is such a major moment in our school's history," she said enthusiastically as the crowd quieted, "Mayor, could you come, please?"

"Mrs. Lewis," the mayor began, as his hands clutched both edges of the podium. "I began this week as any other week...concerned with the city budget; pondering the bilateral concerns of the City Council; and praying that the resources expended impact the children they are meant to reach in our schools. But I met someone today who reminded me that nothing is impossible. That someone is a great builder...He oversaw the construction of one of the Seven Wonders of the Ancient World...He has accomplished literal time travel to get here. He's here with us, today...He has a word for us...How about a hand for the great pharaoh of Egypt—his Honor, Pharaoh Khufu."

Khufu walked to the podium amid tremendous applause and began: "Thank you, Mr. Mayor," he said, with just a hint of his Ancient Egyptian accent. "Whenever I see this many enthusiastic students, I'm excited; for indeed, as in any era, the young people are the voices of tomorrow. In your hands lie the destiny of your city, the nation, and the world....

"Man's incessant quest for knowledge, is what brought me here. Scientists have cured the world of many diseases. You now travel the heavens in airplanes and space ships, where once we thought only the god's could traverse. TV, meanwhile, captures moments in time to be replayed to posterity. And telephones allow one to talk with those thousands of miles away...."

27

The edges of the canopy flapped in the cool breeze blowing over the swimming pool, as James relaxed on his patio lounge chair and surfed the Internet learning all he could about Al Najja. This was a newly emerged terrorist group; not much unlike the more established Jamaat al-Islamiyya, and the Egyptian Islamic Jihad, both of which had been implicated in past assassination attempts.

Al Najja was concerned with Khufu's intrinsic impact on the masses of Egyptians. They feared the emergence of a Rastafarian-type cult that might embrace ancient pharaonic beliefs. Like jihads throughout the Muslim world, their fundamentalist's beliefs precluded room for competing religious tenets.

He sat his laptop on the pool-side patio table and retrieved a printed report he had received from the Egyptian security forces via e-mail concerning Al Najja. The group seemed to have emerged as a direct result of the pharaoh's popularity amongst the Egyptian masses. Paradoxically, Khufu's celebrity with the common people of Egypt had been on the rise even more since he had been outside of the country. But contrary to Al Najja's fears, no religious affectations were arising among Khufu enthusiasts.

In fact, Khufu did not seem particularly religious himself, James marveled. And considering the Ancient Egyptian preoccupation with the gods, and the myriad of gods they had worshiped, it was rather surprising that he was not more inclined toward religion. He had likely felt abandoned by his gods following his encounter with the twenty-first century, James figured.

Furthermore, Khufu now maintained a residence in the US. His condominium in the South Loop of downtown Chicago was finished now. And in this age of jet planes, he could live in both countries, he'd decided. Currently, North Africa and the Middle East were somewhat of a powder keg, and the pharaoh realized he would be more secure outside Egypt's borders for the time being at least.

James got up and walked to the edge of the pool and looked at his reflection in the water before diving in. It wasn't noon, yet, and he had plenty of free time. He would call his wife later, and maybe they'd do dinner and perhaps communicate about that baby they'd been wanting. But for now, he'd just enjoy the pool—he could think more clearly when he swam. And after several laps, he was physically exhausted but mentally stimulated.

He climbed out of the water, dried himself with a beach towel and lay on his lounge chair for a catnap. He ruminated over what might have become of Brooks Edwards. He still hadn't gotten a return call from his long-time friend. At least the medical department at Fisk University had indicated that Edwards was still on staff and going to work everyday.

So what was happening with him? They'd known each other for too long for Brooks to distance himself like that. He must have slighted Brooks somehow, he figured. Well, as long as he was okay—and the office at Fisk had said so—James committed to focus his thoughts on the issues at hand.

Personally, he realized he needed to start spending more time with Marika. He'd made enough money now to retire, if he wanted. And Marika had a job where she was gainfully employed and happy with her work. He was the one who'd been too busy. He'd sunk a lot of time into Khufu, and now the guy was running around the country as if he'd been born in the twentieth century, James chuckled. Khufu was as modern as he was, already.

It was amazing, James thought, how people everywhere were able to adapt to the American life. A guy could be from the Amazon jungle; but give him a few months and he could literally be a trader on the stock-exchange floor.

Khufu was doing a good job, indeed. Book publishers were doing an about face from years and years of error. It was poetic justice for Africans throughout the world. The starting blocks had been moved back, and the world's children would no longer start classical history with Greece and Rome, or even Assyria. Ethiopia, Nubia and Kemet would be the starting points for classical cultures. Khufu was proof in living color.

He sat up and began surfing the net again to see what new was being said about the pharaoh. He'd seen enough about himself. In fact, he rarely read stories about himself anymore. It was always speculation and innuendo anyway. The prying Western media; if there was no story, they would make a story.

Thankfully, they had eased up on the misinformed cloning tales. That was a relief. And James had to admit he was rather surprised at how well the U.S. public, and the world, had taken to the far-fetched reality of cloning. It wasn't something he wanted to become normal, but it also wasn't something man could turn a blind eye to.

Khufu, meanwhile, was apparently in his natural element, James mused, as he surfed the Tennessee online newspapers.

The news that came out of Memphis was excellent. The pharaoh had gone down into the heart of Dixie and challenged ancient Memphis's namesake to live up to the heritage of its moniker.

The wind blew over the water and chilled him momentarily. It reminded him of what Khufu had told him about the Ancient Egyptian use of man-made pools for air conditioning. It was common for wealthy Egyptians to lie around their artificial pools and cool down from the breeze coming across the water. *That's actually how modern air-conditioning works*, James mused. *Air is simply pushed rapidly over water-filled coils which ice up and provide cool air.*

His cell phone rang. The area code seemed to be from Nashville, Tennessee.

"Brooks! What blew you up at this late hour?" James said, startled, not knowing whether to be upset or relieved that his old pal Brooks Edwards had actually called.

Edwards explained how he was having family problems with a college-aged daughter, whom he'd helped move from school after she'd been dismissed for drug use. Since she was on bad terms with her mother, who lived in another city, he'd allowed her to move into his place, which resulted in additional issues because she was now rebelling against *his* rules.

James felt badly for Edwards, because it seemed the guy had never completely gotten back on track since the breakup with his wife. She had been his rock. Through their college years and the tough times, she'd stuck with him; and now everything had fallen apart.

"Hey, you and Khufu are doing a great job," Edwards chimed. "I'm keeping up with the news reports whenever I get a chance."

"Well, we're doing our best," James said graciously. "But what about you? Is there anything I can help you with, Brooks? you know I'm here, brotha."

"I know, man," he said. "Hey, gotta' go, see ya soon, James." Edwards hung up. I guess middle age is catching up with him, James mused. "What a difference a good woman makes...nothing used to rattle that guy."

≈

Khufu pedaled the stationary bike in the exercise room of his Atlanta hotel and reflected on his talks and travels over the past several weeks. He had been on the cover of innumerable news magazines and newspapers in the country and around the world. And now, he was as well known in the modern world as he had been in ancient Kemet.

Wherever he went fans crowded around to get a glimpse of him. And even now, he was pleasantly surprised that word had not gotten around that he was in the workout room, yet. At the moment, at least, a couple of other users of the facility simply smiled at him but stayed put at their own workout stations. His security agents, including Moses, looked pretty menacing, though—they mulled around like Gestapo.

Khufu had recently accepted an invitation to South Africa for a five-day symposium on classical African civilizations. He already knew what he would talk about. He would describe the ancient trade relationships that Egypt maintained with Nubia; the east coast of the continent; and the trade routes with the interior and West Africa.

Craig Kertis, his security chief, walked over and said nonchalantly: "Hey Pharaoh, word's getting around that you're here in the hotel."

Khufu, drenched in sweat, turned around to see a crowd welling up at the exercise room entrance and outside the glass door in the lobby area.

"Thanks, Craig," he said, as he took a towel from him and began to wipe his face as he got off the bike.

The other agents said nothing, but scanned the growing audience with the trained scrutiny of certified professionals. "Let's go," Khufu said. Three agents opened a channel through the crowd as they made their way out the door, and three agents buffered him as they ushered the pharaoh to his hotel room. *There's to anonymity*, Khufu thought.

≈

Moses King couldn't quite believe that what was happening around him was real. He kept figuring he might wake up at any moment to see that he'd been dreaming. Here he was traveling and protecting a historical figure who was probably the most important man alive.

He looked out at the sprawl of Atlanta from his high-rise hotel room and did a check in his mind of his new responsibilities. Craig Kertis had taught him well.

He then walked over to the closet reached into his suit bag and pulled out a fencing foil from its scabbard. He took the sword and in one smooth thrust lunged it forward, bringing it back with the fluidity of a world champion. *Someday I might have to utilize this skill for my very survival*, he mused.

≈

The slight young man in traditional white galabayya robe and head wrap walked down the Cairo street and stopped to look in the storefront window he was passing. On display were six-inch figurines of Pharaoh Khufu. *That is why I dislike the Western influenced governments*, he said to himself. *Everything is commercialized. First they make money off him, and then they turn him into a cult figure. In the name of Allah-the-most-munificent, whom the Prophet Muhammad is his spokesperson, we will not allow the seed of the infidels to take root in our land.*

He had already met with Muhammad Adou and others in Al Najja, and the plans had been set. They would erase the cloned devil from the face of the earth.

He made his way down the street to his parent's flat in Cairo's Sayyida Zeinab district. It was still evening, just after dark. And as was the custom on most hot evenings, the people of Sayyida Zeinab were outside to take in the cool night air. The children frolicked in the nearby neighborhood park, and men and women sitting in separate groups sat on stoops mulling over social issues, family concerns, and neighborhood problems as had probably been done for over a millennia.

He issued routine greetings and sauntered over to a group of men who were talking about local politics and the present conditions of Egyptian life.

"In the 1940s, during the time of the Fellowship of the Brotherhood, we did not have it so hard as now," one elder explained to the group. He wore the traditional galabayya with a turban on his head, and a white beard shrouded his ancient, leathery face. Another man, big boned, middle-aged, and toothless, laughed a sheepish laugh that sounded like the croon of one who had long ago given up dreaming and believing for a better life. He epitomized the urbanized fellahin. He was born there; he had suffered there; and he would likely die there.

The young man smiled politely and only responded when spoken to. He was there with them physically, but mentally he had left them long ago. *These people know only the common things of everyday life,* he mused. *They have no knowledge of the infidels' schemes and are, thus, pawns in the hands of our enemies.*

That is why he had become a revolutionary; to become a voice for the voiceless people. The conversation turned now to his condition of bachelorhood, and they laughed and took barbs at him, suggesting that he marry this one or that one in the neighborhood. But he only smiled. He needed more finances than he had been able to achieve to take a wife. And rearing children was out of the question. He had instead, dedicated his life to Allah. At least he had the prospect of being rewarded with seventy-two virgins in Heaven if he gave his life for the call of Allah.

≈

Khufu could not keep the thoughts of her out of his mind. *She invaded his consciousness again. He was there at the gestation chamber to meet Henutsen as she emerged; she at first looked confused like he had been...before her eyes met his and emitted that glimmer of hope he had come to know so well. Then he awoke.*

It was the same dream. So frequent now, he had lost track of how many times he had dreamed that dream.

He arose and pulled the curtains of the picture window apart to reveal the Atlanta skyline. The lights glimmered like precious stones embedded in some intangible celestial basalt. And then he breathed a long sigh and chuckled quietly at his fate; he was in a wonderful place and a wonderful time, but alone with an unknown future. He had considered trying to reach Dr. Nailah Ali, but he wondered if he could really be fulfilled in the long term with a modern woman.

James had done the DNA sequencing once. Well, he could do it again—but now for Henutsen, Imhotep, Kewab and Khafre. He chuckled quietly. It was ludicrous—but it could work.

28

K hufu returned to Chicago to his new luxury condominium in the city's downtown area. The apartment's thirtieth floor perch provided a breathtaking view that made other high- rises seem within hands reach. Chicago's architectural treasures were a feast to behold.

He had invited James and Marika to dinner, which was catered by *Gordon's*, for the express purpose of discussing his recurring dream. He was sure James would write it off as some Freudian urge to mate, or the like. And *that* was certainly a part of it, he realized. He had been in the twenty-first century for nearly a year now and needed someone whom he could relate to. Nailah Ali was still in Egypt. And he wasn't sure when he would get back there. He certainly wasn't immune to his manly needs for a woman. But his priorities had changed now. A relationship, now, would have to have meaning. Besides, he really didn't think he could truly understand a twenty-first century women. He needed someone with similar sentiments as his. A contemporary woman would only see him as some freak of postmodernism, some anomaly to be studied for her amusement. No, he wanted, he needed Henutsen.

The door-bell rang, and he could see on the monitor that it was James and Marika. They had someone else with them, though, whom he'd never seen before—a good-looking woman. Well, he'd just have to make time to talk with James about the dreams later.

The meal was set up buffet style. And the *Gordon's* caterers had left the food on warmers to ensure it remained hot and ready. The visitors knocked, and he opened the door to the three smiling guests. He had given his housekeeper the day off, and his security team monitored the building and its perimeters, but only came to his apartment if he summoned them.

"James, Marika, how are you? I'm glad you could come."

"Pharaoh Khufu. This is Professor Chaundra Lockhart," Marika said introducing the two. "She's a professor of African Studies at Chicago State University and has been eager to meet you...Professor Chaundra, Pharaoh Khufu."

"My pleasure," Khufu smiled, charmed.

Professor Chaundra returned a pearly smile that could light up a city.

She was, indeed, a very attractive woman with brains to match, it seemed.

"Dinner's buffet style. We can head to the kitchen here and get started," Khufu gestured, exhibiting the characteristics of a good host. "The bathroom's down the hallway there. You can just put your things on the couch here."

Fortunately, he had ordered more than enough food, as James had insisted, under the guise of modern tradition. But now Khufu knew why—the pretty professor.

Meanwhile, James and Khufu headed towards the kitchen, while Marika showed Lockhart to the bathroom.

"Professor Chaundra has traveled to Egypt several times and is interested in Egyptian archaeology," James said. "She's putting a curriculum together for a graduate school program at the university."

"Archee-o-logy. I can barely say the word," Khufu admitted, taking a blind stab at pronouncing archaeology. "Isn't that the area of science where they dig up artifacts?"

"Exactly, it's about studying the intricacies of the lives of people and cultures. Archaeology often consists of conducting digs, but its study of cultures encompasses every conceivable area of the society in question."

"Interesting," Khufu nodded thoughtfully.

"Well, how about we serve you fellas?" Marika announced as the women returned and entered the large specially outfitted kitchen, which had a big marble counter in its center where the food had been placed. "Take a seat at the table, gentlemen, and we'll fix your plates," she said gaily.

"If you insist," Khufu nodded, drying his hands and tossing the paper towel into the garbage, as James followed suit and they headed into the dining room.

The large dining area's floor to ceiling windows provided a stunning view. The towering, gleaming white limestone facade Standard Oil Building and the colossal Sears Tower were just two of the massive skyscrapers that were his neighbors. The two sat and enjoyed the view while the ladies began bringing the food.

"An Egyptology curriculum should make for some goode conversation," Khufu said, after awhile, with a hint of his Hamitic accent.

"Yes, Pharaoh, the current history on Egypt has some gaping holes and inaccuracies that you can certainly address," James said. "Not to mention that we could benefit from your sage wisdom, Father Pharaoh."

Khufu let out a throaty chortle. "Father Pharaoh? Now, I'm supposed to offer sage wisdom to *you*, James? Now that would be the day," he chugged.

The ladies finished serving and took their places at the table, along with the men.

"The noblest employment of the mind is the study of its creator," Khufu said after they'd blessed the food. "Your Christian concept of God is of interest to me," he said looking at Lockhart, as he cut expertly into a piece of *Gordon's* baked chicken.

"What would you like to know?" Professor Chaundra smiled graciously. "I'm very much interested in *Egypt's* religious philosophy as well."

"Out of all the god's of my age, Kemet's creator god, Amen, is the only one found in your religious texts—can you speak to this?" he asked.

"Well, that's one of the connections with the modern world and Egypt that hasn't been talked about much," Lockhart said. "I'm not an expert in that area, but we do close our prayers with the term A-men."

"A-men," James said emphatically. "You mentioned that to the president at the White House, Pharaoh."

"Yes, it's a fascinating but reasonable connection between the eras," Khufu said effusively.

They enjoyed the evening, thoroughly, as they talked about archeology, religion, or whatever hit their fancy…of how Moses, a Hebrew, had been reared by the Egyptians; and how many of the proverbs of Solomon could be traced back to Ancient Egypt.

They all marveled at the similarities and kinship of Judaism, Islam, Christianity and, now, Ancient Egyptian beliefs; noting, for example, that Amen is spelled a-m-i-n when referred to in Islam; Khufu explained things about his era that they had never imagined.

"We used wisdom to manage the populace," the pharaoh said, lowering his voice to cue them that they were about to be privy to a secret. "At some point, I know not when, people began to spread the rumor that cats were divine," he said, gesturing with his hands. "Of course, we know nothing could be further from the truth. But we did not discourage this tale because the cats were a natural protection against rodent encroachments on our granaries. An additional benefit was that cats were cared for by the populace-at-large. And in accordance with a decree we issued, they released the critters to the granaries at night. The result: elimination of our rodent problem—and we had tens of thousands of personal cat managers."

They all broke into laughter at the story.

"So the embalming of the cats was a farce?" Lockhart asked incredulously.

"Well, the cats did serve a divine purpose," Khufu said apologetically. "They ensured that the food supply was unimpeded, securing a prosperous kingdom."

They all laughed some more at the revelation.

"Well, Professor Lockhart has an earlier engagement at the university," Marika said after they had talked some more. "But we can talk more later. You gentlemen are invited to join us this evening for coffee. Want to come along, Pharaoh?" she asked rising from her seat.

"I'd enjoy that very much," Khufu said. "But I'm expecting an important phone call from Cairo tonight and promised to give them my undivided attention. It's a pressing matter...," he explained, rising to see Lockhart and Marika to the door.

"Honey, I'll ride with Chaundra, and we'll see you later this evening, if that's okay with you?" Marika said to James, leaning over to give him a peck on the cheek.

"Sounds like you've got it figured out," James said humorously.

"Khufu and I have some things we need to discuss anyway—I'll see you at home this evening. And you take care, Professor; we'll see you soon," he said.

"Goodbye, you two," Lockhart waved.

Khufu closed the door behind them and returned to the table where he and James ruminated over the meal, talking about travel schedules, fares and cities that needed to be reached by the pharaoh. James could see the *Ebony* magazine building down on south Michigan Avenue, from the window, and agreed that he would contact the editor about doing an interview with Khufu. The publication had run a series of stories in its news digest magazine, *Jet.* But the larger publication, *Ebony*, would reach more homes with its huge circulation.

Then Khufu dropped the hammer. "James, you brought me here. I need you to bring others to the twenty-first century also."

"Bring others back?" James said stunned. "You're saying, you *want me* to attempt to clone *more* Ancient Egyptians?" James asked in stilted English.

"Yes, Khufu said, raising his voice noticeably. I'm alone here. I'm isolated. What would *you* do, if *you* were placed forty-five hundred years into the future and realized there was a way to bring *your* loved ones with you? I need my wives, my children, my friends—so they will have another chance, like I have."

Khufu then recounted the recurring dream about Henutsen. "I keep dreaming that dream, over and over."

"That's a tough one, Ku," James said at last. "Let me explain why. When I began this research, at first, it went against everything in me to go ahead and utilize the science of cloning. But it was as if some cosmic force was beckoning me towards some predestined appointment. I did what I felt was the right thing to do then. And by God it worked out. But I could never risk that again. Do you understand, Pharaoh? We got lucky, man," his voice cracked. "Be-sides, society isn't ready for the ramifications of what you ask—you were a one-in-a-million long shot, Khufu. Leave it at that, Ok?"

"This is a fine time to think about that, *Doctor*," Khufu roared emphatically.

James countered in a reasoning tone. "Khufu, a statute was passed here in the States, after I succeeded in bringing you back, that says the government will arrest any American citizen engaged in human cloning anywhere in the world."

Not hearing or even trying to listen, Khufu shot back: "You can do this, James. You want to make amends? Give me my family back."

"It's impossible?" James said, shaking his head reluctantly and turning toward the couch to get his jacket and briefcase; "I'll tell you what I'll do. I'll sleep on it. That's all I can say. I'll sleep on it," he repeated, hollowly.

≈

"Out of the question," Marika screamed at the top of her lungs. "Are you out of your mind, James? After all we've been through. What are you trying to do to me?" Tears began to stream down her face.

James was staggered. He hadn't expected Marika to take his off-handed remark so strongly. He had thought that she was over the wound she had experienced when he had left to do his research in Egypt. But now he could tell that the scars of that period were still tender. Perhaps she was afraid that he would go away again. But he knew he could never leave Marika again. They had rekindled too much for him to turn around and destroy all they had rebuilt.

"I'm committed to our life's plans, Marika," he said pulling her to him. "Nothing's ever going to come between us again." He had no intent on furthering his cloning research anyway. He was simply speculating on the pros and cons of Khufu's request.

She looked up at him seemingly appeased. "You would give up everything for me, James? I tell you what; Chaundra has a Middle Eastern Studies colleague at Chicago State who's also a minister. Talk to him. See what he thinks about this whole cloning question."

The next day, James called the religious leader, and the Reverend Thurston asked him if he could come by the chapel at Chicago State.

James drove slowly towards the campus, but as he neared the grounds, he began to have a change of heart and suddenly u-turned and was nearly hit by an oncoming car. He accelerated down the street and sped to the nearby expressway entrance ramp and entered the Dan Ryan causeway at breakneck speed. All he could think about was what would become of society now that he had breached an unspoken demarcation. He did not know where he was going, nor did he care.

29

After waiting for over an hour, the cleric realized that the professor had canceled, or something had gone wrong. The campus was, at most, a fifteen-minute drive from Hannibal's address. He dialed James's number, after noting his caller ID, and reached the professor's voice mail. He left a message and then resumed reading the Bible passage that he had intended to discuss with Professor Hannibal. He used his magnifying glass to read parts of Revelation 20:4, as he sat in his chair:

...4 THEY CAME TO LIFE AND REIGNED...A

THOUSAND YEARS. 5 THE REST OF THE DEAD DID NOT COME TO LIFE UNTIL THE THOUSAND YEARS WERE ENDED. THIS IS THE FIRST RESURRECTION.

He then turned the pages to Revelation 3:14, still using the magnifying glass:

14 AND TO THE ANGEL OF THE CHURCH IN LAODICEA WRITE: THESE ARE THE WORDS OF THE 'AMEN', THE FAITHFUL AND TRUE WITNESS, THE RULER OF GOD'S CREATION.

≈

James, meanwhile, found himself driving north on Lake Shore Drive, not far from the pharaoh's building. He retrieved his cell phone and pressed Khufu's pre-programmed number. "Pharaoh, how are you?"

"Good, James, and yourself?"

"I'm not my best," he admitted. "I was supposed to meet with Professor Chaundra's minister colleague and discuss the cloning issue you proposed. But something held me back, I just couldn't go through with it. This situation with you here is more than meets the eye, Pharaoh. This isn't just some lucky stroke. I'm not very religious but I believe you're here for a special purpose."

"Oh really, and what might that be, James? To do your bidding, like a puppet on a string? I submitted my wishes to you on yesterday, and you flatter me about my special purpose? Goodbye, sir," he said hanging up on Hannibal.

Khufu, meanwhile, remained seated on his couch staring out over the waters of Lake Michigan. He knew he wasn't being unreasonable. If there was a chance, Professor Hannibal owed him that.

Meanwhile, his thoughts traveled back in time. *The priests in his era had written in the Great House scrolls of a point in the distant future—translated into English, it would be called the harmonic conversion—a point in history when the god Amen would descend onto earth and live with man.* It sounded pretty similar to the Christian story concerning the millennium, he realized.

In fact, it was the possibility that some harmonic conversion might occur that prompted the pharaohs to have many of their most cherished possessions placed within their tombs at their death.

From what he could deduce from his general knowledge, and now—new-found research—it appeared that the god Amen, in Upper Egyptian, originally meant the "hidden god, or "what cannot be seen." Amen's personification was the hidden or creative power attributed with the creation of the world.

He understood now. He was in this era to clarify his understanding of the eternal gods. Had he passed the test? Would Anubis now weigh his heart on the Scale of Maat? He had come from a religious culture, and had always been interested in the things of the Creator. He thought about how he had closed down the cult temples in the years before his death. He had begun implementing mass reform, but it had begun too late. The cult teachings were too entrenched. And then he had died unexpectedly.

≈

The next morning Khufu was awakened by a call from Egyptian President Fadil Hamadi. The president informed the pharaoh that he needed him to return to Egypt as soon as possible, because he was receiving pressure from certain members of the People's Assembly about the large sums of revenue Khufu was receiving—even though it had been voted on. Now, the opposition voiced their concerns about his being an expatriate, living in America.

Hamadi said that he would send the presidential jet at Khufu's request and would prepare whichever estate the pharaoh decided he'd reside in.

Khufu, frankly, admitted that he had been getting an itch to return to Egypt anyway. He was concerned about the state of Egyptian antiquities and felt that he could be of invaluable service overseeing the restoration and preservation of Ancient Egyptian culture.

Meanwhile, the weather was changing quickly in Chicago, and he wasn't sure he was ready to experience snow, either. "Thank you for the call, Mr. President. I am scheduled to be in

South Africa on next week. How about I return to Egypt following my trip there? If you'd like, your office can issue a press release that I will be en route following the South African trip. Is that fair enough?"

"Very well, Pharaoh. I look forward to seeing you here at home, *Al salaam alaikum,*" peace be unto you.

"*Wa alaikum salaam,*" and peace be unto you, Khufu said to the president. He understood Hamadi's predicament could not be helped. It reflected the normal state of affairs in people relations. Competing needs had to be addressed, and the Parliament simply wanted to keep tabs on the nation's investment, plain and simple.

Khufu, meanwhile, was glad he had been studying Arabic in his spare time but admittedly wasn't half as proficient as he had become in English. In fact, he had begun to think and even dream in English.

He dialed James's number. "James, I'm going to have to cut short my American tour."

"Cut it short? We can work this disagreement out, Khufu," James said grimly, as he sat on the edge of his bed.

"Actually, Professor, urgent matters really do beckon in Egypt. What I'm going to do is return there following the South African trip and cancel all of the remaining engagements that are six months out.

"Following that period, I should be able to resume my travels to some degree."

"And the particulars of your trip to Egypt, Khufu, are?"

"James, my personal business should be of no concern to you. I am an independent sovereign, and I expect you to treat me that way from here on out. If you really have my interests at heart," he paused…"I've already made myself clear concerning my needs."

"I'm not one to get into your personal matters, Pharaoh. I'm just concerned, as any friend would be," James said. "Al Najja is a very real threat, *Brotha*. We've seen what those extremists can do."

"Trust me. I'm a big boy, Professor," Khufu reminded him.

30

The trip to South Africa had been invigorating and thought provoking. And the long stay in America had been breathtaking and enlightening. But now Khufu was home again in Egypt. And as he traveled from the airport, he could see that certain elements of the terrain hadn't changed much over the millennia. The Nile's banks had receded in some places and expanded in others. But for the most part, it wound its same eternal route through the delta. And the rocky desert fringes, though weathered, still maintained their immoveable foundations.

The limousine finally reached palace number one, as Khufu had informally begun to call it. And Omari and two servants hurried out as soon as the auto arrived to retrieve the pharaoh's belongings. Khufu got out, greeted them with a smile, and in his best Arabic said: "Al salaam alaikum." Peace be unto you, "my brothers."

Traditional Arabic embraces followed as each man responded with: "Wa alaikum salaam," and peace be unto you, "Pharaoh Khufu."

Khufu had left several months ago without knowing his staff's names with the exception of Omari's and had decided to make up for lost time, since he could speak some Arabic, now, and realized some of them spoke English, like Omari. He entered the house and summoned all of the workers to the foyer, where he formally reintroduced himself and told them how grateful he had been for their service during his last stay at the residence. He told them he had been studying Arabic, but was sure he would need their help from time to time as he worked to get better at the language. He then dismissed the staff to their duties and strolled down the hallway to his study, where he would soon be joined by the Egyptian president's speech writers.

Khufu was scheduled to speak before the People's Assembly the next day and had been supplied with the professional writers to ensure that the thrust of his talk covered enough to fend off unwanted opposition forces.

Fortunately, President Hamadi is broad minded, Khufu noted. The head of state recognized that contrary to representing a threat to the presidency, the pharaoh embodied an element that strengthened the national character and esteem of the nation. For the first time in memory, Egyptians were proud to be Egyptians, and they viewed the pharaoh as the eternal flame that personified their unending place of honor in the parade of nations.

≈

President Hamadi sent his bullet-proof armored Hummer to pick up the pharaoh the next morning, rather than a regular limousine. The military-style vehicle was the newest accessory in Egypt's arsenal against terrorists. In addition, he had implemented Code Six, which authorized the military and security forces to keep tabs on, and when needed, round up suspected trouble makers. Fifteen Al Najja members had been rounded up on suspicion of conspiracy in the Nadat assassination. The flashbacks of Raheem Nadat's murder weighed too heavily on his mind for him to do anything less, he reasoned.

Meanwhile, the inescapable dynamics that would entail the upcoming parliamentary session energized Hamadi. The synergy of the give and take of politics invigorated him and sharpened his mental acuity.

Khufu was, himself, a marvel to behold; so youthful, yet so wise and refined. He had literally mastered English in less than a year, and already had a commanding grasp of Arabic, the president mused.

The Parliament stood to initiate the session. And Khufu, as the special attendee and speaker, entered to a standing ovation by all parties of the multi-party House. He was dressed majestically in the finest of twenty-sixth century B.C. regalia— the combined red and white crowns that represented the union of Upper and Lower Egypt and the scepter and flail which symbolized the pharaoh's role of shepherd and authority over the nation. The applause was sustained, and the overflow crowd in the upper echelon of the chambers added to the grandeur of this first visit by the leader. A special session that would be broadcast to the nation was in the planning stages, but this visit was the first that Pharaoh Khufu and the Assembly members were to meet face to face to discuss crucial business matters.

Khufu unfolded his prepared speech and began to talk of the sweeping history and culture of the nation. He held the assembly in rapt attention as he told of his escapades as a boy along the Nile. And he evoked laughter and amusement as he explained his utter shock when he finally realized he had not yet reached Duat—having arrived in the twenty-first century instead.

To the opposing factions, within the assembly, he admonished them to keep their focus on the ultimate aims of the nation. He ended by commending the government's leadership for its ongoing direction and management of

Egypt's antiquities and praised their work in promoting the nation's heritage to the rest of the world.

With that, Khufu ended the speech and remained standing for the question and answer session of the assembly.

"Pharaoh Khufu, what is your perspective of the Egypt-Israeli Six Days War, and what would you have done differently given the same set of circumstances?" a parliamentary official asked.

"Every situation is unique, my friend," the sovereign responded. "And in all likelihood I would not have acted any differently than the men in charge. Hindsight is always twenty-twenty, as they say. The tragedy is that wars are waged at the expense of life, and the Six Days War, in that aspect, was no different. *Next question,*" he pointed.

"Pharaoh Khufu, we have an ongoing compulsory education in Egypt. This has taken a huge chunk out of our national budget. What do you see as a positive measure, within the budget, that could be cut from the disbursements in the wake of our dwindling economic base?"

"Compulsory education is certainly the most laudable thing a government can initiate. I would say that the first things you should look to cut are the non-essentials, in all areas. You must look at what you value on a scale of one to ten, with ten being the most valuable, and begin cutting from the least important first. By keeping those essentials, such as education intact, you insure that the nation continues to grow in the areas that will strengthen us internally as a people."

"King Pharaoh," a voice that was obviously a dissenting member rang out. "Currently, the British Parliament has cut back on its funding to the royal family in *that* country, substantially. Given the similar albeit worse constraints that we face in Egypt, don't you think it would be prudent for us to eliminate funding an expatriate pharaoh?" the man said hollowly.

Khufu maintained his calm and began to elaborate on his position: "I think that the rationale used to create an endowment for me was based on modest estimates of a return on the value of my real estate holdings, namely the Great Pyramids. The benefits to the nation, not just over the centuries, but in the modern era account for substantial wealth, I'm advised. I am also told that my pyramid is the only remaining standing structure of the Seven Wonders of the Ancient World.

"It is well known that relative intangibles such as tourism have seen an increase following the publicity surrounding my advent to this era; and that has, in fact, been the case. From what I've been told—and correct me if I'm wrong—tourism and investments in Egypt have increased ten-fold since my arrival."

The majority of the officials and the overflow crowd began to stand and clap rabidly. He was still the king—though titular—he was unarguably the central figure of Egypt's Republic, and rightly so.

≈

"The authorities will have to pay, the young man asserted." He was just a baker's apprentice, but he knew when the government was overstepping its bounds. His boss, Muhammad Adou had been arrested, along with fourteen other members of Al Najja on spurious charges. They had been jailed based on *suspicion* of terrorist activities. *"They had nothing factual on them, that's for sure,"* he murmured.

This was his moment. The moment he had been born for. He was not afraid to die for Al Najja. Alas, he would enter paradise where seventy-two virgins would await him. The plan was simple. He would strap the bomb to his person and detonate it when he shook the pharaoh's hand. Al Najja would then have one more martyr to celebrate.

The infidel, he'll never know what hit him, the young man smirked.

Across town, Khufu was getting ready for his day. He was to visit three schools. Two high schools and an elementary school would be his last stop. He was proud of how things were panning out. He was getting better at speaking Arabic, and he was getting to know the people of Cairo. They were a good people; full of life, quick to smile and eager to lend a helping hand.

The Hummer was already his automobile of choice now. He felt badly about having to take the armored vehicle on tours to schools, though. But it was the only rational thing to do. While several reputed Al Najja members had been arrested, who knew how many sympathizers of the organization were still on the streets.

A knock on the door meant Kertis was ready to go over the security measures for the day. Khufu answered, and the security chief entered prepared for the day ahead. Though calm as usual, there was a certain edge about him that Khufu hadn't seen before. He was all business, and he seemed intent on Khufu understanding all of the precautions and measures. They would form a barricade whenever Khufu would leave or enter the automobile or school. He was not to shake hands with anyone unless it was the school's personnel. And he was to fall to the floor or ground if there was a loud explosion, shooting, or instructions from Kertis or other security agents.

The stop at the first school went well. The students adored the pharaoh and couldn't seem to believe their good fortune at getting to see him face to face. He gave a twenty-minute speech followed by a question and answer session that wound-up lasting nearly an hour, which put them slightly behind schedule for the second school. They made their way to the school, however, without a hitch and were able to begin the assembly immediately upon arrival.

Afterwards, Khufu followed the regular routine of leaving amidst his body guards who shielded him from the pressing crowd of excited students, staff and onlookers. Immediately, upon opening the rear door, of the school, however, a young man walked right into the middle of the agents and stretched out his hand toward Khufu who froze as the body guards seized the youth: In a surreal moment an explosion went off.

31

J ames awoke groggily to the noise of the television set,
while Marika continued to shake him until he assured her
he was awake. The image on the TV was of screaming
Palestinian, no…Egyptian kids, along with erratic, unsteady
camera footage.

"There was a bomb, James! Khufu has been critically
injured and several people were killed."

Meanwhile, the telephone rang and a local radio news
station wanted to know if James could give them a quote in
relation to the bombing. Marika handed him the phone and
sleepily he suggested they call back in an hour, or so, since he
was just hearing about the ordeal via the television reports.

Not knowing who to call first, James decided to press one
of the few numbers he had programmed into his telephone,
Khufu's cell phone number. At least it was worth a try.

It rang once…twice—

"Al salaam alaikum?" peace be unto you, a voice that was
not Khufu's said on the other end.

"Hello. Do *you* speak English?" James asked.

"Yes, I speak English," the voice at the other end said in
an Egyptian accent.

"Is the pharaoh okay?" James asked nervously.

"With whom am I speaking, may I ask?" the voice answered.

"This is Dr. James Hannibal, the geneticist who worked to—"

"Oh yes. I'm sorry, Professor, I simply work in the surgery lab and we are storing the pharaoh's belongings here for safekeeping. He's in serious condition, sir. He's lost a lot of blood. Whether he'll make it is questionable."

"I see," James said solemnly. "What hospital is the pharaoh in, so I might call back, sir?"

"This is the Heliopolis Medical Center. Just ask for the surgery unit," the man said helpfully.

"I appreciate your help, sir. Thank you very much," James said ending the call.

"He's in serious condition, and they don't know whether he'll make it—" James turned to Marika as he picked up the channel changer and clicked through the stations for new information.

He wasn't quite sure what he should do. From the news reports, things didn't look good. Perhaps the only thing he *could* do was fly over to Egypt to offer his moral support to Khufu. He decided to call Robert Luster, to maybe cut through the red tape of commercial flight. If Luster's schedule allowed, they could be in Cairo in no time, relatively speaking.

≈

Luster's jet landed in Egypt some twelve hours from James's first encounter with the bombing scene on television. President Hamadi had a Hummer waiting for them at the airport, and they arrived at the Heliopolis Medical Center to find Khufu bandaged over most of his body. The shrapnel and flash had blinded him, and the explosion had damaged his inner ear on both sides. But he was conscious and could hear when one leaned closely and spoke clearly. He was unable to speak, however, and could only motion feebly with his hands, in futile attempts to communicate.

The pharaoh was not out of the water, yet, but it looked like he'd pull through, hospital officials said. James was, unconsciously, in his paternal role again. He was the one who had brought Khufu into the twenty-first century. And now he felt the onus to protect the pharaoh's life as diligently as possible. He even wrestled with whether he had done the right thing, in the first place, in cloning Khufu's DNA.

Two doctors came in and introduced themselves to James and Luster. They already knew James from television. Khufu needed blood from someone with his O type, they said; preferably an Egyptian, since the entire nation now was reputed to have the bloodline of the pharaohs. James, meanwhile, offered his encouragement and told the doctors that he was there to help in whatever capacity they needed.

≈

By the next day Khufu seemed to be doing better and that was without the blood transfusion. He was trying to talk, and his movements were a little stronger. Still, he was being fed intravenously as he had been since the operation. But at least he was heading in the right direction.

Hannibal and Luster arrived at the hospital encouraged by Khufu's progress. The president had put them up at Koubbeh Palace, Egypt's official guesthouse, and provided the armored Hummer for their transportation.

"You've done some good things, man," James said to Khufu, as he placed his chair next to the bed. "You were helping the kids, right? The god Amen wouldn't argue with that, would he? Maybe that's what you've been put here for.

To do some good; God knows we need more good on this crazy planet."

With that, James could see Khufu raise his hand to acknowledge his presence, and perhaps his words.

Khufu, without success, tried to raise his head...then spoke. "James. I need to tell you this," he said with difficulty, as he settled for resting his head on the pillow. With much effort he began, speaking in broken words: "A tra-jec-tory of progress mark-ed Kemet's cul-ture from the earliest times. Slow-ly, we began to realize that a contin-u-ation of such advancement would inevi-ta-bly lead to, there-to-fore, un-imagin-able possi-bilities; so, utilizing possi-bility thinking, we con-struct-ed the pyramids as literal time cap-sules. Many of our priests believed—and now *I* know they were correct—that one day a soci-ety would arise with the know-ledge to re-a-waken us, allowing us to re-a-lign with our Ka and continue to live in the earth; so, they mum-mi-fied our bodies and had them placed in struc-tures that would withstand the test of time. I, per-haps, am early, but your DNA sequencing shall reach perfection in the millennium—you...have opened the door—to the har-monic con-version."

James clasped Khufu's hand. "It's not over yet...hang in there big boy...it's not over yet." But it *was* over. Khufu's hands went limp...his head rolled to the side. He was gone.

≈

Two prominent-looking black men, in Diaspora business suits and sunglasses, along with Dr. Brooks Edwards, paused in front of Cleopatra's Needle, an Ancient Egyptian obelisk in New York City's Central Park. They were pointing out the major misnomer about the edifice—the Greek Cleopatra had nothing to do with the monument. It had been built centuries earlier in honor of the great African pharaoh Thutmoses III.

Edwards was then heard to mention the men's names—
"Thutmoses and Rameses." The two, meanwhile, gave each
other a high five as they said:

"We're back, man."

CPSIA information can be obtained
at www.ICGtesting.com
Printed in the USA
LVHW09s2000011018
591979LV00001B/12/P